TORMENTED

LEE MOUNTFORD

For my beautiful wife, Michelle, and amazing daughter, Ella.

FREE BOOKS

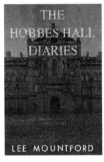

Sign up to my mailing list for free horror stories...

Want more scary stories? Sign up to my mailing list and receive your free copy of *The Hobbes Hall Diaries* and *The Demon of Dunton Hall* (prequel to The Demonic) directly to your email address.

And that's just the start—as a *thank you* for your support, I plan on giving away as much free stuff to my readers as I can. To sign up just go to my website (www.leemountford.com) and get your free stories.

1
———

ADRIAN JAMES LOOKED down at the floor as the person at his feet begged. *It was a person he knew well.*

'Please,' the dying person pleaded.

Adrian wasn't listening—nothing was going to stop what was about to happen.

Because it had already happened before.

The act of taking the life was every bit as difficult and soul-destroying as he remembered it being the first time around: the pleading, the struggling, and the weak resistance which he easily overcame. Adrian snuffed out the flame of life, and the body lay still.

The room they were in, illuminated only by faint candlelight, fell silent after the death rattle—the last wheezing breath—petered out of the corpse.

After the deed, Adrian slumped to the floor, feeling incredibly drained. He studied his hands—murdering hands that he'd just used to kill.

Was he a monster?

Adrian felt something squirm inside, a knot in his gut that tightened and tightened. Then he purged, spilling the contents of his stomach across the dirty carpet floor.

When his vision finally cleared, he looked up at the walls of the room. Once white, they were now dull and yellowed.

Then the paint started to discolour even more before his eyes.

Something was wrong here.

This wasn't how he remembered things.

Dark pools of black formed in places along the walls, and from these pulsating pockets, sickly yellow tendrils ran free, weaving their way around the remaining space, spreading and covering the entirety of the walls.

A sickness running wild.

Adrian was crying now, wailing uncontrollably. What had he done? He was a monster, there was no question of that. A killer.

A murderer.

He hugged himself and fell to his side, curling up into a foetal position as he continued his sobbing, feeling the wet, sticky patch of vomit beneath him.

Then he felt a breeze around him and detected a foul smell—worse than the one that already emanated from the carpet.

Adrian looked up just in time to see the surrounding room completely disintegrate before his eyes like it was never there. Blown away as if made of smoke. And what lay beyond terrified him.

He screamed.

This wasn't real—couldn't be. It was madness.

The ground beneath him—hard and black—stretched out, on and on, a seemingly never-ending landscape. It was a smooth, rocklike formation that secreted a thick red liquid beneath his weight. Enormous, jagged mountains broke from this ground and clawed up at the dark sky, and these themselves were dwarfed by terrible, perfectly cylindrical black towers.

This alien landscape, however, was not bereft of life.

Beings that defied sanity roamed, feeding off each other. Grotesque titans scooped up smaller, helpless monstrosities and thrust them into what appeared to be mouths. One being was so vast it stood level with the mountains as it screeched into the star-filled sky.

Other creatures, which were closer to Adrian, emerged from the ground—large, moaning mouths on long bodies lined with rolling eyes. They devoured anything that was within reach. One of these snake-like beings was ripped from the ground by a rolling, formless mass, then mashed and torn apart inside the gelatinous thing.

A screaming, humanoid figure—one that seemed human, only devoid of skin—was pinned down by a twisted horde of much larger creatures. Without legs, they pulled themselves along the hard ground on stumped midsections and toyed with the person—a man—tossing him around and dropping him from heights that should have ended his life.

But he did not die.

He simply moaned and screamed in agony. Then the monsters got to work. Not content with just pulling his exposed flesh from his body, they thrust engorged stalks that protruded from their underbellies into him, piercing him.

Adrian watched this horror unfold and continued to scream at the madness that surrounded him. Immense noises echoed, booming through the air, completely drowning out his own howls.

Then he heard something else amongst the chaos, something more focused. Something meant just for him.

He felt it inside his mind.

Something was communicating with him, and him alone.

It was not via a language he understood, yet he could still detect the intent.

This thing hungered for him and his fears.

For his guilt. For his madness.

Adrian felt this pull and turned himself around to face the direction it was coming from. A vast, raging body of thick liquid —a sea of boiling rage—was spread out before him. Whatever was communicating with him, he knew it was deep within that watery expanse.

And it called to him and tore at his mind.

Adrian fell to his knees, then rolled onto his back, continuing his screams. The sky above was a never-ending cosmos, and not one he recognised. Even the stars that sat high up behaved differently—pulsing, twisting, and moving. They coiled together, swirling and mixing to form something that was familiar to him somehow.

The thing inside of his head now seemed fearful, scared of the cluster in the sky.

He then realised what this formation of countless stars—the slightly elliptical shape that contained an iris within—reminded him of.

It was an eye

A great, cosmic eye.

It moved, and Adrian knew it was focused directly upon him.

ARLINGTON ASYLUM, ENGLAND - SEPTEMBER 1954

ADRIAN JAMES SCREAMED OUT AGAIN, but this time he could hear himself clearly, no longer clouded by that sinister voice inside of his own mind.

His panicked cries reverberated around him.

The other nightmarish sounds were no longer there.

He thrashed and kicked, but his arms and legs would not cooperate.

Adrian then opened his eyes, immediately seeing different surroundings. No longer in that cosmic madness, he now recognised a more familiar environment.

It was a small, dimly lit room containing only himself, the bed he was lying on, and a small, dirty toilet to his left. A single window sat directly above him lined with thick iron bars, and the dull light of the morning beyond seeped through. The walls were bare brick, grey and streaked with watermarks.

He looked down, breathing rapidly, still fighting and squirming, trying to get his bearings which were slowly returning. He was dressed in ill-fitting cotton overalls, once white, now yellowed and damp with perspiration. His arms and legs were restrained with wide, leather straps.

Memories started to flood back, finally overwhelming the lingering nightmare that refused to disappear.

Adrian then heard a metallic sound from the iron door ahead of him as it was unlocked.

The door creaked open and four men entered.

Two were dressed in simple white uniforms and took their positions at each side of the room, arms folded across their chests. Of these two, the man farthest to Adrian's right loomed over him, a giant looking down. He wore a sneer and his dark eyes bored into Adrian.

That was Jones.

The man to the left was Duckworth, less imposing, but still not someone Adrian wanted to cross.

The other two men present were the more senior figures. One was a doctor—Dr. Reid. He was a serious-looking man in his early fifties who wore thin, round glasses and had a neatly trimmed goatee and closely shaved head. As ever, he wore a three-piece suit, this one a light brown.

The other man was older and dressed in a fitted black gown, one that had a faint embroidered pattern. It also had a high neckline that was finished with a clerical collar. This man was well into his sixties, and his grey hair was combed with a neat side part.

It was Director Templeton—the man who ran the facility.

'Now, now,' the director said. 'All this screaming. What in the world is wrong, Adrian?'

Adrian's memories then flooded back completely, and he realised that the fantastical, horrific things he had witnessed only moments before were nothing more than a dream.

A nightmare.

He knew *exactly* where he was.

It was where he was supposed to be—Arlington Asylum.

'Nothing is wrong, Mr. Templeton,' Adrian finally said. His strained throat—sore and raw—hurt when he spoke. 'I'm fine.'

'Good,' Templeton said and stepped forward. 'I'd hate to think our treatment was doing more harm than good. And I'm quite certain we are on the verge of a breakthrough with this medicine.'

Adrian heard the screams of the insane rattle around from beyond his room as Director Templeton's lips spread into a wide smile.

'Now,' Templeton went on, 'tell me what you remember.'

2

'WHAT I REMEMBER?' Adrian asked.

The director nodded. 'Yes. You were screaming quite severely in your sleep. Bad dreams?'

Adrian ran a hand over his face and could feel the dampness of sweat. He looked down at his palms to see them glisten. 'You could say that,' he said.

'Then tell me about them.'

Adrian looked up at the older man. Director Templeton had a gentle face with grey eyes set into skin that had started to sag with age. The man had a quality about him that drew Adrian to him, one he felt he could trust. This had been true ever since their first meeting, back when Adrian had almost...

'Please,' the director pressed. 'It would help us greatly to know.'

Adrian shrugged. 'It was just a dream. Is it important?'

'Why yes,' Templeton replied. 'The medicine we gave you often spikes the brainwaves, we believe. Dreams are a fantastic indicator of how well it has worked. This was your first dose, and I am keen to know how effective it was.'

Adrian paused and shifted on the uncomfortable bed, going over the nightmare in his mind. Not that he particularly wanted to. 'I dreamt that I killed somebody,' he said, sombrely.

The director nodded, and Adrian even saw Dr. Reid raise his eyebrows. 'And how was that?' Director Templeton asked.

'What do you mean?'

'What I say. How did it feel?'

That was indeed an odd question. 'Horrible,' Adrian said.

'Just horrible? Anything else?' Templeton pushed.

Adrian shook his head, but that was a lie. When he replayed the act of killing over in his mind, he could not deny that he felt a certain sense of power with it. His face flushed with shame. Was that actually how he had felt when he'd carried out the foul deed?

'You can be honest with me, Adrian,' the director said. 'This will only work if we are honest with each other.'

'I am being honest,' Adrian lied. Whether he trusted Director Templeton or not, he was not going to admit to those feelings.

He was not a monster. At least, he desperately wanted not to be.

'Okay,' the director went on. 'Tell me, this dream. Was it a memory?'

This man certainly didn't miss a beat.

Adrian looked down and nodded.

'So, am I correct in thinking this was the incident that you have told me about already?' Templeton asked. 'The one with your father?'

Again, Adrian nodded, even though it was not true. The dream was of a different memory.

'Can you tell me about what happened when you killed him?'

'I've already told you,' Adrian said. 'It's why I'm here. You know everything about what happened.'

'But what happened in the dream, Mr. James? I am keen to know how accurate it was.'

'It was accurate,' Adrian said, growing tired and annoyed. 'It happened pretty much as I remember it.'

'And what about the details?'

'The details are the same,' Adrian snapped, raising his voice. He shifted again on the bed. The restraints dug into his skin, and the mattress of the bed, thin and lumpy, was hard beneath him.

'Okay,' Director Templeton said, holding up his palms in supplication. 'That's okay.' He then looked up to the large orderly. 'Mr. Jones, could you please release Adrian here from these dreadful restraints? He is quite clearly uncomfortable.'

'Are you sure?' Jones asked, his voice deep and soulless. The man was well over six feet tall, possibly pushing six and a half, with a broad frame. He had short black hair to match his dark eyes, a misshapen nose, and he carried himself with authority. Adrian had wondered if perhaps Jones had a military background. The man nodded at the director and bent down over Adrian, engulfing the patient in his shadow. Adrian winced as Jones grabbed him, causing the bigger man to smirk. The restraints were released, and Adrian felt the tingle of blood coursing through his veins again as the circulation was able to flow unobstructed.

'Better?' Templeton asked, and Adrian nodded.

'Thank you.'

The director waved his hands dismissively. 'Think nothing of it. Those straps were for your own good, I hope you know. The medicine has been known to cause extreme reactions. Dreams like the one you've had are common, but some are more potent than others. Some people have actually thrown themselves from the bed, such was the ferocity of what their mind was showing them.'

Adrian nodded, rubbing his wrists.

'Now, is there anything else?' Templeton asked.

'What do you mean?' Adrian replied.

'In the dream? Was that everything?'

The older man seemed to know much more than he had any right to. 'There was something,' Adrian admitted.

Templeton smiled and leaned forward eagerly, the flat springs on the bed squeaking as he did. 'Go on,' he said.

Adrian realised that every eye in the room was focused on him, and Dr. Reid was looking less than impressed. Adrian had already had some dealings with the doctor and found him to be cold, but clearly the man was knowledgeable in his field. Adrian noted an ever-so-subtle shake of the head from Reid. Did he think this a complete waste of time?

'Well,' Adrian started, 'after I killed... him, the room I was in changed, somehow.'

'Please explain,' the director pressed.

'I can't,' Adrian said. 'It just sort of, flaked away, like it wasn't even a solid structure. And then I was somewhere else.'

'And can you describe where you were?'

A humourless chuckle escaped Adrian's lips before he had a chance to stop it. How on earth was he supposed to describe the nightmarish vision that his mind had thrown up? He gave an attempt, regardless.

'Well, the whole landscape was... different.'

'Different, how?'

'I know how this will sound, but I don't think it was on this planet.'

The director raised his eyebrows, but he did not look skeptical. In fact, he looked pleased. Dr. Reid, however, was visibly less-so.

'Do we really have time for this, Isaac?' the man asked.

'It is Director Templeton,' the director said, calmly exerting his authority. 'And yes, we certainly have time for this. It is of the upmost importance.' Reid shook his head, this time not caring to hide the gesture, but the director didn't even look back to notice. Instead, his gaze was fixed expectantly on Adrian. 'Please,' he said, 'go on. Tell me about this... other place.'

'It was horrific,' Adrian said. 'The ground was like black rock, but felt a little different under my feet. There were huge mountains and these gigantic pillars that touched the sky. The size of them was hard to comprehend.'

'Anything else?'

'There were these... things.'

'Things?' Templeton asked, and Adrian nodded, not sure how best to describe them. Then another, more fitting word sprang forward in his mind.

'Monsters,' he said. 'Nightmarish monsters of all sizes. Some in the distance were as big as the mountains themselves. The whole place just felt evil. And the sky was different too. A little like looking up at the night as we know it, but the stars moved differently. And I swear that they pulled together at one point, swirling about each other like some unfathomable eye that hung in the space beyond.'

'This is good, Adrian,' Templeton said. 'And was there anything else? Anything at all?'

Adrian thought, and then remembered the boiling sea.

And he recalled that feeling he had, as if something were making contact.

'I think so,' he said. 'There was this expanse of water, if that is the right word. And I somehow felt that there was a presence beneath it. Something that was reaching out to me, in my mind.'

The director's expression grew even more eager. 'How so?'

'It felt like it wanted me. I don't know how else to explain it. It knew I was there, and it wanted to... claim me.' Adrian shook his head. 'It's hard to explain.'

The director gave Adrian a reassuring smile. 'Very good, Mr. James,' he said. 'I think that is enough for now. I can imagine this is difficult and more than a little distressing.'

'I guess so,' Adrian said. The director then got to his feet, groaning slightly as he did, the action clearly taking some effort. Adrian heard the popping of the man's knee joints as they took on the strain of the rest of his body.

'Is that normal?' Adrian asked, 'Dreams like that, I mean? Does it always happen after taking the medicine, because I've never experienced anything like it before. I never knew I had that kind of imagination.'

'They are normal,' Templeton reassured. 'But, Adrian, do we ever really know ourselves? That is the question I am trying to answer here, and this new medicine will help me do that. If successful, the patient will be at ease with who they are. Once that happens, I feel that in most cases our work will be done—there would be no more need for treatment.'

'And it will work for me?'

The director nodded. 'I am sure of it. And once it does, all of that suffocating guilt you now feel will be gone. You can live out your life without regret.'

It was a soothing notion, one Adrian had heard before. It was the same promise that had drawn him here in the first place. Still, he wasn't certain he deserved that kind of relief or absolution.

He actually felt that this place, Arlington Asylum, was exactly what he deserved.

Adrian's four guests then moved towards the door, but Templeton looked back over his shoulder. 'That is all for now, Mr. James, I appreciate your candour on this. You are free to wander the ward as you see fit and we will catch up soon. Have a good day.'

Adrian only nodded in response as they exited the room, leaving the door open behind them.

The truth was that there were no good days in this place, only repetition and misery that repeated in an endless cycle.

This was his life now.

This was his punishment.

3

ADRIAN WALKED down the long hallway, heading towards the Communal Area—a large room where the inmates in the ward were able to assemble and, if their mental capacity allowed, talk and socialise. He knew in that regard he was lucky. It was a privilege awarded only to Ward B residents.

His ward.

From speaking with other inmates, he knew that the other main area, Ward A, was a place even worse than his current one. Patients there were afforded no time of their own, always under constant observation and therapies. Though Adrian knew that these treatments amounted to little more than torture.

Adrian passed the room next to his own and looked in to see his neighbour, Tom, asleep on his bunk. The poor old guy looked worse and worse with each passing day, so Adrian decided not to wake him.

All the doors to the rooms he passed were the same: rusty iron with small, square viewing hatches cut into them. Most of these doors were now pushed open, indicating the rooms were likely empty. The corridor itself was narrow with dirtied white-tiled walls that ran up to the high ceiling. The floor covering consisted of old, hexagon-shaped tiles, coloured with a slight tinge of green that could just be made out beneath old stains. The area was poorly lit, lending the narrow corridor a claustrophobic feel.

Adrian didn't know too much about the facility he was housed in, other than the name of it, and that Director Templeton ran it, but he understood that whatever funding or financing the asylum had was insufficient. Very little of the budget seemed to go towards the upkeep of the building, that much was obvious, and the management, such as it was, were happy enough to let the place go to rot and ruin.

He followed the corridor around to the left, passing more rooms as he walked. Sometimes, even though the doors were open, he saw patients inside who had apparently decided not to leave the safety of their four walls for now. One such man—Malcolm—sat on his bed, rocking back and forth and scratching at the skin on his arm that looked red-raw.

Malcolm had been here for months, longer than Adrian, and hadn't shown any signs of improvement during his time here. If anything, his state of mind seemed to be declining, and there was talk that he may soon be transferred to Ward A.

Adrian carried on to a large metallic double door at the end of the hallway. It contained wide vision panels in the top half, the glass within crisscrossed with wire. One door leaf was open, and Adrian could hear the buzz of voices within, somewhat drowning out the usual background noise of pained moans and cries.

This was the Communal Area.

The large space had maybe thirty people inside, but was so big that it still did not seem full. The ceiling was much higher than that of the corridor, arched and supported on old timber beams. The windows on the far wall were tall and thin, six in total, lending the space some natural light. All were covered with rusted iron bars, reminding everyone inside that there was no way out.

Not that anyone would try, given the number of orderlies present.

Most of them—all dressed in their plain white uniforms—stood watching from their positions against the walls, but some walked between the patients, making sure nobody stepped out of line.

And Adrian had seen first-hand what happened when any of the patients acted up. While none of the orderlies were as bad as Jones, even the less sadistic were still swift and brutal in their methods of maintaining order.

Looking around the gathering of lost souls, many of whom milled aimlessly around the basic tables and chairs that were dotted about the room, Adrian spotted the group he had chosen to interact with most during his stay here.

He made his way over to them, careful not to bump into the subdued, zombie-like patients that stood in his way. They were obviously heavily medicated, to the point of being completely placid, and Adrian wondered if all of them were taking the same medicine that was administered to him.

Watching these patients aimlessly roaming the space caused Adrian to wonder if this was what he had to look forward to.

Was this the 'cure' that the director had promised him?

After all, you couldn't feel pain and torment if you couldn't feel anything at all.

Which actually sounded appealing.

He reached the table where his four friends, if that was

the correct term, were seated. In truth, this was merely a group that had formed through nothing but circumstance—all seemed relatively compos mentis when compared to most of the people here. It was perhaps this fact, more than any other, that drew them to each other.

Other than Adrian, the newest member, the group consisted of Seymour, Jack, Trevor, and Sean. It was Trevor—a sleek man with short, mousy hair—who spotted Adrian first. He raised a hand and waved in greeting—a meek gesture that was quickly withdrawn, fearing the gaze of others. Trevor, it seemed, was his usual self today: a timid shadow of a person.

But he could be different. There was another side to him that Adrian had seen only once before.

Another personality altogether.

Mother.

Adrian took a seat next to Sean, given it was the only space available. Sean was a stick-thin, haggard man who had a severe opium addiction, and he was struggling with being cut off from his one true love in this world.

The man's teeth—the ones that were left—were a mixture of black and yellow, caused not by the opium, but by his complete disregard for any kind of personal hygiene. A result of many years of neglect. His condition and reliance on the drug was so bad that when he tried to eat, he often regurgitated any food back up, along with streams of green bile. To Sean, it was not food that gave him sustenance, but the opium, and without it his life in here was hell.

Then there was Jack, a giant of a man—even taller than Jones—who was also the most gentle soul Adrian had ever met. He had no hair at all on his head, not even eyebrows or facial hair, and had a thick browbone that protruded out over his eyes like a small canopy. He had kind eyes that often seemed lost—like a puppy—and of everyone here, Jack was the one Adrian felt most sorry for.

In addition, Jack seemed to be mute and had never uttered a word in all of Adrian's time here.

As Adrian sat down, he was greeted by the last member of the group, Seymour, and he knew the welcome would not be a pleasant one.

'Good morning,' the large man said. Seymour was not tall, but round, and his clothing struggled to contain a stomach that pressed against the thin cotton beneath. He had messy brown hair that was beginning to grey, and his gelatinous chin wobbled as he spoke.

'Good morning,' Adrian replied, waiting for the inevitable additional comment.

Seymour didn't disappoint.

'You look terrible, old boy,' Seymour said, with a chuckle. 'Even for someone as ugly as you.'

It was typical of the fat man, always quick to tease and put others down.

He was also quick to anger.

'Anyone hear the noises coming from Malcolm's room last night?' Trevor asked, quickly changing the subject.

Malcolm Peters was the man Adrian had seen on his journey to the common area, but he hadn't heard the screams in question. Of course, he had been unconscious all night, lost in his terrible dreams following the dose of medication.

'I did,' Seymour answered. 'Fucking horrible sounds. I reckon he was in pain.'

'Anyone seen him today?' Sean asked, scratching irritably at a red patch of skin on his arm.

No one verbalised an answer, but all shook their heads.

'Heard they'd upped his medication,' Seymour added.

'Guess that means it won't be long until he disappears as well. Just like the others.'

'You mean it won't be long until he's better and released, just like the others?' Trevor asked.

Seymour laughed. A big, full-on belly laugh. 'Don't be so stupid, boy,' he said. 'People don't get better here. And they're never released.'

'Of course they are,' Trevor shot back, but his voice was small and weak, as it normally was in his more placid state. 'The treatments here work.'

Seymour shook his head with a smug look of superiority. Adrian didn't like Seymour, but he did tend to agree with him on this point. A small part of him did indeed cling to the hope that this miracle medicine Director Templeton was developing would work, but he was well aware that it was all experimental. The chances of people leaving here, actually cured of their mental conditions, were slim at best. He had come to that conclusion a while ago.

And he'd also made peace with it.

After what he had done, he didn't deserve to be cured of his guilt.

He deserved to be right here amongst the misery.

'Trev,' Seymour said, 'come on, think about it. In all your time here, can you remember a single person being released?'

'Yes,' Trevor said, with a little more conviction. 'Angus Frey and Edward Simmons. And Alfie, only last week. They've all been released and are all cured.'

'All have disappeared,' Seymour said, 'but not all cured. And certainly not released. I can't believe you thought...' but then Seymour trailed off, alerted by someone behind Adrian. Seymour's eyes dropped and his shoulders slumped. Adrian turned to see one of the orderlies—Duckworth, the one from his cell earlier—walking up to the table.

'All getting a little excitable over here, wouldn't you say?' Duckworth asked. He had a mop of red hair and pale skin, but was well-set. No one answered him or even made eye contact. Adrian could see that Duckworth had his cosh—a lead club wrapped in leather—already in hand, and he was patting it repeatedly into the palm of his other hand. Everyone remained silent, hoping the orderly would be happy that he'd proven his point and just walk away. Thankfully, luck was on their side.

'Keep it down,' the orderly said and moved on, much to everyone's relief.

Adrian looked over to see Jack hunched over in his seat, his head bowed, and he rocked back and forth. Adrian laid a hand on his shoulder to calm him.

'It's okay, big man,' he said. 'He's gone now.'

Jack smiled, and his rocking slowed.

Adrian was then about to change the topic to something a little less excitable, but wasn't given that chance.

'There he is,' Seymour whispered. Adrian turned and saw Malcolm entering the large room through the double doors.

He looked like hell.

Worse than normal.

Already a tall, gangly man, Malcolm's skin was now ashen, almost grey, and he had dark purple bags beneath his eyes, one of which always hung lower than the other— seemingly a genetic defect.

And he looked even thinner than usual, too, which was saying something for him. His cotton clothing hung loosely off him as if several sizes too large. He also seemed unsteady on his feet as he swayed over to an empty seat and plopped down into it.

'Does that look like a man who is getting better?' Seymour asked, but no one answered.

Adrian felt his gut lurch, and a sudden, queasy feeling washed over him. Last night he had started the same treatment Malcolm was on, and this could well be a glimpse of what he had to look forward to.

Still, that might not be a bad thing.

He thought back to his dream last night.

Not the nightmarish landscape, but what came before.

Activity at the entrance of the room drew their attention as dinner was wheeled inside. Large silver troughs contained the bland, runny slop that they would soon gulp down.

Orderlies began heaping the gruel onto paper plates.

'All right,' one of them shouted, raising his voice above the general noise of the room. 'Anyone who wants to eat, make your way over to the food here in a civilised manner. And make sure you queue—we aren't fucking animals. If any of you step out of line, you'll not eat for a week.' He raised his cosh high in the air. 'In fact, I'll make sure to crack your jaw so hard that you won't be eating for a month. Understand?'

No one needed to reply, and the man didn't wait around for an answer. The patients in the room gradually got to their feet and started to filter over to their awaiting meals.

'Adrian?' Trevor asked as the group stood up. 'How was it?'

'How was what?' Adrian asked.

'The medicine. Did you... did you dream?'

Adrian nodded. 'Yes, Trevor, I did.'

'Same happened to me,' Trevor said. He'd started his

treatment a couple of weeks ago and had received multiple doses so far. 'They get worse, but the director told me it's one of the ways they know it's working. He says it's a sign that it's helping my mind.'

Adrian didn't know exactly what this medicine was, or what it did, but he wasn't as optimistic as Trevor. However, he didn't have the heart to crush the shy man's hopes. 'That's good, Trev,' he said, and the man smiled in response.

'Yeah,' Trevor said, still smiling. 'It is.'

But his voice faltered, and it was clear that he hadn't entirely convinced himself.

4

Dr. Thomas Reid was not happy.

He walked alongside Director Isaac Templeton as they made their way back towards the Administration Ward. They passed from Ward B, through the secured door, and then into the Main Hall, which also served as a reception area to the facility. It was a wide-open space with a cluster of desks towards the back where a smattering of administration staff worked, writing up reports and filing paperwork. The front section of the hall had an unmanned reception counter that had not been used for many a year and had gathered piles of clutter that threatened to spill off to the floor. Dr. Reid knew that Arlington Asylum was not open to the public, and hadn't been for a long time, but the layout of this reception area suggested it once was.

The two distinct areas were demarcated by timber partitions on either side of the room that extended a few feet inwards, leaving a wide opening between. The main walls of the hall were lined with a similar style of oak panelling that ran up to a moulded rail set about five feet from the floor. Above that, the walls were finished in flaking plaster. The ceiling above was arched, giving the area a grandiose feel. In its heyday, it would have been quite impressive.

Both men walked from one side of the Main Hall towards the door to the Administration Ward on the opposite side, weaving between desks as they went.

'You know,' Dr. Reid began, deciding to air his concerns, 'I still don't know very much about this medication that's being administered.'

'Yes, I am aware of that,' Director Templeton replied.

'Well, as the head physician here, don't you think it is something I should be made aware of?'

'You have your role here,' Templeton replied, dismissively. 'This is something that doesn't concern you.'

'Well, it should concern me,' Reid answered, raising his voice slightly. Being kept at a distance had been annoying at first, but now it was becoming infuriating. 'Again, you appointed me as Head Physician. It is my job to know what is going on with my patients.'

Director Templeton stopped and turned to face Reid. As he did, Reid could feel the eyes of the surrounding staff look up from their work and settle on the pair. 'Correction,' Templeton said. 'These are *my* patients, Dr. Reid. Every single one of them. They belong to me. And you are here under my employ, so you do as ordered. Do you understand?'

Reid clenched his teeth, and his first instinct was to retaliate. After all, what did this man—a God-damn priest— know about healing the mentally ill? Reid was the only qualified person working in the asylum, as far as he could tell, and the only person with any real authority to determine what was best for these patients. He was the one who should be running the show.

But he let his teeth unclench because he wasn't running

the show, was he? There was a reason he was working here, relegated to this private hell-hole of an asylum. He needed to get his career back on track, and this was the only place that gave him the opportunity to do so. He had to be careful not to ruin this chance, at least until he had rebuilt his reputation sufficiently to move on.

But he needed results, some breakthrough that would put him at the forefront in his field again. It was fair to say that whatever organisation Templeton represented cared little for the patients in their care, so he could certainly indulge in more radial methods and treatments here. Indeed, many of the patients were held against their will, without showing any symptoms of mental issues beyond the stress of being held prisoner.

'I do understand that,' Reid conceded and turned to walk on, hoping Templeton would follow along away from the ears of the staff. Fortunately, Templeton did just that, so Reid continued. 'I don't mean to be disrespectful, or ungrateful, it's just that I don't think I can do my best work if things are kept from me.'

They arrived at the door to the Administration Ward, which was smaller than the others and contained a few spare offices, some small padded cells used to isolate patients, a library, a room that had been converted into a Chapel, and separate offices for Reid and Templeton.

Templeton did not answer the question at first, but instead pulled free his ring of keys and selected one that would open the door before them. Once through, and the door locked behind them, Templeton turned to Reid and gave his reply.

'You are afforded plenty of patients on which to carry out your studies and claw back what little reputation you can, but this facility has a greater purpose, one that I am fulfilling. One that will, believe it or not, change the world. And until I know I can trust you completely, I will simply leave you to tinker with your outdated and misguided methods.'

'If you really believe that,' Reid asked, 'then why bring me on board in the first place? Why do you even want me here?'

'From time to time, we will need the expertise of someone like yourself. But, more than that, when you realise what it is we are doing here, I am hopeful you will see the potential we have and commit yourself to the cause.'

'Then tell me what the cause is,' Reid said. 'How can I commit to something I am not aware of?'

Templeton just smiled. 'In time,' he said, infuriating Reid even further. 'Prove yourself first, then all will be made clear.'

'And how exactly am I supposed to prove myself?'

'Continue your work for now,' Templeton answered. 'And when the time comes, do not disappoint.'

Dr. Reid raised his eyebrows in surprise. Director Templeton was much older than he was; shorter, too, and supposedly a man of God, but Reid was almost certain the old man had just issued him a veiled threat. Templeton then patted him on the shoulder and walked off towards his office, leaving Reid dumfounded.

5

ADRIAN LOOKED *down at the beaten and bloodied man; his pitiful face had already begun to swell and bruise. He spat blood, some of it coating Adrian's shoes.*

'Say it,' Adrian seethed, fists still clenched. 'Say it to me now.'

The man crawled forward, like a dog, and grabbed at Adrian's ankle.

This man was his father. Someone who, over the years, had beaten and abused both Adrian and Adrian's mother. He'd worn them down to hollow shells of the people they once were.

Snuffing out the people they could have been.

But Adrian was bigger now, an adult in his own right, and he'd finally had enough. So, in the dark and dingy home, one that his father had stripped of warmth over the years, Adrian erupted. After being called a 'worthless mistake' yet again, he snapped and assaulted the old drunken monster, smashing his fists into his father's face.

The suddenness and ferocity of Adrian's attack overwhelmed his father, who made a futile attempt to fight back. Adrian's mother screamed at him to stop, telling him not to go too far, but when the man fell Adrian unleashed a flurry of kicks to his father's head and watched as the cartilage of the man's nose crumpled and splintered.

Expelling all of his pent-up rage felt good—exhilarating, even. So, he kept going, indulging in the violence, and taking a kind of sadistic glee in the power he felt making the man suffer who had caused him such anguish.

'Say it to me now!' Adrian screamed again. 'I dare you!'

He wanted his father to beg for forgiveness and plead for his life. Instead, the old bastard simply looked up at him with his one good eye and spluttered out his reply.

'Worthless fucking mistake,' he said, managing a pained smile.

Despite Adrian's mother's protests, Adrian allowed himself to fully embrace the anger that fuelled him. He grabbed the man by the throat and squeezed with all he was worth. His father fought back—a pathetic and weak attempt—but soon his face went from being beet-red to a shade of blue, and his eyes bulged from the sockets. With a wheeze, his life was finally choked away.

'Good,' a voice said as the walls around Adrian started to change. They peeled and flaked away to reveal a world outside that was not his own. A nightmarish place. He heard his mother's terrified cries as something took her—a twisted, monstrous being—and crushed her skull.

Adrian screamed.

ADRIAN WAS PULLED from unconsciousness and back into reality.

It took him a moment to realise why.

The asylum was never exactly a quiet place—the cries and moans of residents around the facility were a constant background noise that took him days to get used to after he had first arrived. But the noises that woke him now were different.

Something was happening.

Adrian lifted his head from the hard pillow and stared over to the closed door of his room, as if doing so could help visualise just what was going on in the hallways beyond. But it didn't help, because while he could understand and make sense of some noises he heard—panicked yelling and angry shouts—there was another, terrifying sound that made no sense to him at all.

It seemed... inhuman.

Guttural groans and roars that were unfamiliar to him. The sounds were getting closer now and were punctuated by a howl of someone in tremendous pain. That was followed by some kind of gurgling and spluttering.

The chaos of what was happening in the corridor moved closer and was soon outside of his room. Something clashed against the sturdy metal door hard enough to make it rattle in its frame. More pained cries, and then the viewing hatch was knocked open.

Mouth agape, Adrian gazed out into the darkness, not daring to move. The noises outside plateaued, and he could hear somebody struggling desperately, gasping and groaning. Whoever this man was, his pained pleas were soon overwhelmed by a monstrous growl.

Adrian was terrified, but he was also desperate to know what was going on. Surely the thick door between them would keep him safe from harm? He got to his feet and, ever-so-slowly, made his way over to the now-open hatch. He heard a horrible crunch from beyond and yet another cry of agony, then a prolonged ripping sound as the cries heightened before blurring into a wet gurgle.

Adrian reached the hatch and carefully peered out.

Before he had the chance to take anything in, a blood-covered face slammed into the opening, causing him to yell and jump back in shock.

Adrian looked at the terrified face in repulsion. This man was one of the asylum's orderlies, but it was hard to be sure as to which one because his jaw was missing completely; it had been ripped off, leaving jagged wounds and exposed red flesh and tendons beneath. His tongue lolled down through the door's hatch and into Adrian's room. It writhed and twitched, almost with a life of its own.

Adrian made eye contact with the orderly, but immediately regretted doing so. The eyes seemed to plead for help, but the only sounds the man could make were incomprehensible moans. As quickly as it had appeared, the face was yanked away, and Adrian heard more growls. Then a pained, high-pitched cry.

He was scared, but couldn't help himself; Adrian slowly moved forward and peered out to see the dark corridor beyond. He could make out a tall, spindly figure in the darkness, holding what appeared to be the orderly's head in its long, claw-like hands as the detached body was dropped carelessly to the floor. Whatever this thing was, it was almost seven feet tall and its skin was pulled tight over oddly shaped bones that protruded beneath.

Adrian drew in a sharp gasp of breath as fear gripped him further, and as he did it appeared the demonic thing outside heard him. While still holding the severed head, it turned, allowing Adrian to see its face: melted and warped, the features like that of some horrific painting. One eye hung considerable lower than the other, almost in line with the corner of its unnaturally wide mouth, which opened like that of a snake, revealing rows of long, serrated teeth. The edges of its thin lips turned up into a smile as it raised the detached head up and pushed it into its open maw.

The demon made a sound reminiscent of a chuckle as the jaws clamped down over the cranium and started to exert force. It didn't take long for the head to crunch and compress, eventually popping completely, causing a shower of gore and grey brain-matter to burst free.

Another sound came from the tall, gangly thing outside of Adrian's room. It was a kind of huffing, snorting noise. The thing's shoulders bobbed up and down and its smile increased as it began to chew.

Adrian realised that it was laughing.

Then Adrian heard approaching voices, and he turned to look farther back down the dark corridor. In the distance, he could see bodies littering the floor—other orderlies who had met a similar fate as their friend. The approaching group seemed to be coming from that direction, but had not arrived in full view as yet. The chewing, demonic thing outside evidently heard the same voices and running foot-steps, too, as it turned in the same direction. It began to backpedal, but before running off into the darkness completely, it cast Adrian one last look.

It may have just been Adrian's imagination after seeing something so horrific, but he was sure he recognised a familiarity in that melted, twisted face.

Malcolm?

Adrian heard the monster's thumping footsteps move down the corridor as it fled. A group of orderlies finally emerged, sprinting after the thing, armed with knives, coshes, and sticks.

And one of them had a different kind of weapon altogether.

In his hands, he gripped a thin pipe that was fitted with

handles and a nozzle at the end. A rubber tube ran from the back of the shaped metal pipe and connected to a small tank that was strapped to the man's back. From the end of the nozzle, Adrian saw a small, blue flame.

Could that weapon really be what he thought it was?

If so, why the hell did an asylum need to be equipped with something like that?

'Get it,' an orderly yelled as they sprinted in a huddled group down the narrow hallway. One orderly bringing up the rear saw Adrian's open hatch and locked eyes with him through it. The man quickly slammed the cover shut, cutting off Adrian's view of what was happening.

Adrian then heard the voices and clattering footsteps disappear as they moved further away.

It seemed the chase was on.

Adrian stood before his door in silent disbelief.

What had he just seen? And could that thing have really been Malcolm?

Unable to make sense of it, he eventually made his way back over to his bed and dropped down onto it. He lay back and pulled his knees up to his chest, feeling himself shaking with fear and adrenaline.

He listened, trying to make out any sounds in the distance that would give him a clue as to what was going on, and he could hear wild cries, screams, and roars. Whatever was happening, Adrian knew there was violence involved.

And amongst all of that, the patients in the facility seemed particularly agitated tonight, and their mad bellows were also clearly audible.

Adrian had no idea of the hour, but he knew he would not sleep again that night.

6

It was late, but Reid could not sleep. He was seated in his office, a rather small, cramped room which housed his chair and writing desk in the centre, spare chair near the door, and tall bookcases lining the walls. Each case was crammed full of files and medical journals, while his desk itself was a sea of loose papers, parchment, and notes. As precise and meticulous as he believed he was, his office was in stark contrast to that—organised chaos was how he liked to describe it, with more emphasis on the *chaos* than the *organised*.

He was trying to focus on the job at hand—of writing up a report on a patient. Reid had a treatment in mind for the man, and it was the same treatment that had derailed his career and landed him in this God-forsaken place. Though it was not the report that was keeping him awake.

The altercation with Director Templeton was playing on his mind, specifically the things the man had said to him.

Prove yourself. Do not disappoint.

All vague riddles and threats, with nothing of substance behind them. What the hell was expected of him here?

He tried to concentrate on the words he was scribbling in his ledger as his eyes had started to ache with tiredness, but he knew it was pointless trying to rest them, as his mind was just too active. To help, he had switched off the light in his office and was now writing by the gentle, flickering glow of his table-mounted lantern. He'd owned the lamp for many years, even brought it with him when he'd started at Arlington Asylum, and found that the soft hue it gave off was much more forgiving on his eyes than the sharp illumination from the electric lights fitted throughout the facility. It also usually helped his mind to settle.

But not tonight.

He was not the kind of man to take kindly to threats—obscure or not.

Ignore the old fool, Reid said to himself. *Concentrate on your work, then you can leave this place behind forever.*

He tried doing just that and went back to a report which outlined the treatment he was planning to try on one of his patients—a young man, only seventeen, who had been picked up after living on the streets. He suffered from fits of violence, and with no warning he would erupt and lash out at anyone around him. Afterwards, when the episodes subsided, he always showed great regret for his actions, and Reid felt that he was the perfect candidate to try the procedure on again—the one that had almost ruined him last time.

It was less of a risk now.

If he failed, no one would care. He could simply try again. Not like last time, with Elton Breyer.

The procedure that was supposed to push him into fame and renown had not gone as expected.

Elton had been tied down to Reid's table, fully awake and cognisant. Reid knew exactly what he had to do, and how much pressure to exert, but knowing something and actually carrying it out were two different things. Reid remembered taking hold of the instrument—which was long and thin, with a sharp end and made of lightweight aluminium—and bringing it down to the inside corner of Elton's left eye. The young man's blue irises had looked up to him as he did, wide with fear at the approaching pick. Reid felt the instrument slip in beside the wet eyeball and could see the fleshy orb push slightly to the side, making room for the new object that had invaded its space.

Reid had then brought up a mallet and started to gently hammer the pick into Elton's head. It had slipped inside easily, moving down farther and farther until Reid had felt resistance.

He had reached the brain.

With a steady hand, he had hammered the pick again and penetrated the rubbery matter. Elton had let out a moan, and his body had begun to convulse. Reid had kept hitting the instrument, pushing it down farther, and Elton's convulsions had become more severe. Finally, Reid had stopped, keeping the pick in place at what he thought was the correct depth. Then he had gently moved it from side to side, hoping to successfully sever the connections to the prefrontal cortex and frontal lobes of the brain.

This procedure, known as a transorbital lobotomy, should have put an end to Elton's violent episodes and made him much more docile. While not conceived or developed by Reid himself, it was still considered an untested and unpractised procedure, and therefore looked down upon by the stuffy old medical elite—especially here in England. However, it was much easier and simpler to perform than a conventional lobotomy, saving time and money, and Reid had ambitions of taking this idea and pushing it to become common practice in his home country —and collecting all the plaudits that were owed to him as he did.

But things had not worked out that way.

Instead, Elton had died on his table and Dr. Thomas Reid's promising career had gone into free-fall.

But he was determined to prove that the procedure was not only viable, but also the best way to treat most mental ailments.

Which meant he needed to try again.

And he had scheduled his first re-attempt for the very next day. If successful, he intended to try again and again, and hone the procedure until he was able to carry it out flawlessly, each and every time.

Then he could leave Arlington Asylum behind, and the clueless Isaac Templeton—a religious idiot playing at medicine—could go to hell.

Reid dropped his pen and let out a sigh. That was enough for tonight. While he was a man who did not need a lot of sleep to operate well, he was in danger of overdoing it and leaving himself too exhausted tomorrow to be at his best. And when he was overly tired, Reid tended to think of his wife and son, and he could not afford to let himself do that. He removed his glasses and rubbed the bridge of his nose.

Time for sleep, at least for a few hours. And even if sleep did not come, he could at least rest his tired eyes.

He then got to his feet and turned off the lantern before leaving his office and locking it securely behind him. Like every other area of the asylum, his personal quarters were just off the Main Hall. That area acted as a hub, and the other wards were connected to this central section like the arms running from the head of an octopus. The building itself was all single storey, with no stairs or elevators to speak of.

Though that wasn't true, was it? There was an old-looking service elevator at the back of the Main Hall, one that Reid was not allowed to use. He knew it went down, but to where he had no clue, and Templeton would not tell him.

Secrets upon secrets, in a structure that almost seemed designed to be hidden from the world: sunken into a surrounding forest, with only one road in and out.

A road that was not much travelled anymore.

Hell, even the administrative staff who worked in the Main Hall seemed to live on site. At times, this place felt more like a prison than a place of work. He was allowed to leave, but excursions needed to be arranged with Templeton, who held the key, and it was made clear that the facility was not to be discussed with anyone outside of its own walls. Another threat from Templeton, this one followed with a promise of expulsion.

And given that Arlington seemed to be his last chance at professional redemption, Reid could ill afford to go against the director.

Reid made his way towards the Main Hall, savouring the quiet. At this time of night, things were usually silent in the area—the cries of the insane insulated to their own wards.

And he expected that tonight would be no different.

But as he got closer to the Main Hall, he heard it.

Voices.

Screams.

They were panicked, and as he got closer, he could make out the sounds of a struggle. Screams bellowed, and muffled orders were barked out.

Above it all, a horrific screech.

Reid stopped, not knowing if he should run back or

continue forward. Curiosity got the better of him and he jogged onwards.

What on earth could make a sound like that? His first instinct was that there was an animal loose in the asylum. How that had happened, he had no idea, but what else could explain it?

He reached the blank iron door that separated the zone he was in from the Main Hall and unlocked it. Whatever was happening beyond seemed to be in full flow. He gently pushed the door open, just in time to hear an ear-piercing scream as someone wailed in agony.

Reid peeked through the opening and could scarcely believe his own eyes.

A group of orderlies had surrounded... something... and were trying in vain to subdue it. They seemed to be failing in their efforts, however, and Reid saw who it was that was crying out in agony. One of the orderlies was without his arm, and blood pumped freely from the stump at his shoulder. The severed appendage was on the floor close to the creature that they had all surrounded.

And Reid had no idea what it was.

Humanoid in shape, certainly—with arms, legs, a torso, and head, but it was not human. First of all, it was far too tall, and its limbs were stick-thin. It evidently possessed a power that belied its slight build, however, having pulled a man's arm clean off. Reid was too far away to make out its face or finer features, but its thin skin looked to be black, or at least a dark purple.

Reid then saw Jones run into the room, coming from Ward A.

'What do we do?' one of the other orderlies yelled, desperate for help and instruction, clearly at a loss as to how best handle a situation such as this. Jones circled round to another of the men, one who was equipped with a strange weapon, one that was connected to a metallic tank on his back.

Jones relieved the man of the instrument and quickly put it on himself. 'We kill it,' he said.

'But what about the director? Will he allow us to do that?' another asked.

Jones raised the end of the weapon and aimed at the feet of the approaching beast.

'I'll explain it to Templeton,' Jones said, before a stream of orange and yellow liquid flame burst free from the metal nozzle.

The creature was immediately engulfed in searing fire that swam up its body, coating it completely. The monster roared and screeched and continued to run towards Jones. The orderly, however, was not easily fazed and circled the creature before letting loose with another burst from the weapon. Flames engulfed it completely now, so fierce that Reid could barely make out the black of its skin beneath the yellow and red flames.

Eventually, the thing's screams faded, and it dropped to the floor—lifeless. The smell of burning meat flooded the air.

'Give it a minute,' Jones commanded in a confident voice. 'Then put the fire out. I'll go and speak with the director.'

'The changes are getting worse,' one of the orderlies said, as others rushed to the aid of the man who had been stripped of an arm. 'We can't go on like this.'

'We can, and we will,' Jones replied, taking off the weapon and thrusting it into the arms of the complaining man. 'We are all here for a reason, and that reason doesn't change. If anyone has ideas about leaving, they will answer to me. Understand?'

No one presented an argument.

Satisfied, Jones walked away from the room, leaving his colleagues to put out the fire before it spread further.

Reid quietly pulled the door closed before he was seen.

His mind struggled to comprehend what he had just witnessed. Monsters did not exist. He was a man of science, unwavering in his beliefs, so how did he reconcile his mind with what his own eyes had just shown him?

He felt his heart beating quickly in his chest and realised he was sweating. A nervous energy flooded him.

And something else concerned him as well; something an orderly had said after they put the creature down.

The changes are getting worse.

It was clear from what was said that Director Templeton was aware, at least to some extent, of what was going on here.

Reid knew he needed answers and resolved to confront Templeton about this as soon as he could. He headed back to his office in a daze and decided to stay there for the night.

First thing tomorrow morning, he would pay the director a visit.

He fell into his seat and dropped his head into his hands —just what in the hell had he gotten himself involved in?

7

THE VERY NEXT DAY, after a night without any sleep, Reid saw Director Templeton enter the Administration Ward and make his way straight to the Chapel—which was a morning routine for the director. It was here Reid planned to confront Templeton about what he had seen the previous night.

The image of that inhuman thing—and what it had done to that orderly—had stuck with Reid ever since he'd witnessed it the previous night. Reid had used the time throughout the night to try to explain just what it was he had seen, and the best he could come up with was that the thing was indeed human, but had somehow transformed or mutated. He'd skimmed through his medical books in his office to try to find a known condition that could explain such a transformation, but had come up empty-handed.

Nothing could explain what he had seen. At least nothing that he was aware of.

However, he had a feeling that Templeton may have a little more knowledge of what was going on around here.

Reid opened the door to the Chapel and stepped inside

to see the director seated in one of the rows of pews at the front of the room. The walls here were white plaster, and on their surfaces were pictures and effigies of biblical figures. The ceiling was not as high as in other areas of the building, and the floor was an ugly white tile, giving the room quite an underwhelming feel. On either side of a central aisle, rows of uncomfortable-looking wooden pews stretched back from the front. At the head of these seats was a simple altar —a table covered in white cloth. This shrine housed a large, ornamental crucifix that stood centrally, with an open Bible beneath it. Either side of the thick book burned sticks of incense, filling the whole room with a pleasant aroma of jasmine.

Other than the assorted ornaments and effigies, the only other thing of note was a large mirror that was affixed to one of the walls.

Whether this room had always served as a Chapel, or whether it had been converted for such a purpose, Reid did not know.

Nor did he care.

Templeton did not hear him enter, or made no show of being aware of his presence, and continued to sit with his head bowed. Reid made his way over to the director, walking down the central aisle, and took a seat next to him.

'I never took you for a religious man,' Templeton said with his eyes closed. 'Care to join me in prayer?'

'No,' Reid answered, 'I'm not one for superstition or make-believe.'

Templeton let out a small laugh. 'To each his own.'

'At least,' Reid went on, 'I thought I believed that. I was certain that all things supernatural, including demons and monsters and the like, were just made-up stories, the product of a weak or retarded mind.'

'It sounds like you may have had a change of heart?' Templeton said. His voice was flat, unreadable, and still he did not open his eyes.

'Hard to say,' Reid said, letting some of the frustration he was feeling show through in his tone. 'But after last night, and what I saw, I don't know what to think anymore.'

'Is that right?'

Templeton showed no emotion at all, other than perhaps a slight, amused curiosity—which only angered Reid more.

'Yes,' he said, 'that is right. And do you have any idea what it is that I saw?'

'Does it matter?' the director asked, the question throwing Reid off his train of thought. 'If you saw something that has made you question the very beliefs you held as sacred, then surely there is a more important question to be answered?'

'Really? And what would be more important than getting to the bottom of it? You don't think the truth is important?'

Now Templeton opened his eyes, and he turned to face Reid. 'Oh no,' he said, 'do not misunderstand. The truth is the only important thing in our lives. But I'm afraid people cling to truths that are, in fact, outright lies, and they live their lives never actually knowing real truth. Just as you have been doing.'

Reid shook his head. 'More riddles? Really?'

'Not riddles, Thomas,' Templeton said, using Reid's Christian name. 'I am simply asking a valid question. You say you saw something that has perhaps changed the way you view the world. Instead of contemplating that, and what it means to you, you rush to me for answers. But you need to provide your own.'

'I am getting tired of all this vague rubbish you spout, Director,' Reid said, raising his voice.

But Templeton just shrugged. 'Then do not ask anything of me. Go about your business.'

'Go about my business?' Reid was yelling now, and he got to his feet, looking down on the other man. 'Do you know what I saw last night? I saw something in the Main Hall that was, as far as I could tell, not human. Roaming around, attacking the people that work here, and in the end it was put down by a weapon that has no business being kept in a place like this. Yet there it was, spraying its flame and killing whatever the hell that thing was. A little coincidental that such a thing was here when needed, no? And I know that you know something about it, because the men practically said as much. Now, I want you to give me some straight answers for once and tell me just what the fuck is going on here.'

Calmly, Director Templeton rose to his feet and looked Reid directly in the eyes. 'No,' he said simply, and smiled. Then he turned to leave.

Yet again, Reid could not believe the audacity of the man.

'What do you mean, *no*? That isn't an acceptable answer,' Reid said.

'I'm afraid it's the only one you are getting,' Templeton shot back.

'Not good enough. If you don't explain this to me, then I'm leaving this place for good. You will be on your own here.'

'That seems fair,' Templeton said. 'I'm sure you will find a plethora of opportunities just waiting for you when you do. Best of luck for the future.'

'I want answers, Templeton!' Reid screamed.

Templeton reached the door to the room and turned back to face Reid. 'Then find them, Doctor. I am not stopping you.'

'Find them? Why not just tell me?'

'Because truths that are given and not earned are not really valued. What we are doing here is hard to accept. We are learning truths about the things that govern our reality, our very existence. Something that transcends your science.'

At this, Reid had a realisation. He looked around the room they were in, the one Templeton visited every morning, and then at the robes Templeton always wore.

'God,' Reid said. 'This is something to do with God, isn't it? What, you think you are somehow able to communicate with him?'

Templeton let out a loud laugh and shook his head. 'I'm afraid you haven't got it worked out just yet, Thomas. But keep looking. The truth will reveal itself to you, I have faith in that.'

And then he exited the room.

'Goddamn it!' Reid huffed.

His attempt to extract the truth from Templeton had left him feeling more confused than ever.

No answers, only more frustration.

Then he remembered what Templeton had told him about answers: *Find them. I am not stopping you.*

Fair enough, Reid thought to himself, intending to do just that.

8
————

ADRIAN AND HIS GROUP—JACK, Trevor, Sean, and Seymour —were all seated in the Communal Area yet again. It was a change to the four walls of his room, but was fast losing its appeal—every day the same cycle.

Rinse and repeat.

And while not usually an environment of fun or jubilance, it felt especially on edge this morning as the group discussed what they had heard the previous night.

Only it was different for Adrian—he hadn't just heard it, he had seen it. However, he'd decided not to divulge that fact and let them speculate on their own. After all, what good would it do to explain that a creature beyond their understanding decapitated an orderly and then devoured the severed head?

'I heard it, sounded like people were dying,' Sean said. 'What do you guys think it was?'

Jack wrapped his long arms around his chest and hung his head. The conversation, coupled with what he had no doubt heard last night, were clearly upsetting to him.

Adrian caught his attention and gave him a friendly smile. Jack noticed the gesture and returned it with one of his own.

His smiles always seemed sad, somehow.

'Someone got out,' Seymour answered, confident in his own assessment. 'Tried to escape. Can't say I blame them.'

If only they knew, thought Adrian.

He guessed that most of the patients in the ward would have been aware of the commotion that had taken place, but Adrian doubted any had witnessed what he'd seen. It was only through sheer chance—having his hatch knocked open—that he'd seen anything at all, and the violence that had unfolded stayed with him, replaying itself over and over in his mind.

The orderlies, too, looked different today. Usually, these men tried their very best to be intimidating and imposing—and if not, they showed outright indifference—but today they seemed... a little timid. When one especially agitated inmate started to act up, the orderlies were much slower in dealing with him than usual. Instead of instant action, they seemed hesitant, looking to one another for reassurance before diving in.

Adrian had to wonder if the thing from last night was still prowling around here somewhere. In truth, he was surprised that he and his fellow patients had been let out of their cells this morning, same time as usual. Surely if that thing were still on the loose, then they wouldn't have been allowed to out of their rooms, would they?

'I hate this place,' Sean said, once again picking at the angry red scabs on his arms. The man's body was dotted with sores, caused not by needles, but by the continual scratching of his skin, clawing at an itch that could seemingly never be sated. And he constantly fidgeted as well—his left knee always bouncing and his fingers constantly picking at something. Adrian had no idea how long it took someone to get through opium withdrawal, but Sean was deep within it and showing no signs of coming out of the other side. 'I've seen and heard some strange things in my time here, but nothing like that.'

'Could it just be that someone got free?' Trevor asked, with a quiet voice.

'Of course,' Seymour asserted, 'and caused himself a little trouble, I'd wager.'

'A little trouble?' Sean asked. 'Mild way of putting it. What I heard didn't sound like any man.'

'You'd be surprised at the sounds the mad can make.'

'The mad?' Trevor asked. 'You mean, people like us?'

'I ain't mad,' Seymour said, gritting his teeth. 'So don't lump me in with the rest of you.'

'I didn't mean that,' Trevor said, tentatively. 'It's just... aren't we all in here for the same reason?'

'No,' Seymour shot back. 'Most of us ain't in here by choice. I don't wait around and hope for some miracle that will never come, like you. I was taken and thrown in here against my fucking will. Ain't nothing wrong with me. And I'm sick of being stuck in this place with the rest of you crazies. You mark my words, I'm getting free of this shit-hole.'

A smile formed on Adrian's lips as he realised that Seymour was just as scared as the rest of them. The source of the large man's anger now made a little more sense to Adrian. It was fear. Getting angry was the only way he could deal with his situation.

Adrian felt a small sense of pride at connecting the dots.

In another life, maybe he could have been on the other side of the fence, helping people in need instead of being one of the infirmed.

'Something funny, boy?' Seymour asked, venom cutting through his voice.

Adrian stared at him, not wanting to back down, but not wanting to start any unnecessary trouble, either. He shook his head. 'No, nothing is funny.'

'Then what the fuck are you smiling at?'

'Nothing,' Adrian said.

Seymour was used to bullying the rest of the group, who would all fall in line when confronted, as Adrian had seen with Trevor. But Adrian was the new boy, and he got the feeling Seymour was still sizing him up, trying to figure out if he was a threat to Seymour's alpha-male status, or simply a follower like the others.

Then there was Jack, of course.

Seymour never bothered the giant, but then again Jack was always silent. However, Adrian got the impression the docile man was always listening.

'I don't believe you,' Seymour said, leaning forward and poking a fat finger into Adrian's chest. 'Now apologise, or I'll rip off your jaw.'

Adrian stayed silent at first, just wanting to defuse the whole situation. The orderlies may not be as quick to dive in today, but that didn't mean they would ignore this little exchange for long. 'If you keep this up, we're going to wind up in trouble,' he said.

'Then wind your neck in,' Seymour spat back, red-faced.

'Can we just leave it, before someone hears?' Trevor pleaded and looked around the room, nervously.

Seymour leaned back in his chair, but still looked furious.

'Apologise,' he said to Adrian.

Adrian cast a glance over to Trevor, who was looking back with pleading eyes. He then turned to Jack, who was still looking down to the floor with a sad, nervous expression. And Sean was pretending to ignore everything, instead concentrating on the sores on his arm, drawing blood as he picked at them.

Adrian took a deep breath, then exhaled. 'I'm sorry,' he said, slowly balling his hands into fists, an involuntary reaction that he hoped no one noticed.

Seymour's round face broke into a wide, self-satisfied grin, obviously pleased with the power he'd exerted over Adrian.

'Good,' he said. 'Just make sure it doesn't happen again, boy.'

Adrian turned away, seething inside. Seymour had bullied and belittled Adrian—embarrassed him and knocked him down—and Adrian hated it. Seymour had briefly instilled in him the same sense of worthlessness that his father used to on a constant basis.

And Adrian had to fight to keep the monster inside. He couldn't allow it to show itself again. Thankfully, the orderlies wheeled in the trays of food—dinner time. It would give him something to focus on other than strangling that fat fucker Seymour. Because he knew that giving in to those urges would be wrong.

He wouldn't be that person, he would not turn into his father.

So he let it lie.

For now.

9

BRIAN HODGSON HAD BEEN FOUND LIVING on the streets three years ago.

He was the mental age of a child, despite being forty-two. With no one to care for him, or care *about* him, he had been a prime candidate for Arlington Asylum.

And while the notes did not say exactly how he was brought in, Thomas Reid knew that if the man had any capacity to object, it would not have mattered. Reid set the notes down and observed his subject.

Brian was currently submerged in a tin bath, which was filled with ice-water up to his neck. He had been this way for over twenty minutes, with orderlies on hand to make sure he stayed inside the freezing-cold water. Brian was a docile man, however, so the chances of him disobeying instruction was doubtful.

His teeth chattered together as he drew breath, and Reid noted a blue tinge on his lips.

Reid had no confidence that this treatment would prove successful, but wanted to see it through regardless, just to satisfy his own curiosity.

That was one of the perks to Arlington Asylum—there were no restrictions over the treatments and therapies he performed, and he was given free rein to indulge his theories. Reid had worked in other facilities like this, and none in truth really cared for the patients they treated—looking at them as little more than objects to use for further study—but even those places had a chain of command and someone to answer to.

Not here, however.

Reid took out his pocket notebook and scribbled an entry, outlining the patient's progress.

Not that there was much to report.

He was cold.

Brian had never been a violent patient, and his mental capacity was something that, Reid felt, was just part of who he was now. Perhaps it was due to difficulties in the womb, or a problem at birth that had affected his brain development, but it was nothing that Reid thought could be fixed. Still, Reid was not pursuing this line of treatment to see an improvement in the patient—he was more interested in knowing just how much Brian could bear, and if his tolerance differed from patients with other afflictions. Did his docile state mean he would willingly accept more punishment—even holding out until it killed him—rather than complain or fight back?

'Keep him in for another twenty minutes,' Reid said to the orderlies. 'Then get him out and return him to his cell.'

Reid left the room and continued to the next.

Today was the day Reid was supposed to be trying his second-ever transorbital lobotomy, but last night's events, coupled with his lack of sleep and the non-productive talk with Director Templeton this morning, had meant he was not in the right frame of mind for something so important. So, he had postponed it.

Not that it mattered.

The patient wasn't aware of what was coming, so Reid didn't need to rearrange much.

His next stop on Ward A was to see Patrick Evans, a man who had to be kept in a restrictive jacket due to his insistence that his entire body was crawling with maggots and other insects. The state of his skin from scratching in an attempt to free himself of the imaginary bugs was disgusting: angry, red scars and cuts dominated his flesh. An earlier treatment Reid had sanctioned was to actually cover the man in bugs to see what he would do. The results were explosive, and he hit levels of frantic panic that Reid had rarely seen before. Since then, Patrick's default state of constant agitation was much higher than before that experiment. All in all, a rather pointless exercise.

Now Reid was trying a different method—a treatment that had, at best, mixed results. Again, Reid held out little hope of any success, but wanted to see it for himself.

He walked into the small dark room, hearing the screams of pain before he entered. A single light overhead shone down onto the bald, writhing man who was strapped into a high-backed wooden chair. Wires were connected to his naked, malnourished body, and they ran to a trolley-mounted control box to his side that an orderly was operating. With each twist of a knob on the panel, jolts of electricity were sent coursing into Patrick's body. He shook violently as another shock was administered, and Reid could see the veins in the man's scarred neck bulge out through the skin.

'Please,' Patrick begged, barely managing to strain the word out as his body locked up again.

This electroshock therapy had been administered inter-
mittently on him for over an hour. Reid again brought out
his notebook and jotted down what he saw. The real results
would come after the treatment, however, and Reid had
poor Patrick scheduled for two weeks of this, in three hour
stints every other day. If he survived, perhaps he would be a
changed man and be free of those bugs forever.

Reid stayed with the man for a little while longer,
watching his treatment and suffering with interest, but even
so it was a struggle to keep his mind focused today. There
was a constant, dull ache behind his eyes, and a terrible
headache was brewing that he knew would, in time, turn a
bad day worse.

The men under his charge, the orderlies who worked
and lived at Arlington Asylum, seemed off today. Or some of
them did. And he recognised that it was the ones that had
been present for the previous night's events with that...
thing who were not quite themselves.

The only one who seemed business-as-usual was Jones,
and to see him work, one would never imagine he had been
through such an ordeal as Reid had witnessed.

After confirming that the electroshock therapy was
progressing well, Reid left that room as well, then turned to
head to the next. Up ahead was a small cupboard used to
house cleaning equipment and some old medical tools that
were rarely ever used. Upon his approach to this cupboard,
Reid noticed that the inward-swinging door was ajar, and he
could hear voices within talking in hushed whispers.

Ordinarily, Reid would have no interest in the idle chit-
chat of others. He didn't care enough about their problems
to make it his business, but right now things were different.
Reid slowed his walking so that his steps were as silent as he
could make them, inched close to the side of the door

without revealing himself, and listened. He heard the voices of two people inside—orderlies, he assumed. And, from the sound of it, both had been present during the fantastical and gruesome events of the previous night.

'I tell you,' one said, 'they aren't in our control anymore.'

'Don't be ridiculous,' the other argued—his was a much deeper voice. 'This is why we are here.'

'To be killed?'

'If that is what is needed, then yes.'

'Your life means that little to you?' the first man argued.

'You know why we are here, and what we pledged ourselves to,' the second replied. 'Am I to take it that you are doubting your promise and your beliefs?'

'It's not that,' the first said. 'It's just-'

'It's just nothing,' the second man cut in. 'We all serve The Church, and therefore the director, too, while we are here. If you give me cause to doubt your devotion, then I will have to take this higher.'

'No, there is no need for that. It's just... last night I was terrified. Weren't you?'

'A little,' the second man admitted. 'But more so, I was excited.'

'Why?'

'Don't you get it? What we saw last night, and the other things we have seen here, it is all proof. Proof that validates everything we believe in. How can we doubt The Church now?'

'I... I guess,' the first man said.

'Keep your faith, brother, and all will be well. Now, let's go, I need to assist that idiot Dr. Reid today.'

'Do you think he will come to see the truth?'

'Perhaps. If not, then he may end up like his predecessor.'

'Or worse,' the first man said, with an actual hint of humour. They both chuckled.

Reid heard shuffling inside and decided he had heard enough. He spun on his heels and, as quickly as possible without making a sound, moved back down the corridor and rounded the corner. When he was out of sight, Reid leaned against the wall and tried to make sense of what he had just heard.

The Church? It did not sound like they were talking about any religion he was aware of.

And a predecessor?

If Reid hadn't felt in enough trouble after seeing that creature last night, it now seemed that this whole facility was wrapped up in something very strange.

Enough was enough, he was going to get to the bottom of it all.

And he was going to do it now.

10

───────

AFTER LUNCH—MORE grey slop that tasted of nothing—
Adrian was tempted to go back to his cell for the remainder
of the day, if only to keep away from Seymour. The fat man
seemed pleased to learn that Adrian, like the rest of the
group, would bend to his will, leaving him as the sole alpha
in charge.

'Worst thing about this place?' Seymour asked, to no one
in particular, just enjoying holding court. 'No women. Men
everywhere. Wall-to-wall cock. Man like me? He needs the
attention of a lady.'

Trevor winced at this. Adrian sensed this was not a
conversation the meek man wanted to have, and he knew it
was Trevor's relationship with a certain woman that had
landed him in Arlington Asylum in the first place.

'Sean?' Seymour said, keen to engage the rest of his little
flock. 'Do you know what I'm saying with this? You miss the
touch of a woman as well?'

Sean nodded but did not look up from his work—
peeling the skin from an angry sore on his arm.

'Come on, man, give me something back. What's your favourite thing to do with a woman?'

Sean just shrugged. 'Don't know.'

'What do you mean, you don't know? You must know. Their tits? Or do you go straight to the good stuff?'

Sean didn't answer.

'Have you even been with a woman, boy?' Seymour asked, clearly enjoying tormenting Sean and making everyone uncomfortable. Sean, again, did not answer.

'Don't tell me men are more your thing? Because that would explain why you are here. Is that it? You a fan of cock?'

Sean shook his head. 'No.'

'Good,' Seymour replied. 'So answer me. Tell me some of your conquests. We need to do something to pass the time here.'

'I don't want to, Seymour,' Sean said.

Seymour's eyes opened wide in realisation. 'You don't have any, do you?' He let out a big, full-on belly laugh, and Sean's face flushed. 'You've never even tasted a woman, have you? That is pitiful. Jesus, what is it with you? That poison you pump into your veins make you limp? Pathetic worm.' Seymour wiped a tear away from his eye. 'Unbelievable. Now, I'll tell you what really gets me going,' he said as he leaned in close and his voice took on a sinister tone. 'When she doesn't want it. She'll try to fight back, but that won't help her any. You just force it, you see. Split her in two. Nothing like that sense of power.'

He chuckled, and Adrian's already low opinion of the hideous man now dropped even farther. He felt a surge of anger grip him, and his thoughts were cast back to his mother, and the things she suffered at the hands of his father. When Adrian looked over to Seymour, that was who he saw.

The anger rose, and he knew he could not control it.

Then Trevor let out a chuckle.

'You like to talk, don't you, fat man?'

His voice was different from normal—though he was usually weak and timid, he now sounded... insidious.

And more feminine.

They all turned to face him and saw a dead, hollow smile on Trevor's face.

Adrian held his breath—it looked like Mother was here.

'Shit,' Sean muttered.

Trevor flipping personalities was the last thing they needed right now.

'Hello, boys,' Trevor said.

Adrian had seen this before, and he knew that Trevor was adopting the personality of the woman who had traumatised him so much in life. 'What have I missed?' Trevor asked.

No one said anything, not daring to make a sound. Trevor turned to Sean. 'How about you? Are you going to show some manners and answer me? Or are you thinking about when you can get your hands on more of that sweet opium? I have news for you, you pathetic worm, that ain't ever happening.'

Sean looked away, so Trevor instead turned to Jack. 'And you. Still with us, big fella? Or are you away with the fairies again?' Like Sean, Jack stayed silent, so Trevor turned to Seymour. 'And what about you, fat boy? Cat got your tongue? Care to tell us more of your stories of conquest and of the women you forced yourself onto?'

Seymour followed suit and said nothing, either. Usually so quick to anger, even he did not want to provoke what

Trevor had become. Adrian then noticed Trevor's gaze fall on him, just as an orderly walked over to them.

'Come on, Adrian, don't let me down. Someone here must be man enough to let me play with them? You're the worst of all, aren't you? Filthy little monster, just like your father. What do you say to that?'

Adrian wanted to say a lot, but he knew that Trevor, or this version of Trevor, was goading him, trying to provoke him into talking back. Because once you spoke back to Mother, that's when the trouble really started. So Adrian, like the rest, stayed silent.

'Pathetic,' Trevor said.

'What's going on here?' the orderly demanded, now standing beside them.

This was not going to end well.

'Well, who is this?' Trevor asked, turning to look up at the orderly.

'None of your fucking business,' the orderly replied. He was tall with black hair slicked over to one side. The man brought up his cosh under the jaw of Trevor. 'Understand?'

Trevor chuckled. 'Well, someone needs to learn some manners, don't they?'

And that was it.

Trevor leapt up out of his seat with frightening quickness and clung to the orderly like a lion tackling a gazelle. And, like a lion, Trevor bit down on the screaming orderly's face. They both tumbled to the ground in a heap as the noise level in the Communal Area rose—the outburst drawing almost everyone's attention. People gathered around as Trevor quickly got himself on top of the orderly and bit at his cheek, pulling away flesh. A tear that ran with blood formed in the skin. Trevor then dug a thumb into the unfortunate man's eye as his screams increased.

Trevor, meanwhile, just laughed manically as he went to work.

It didn't take long for other orderlies to arrive and intervene, violently pulling the attacking inmate from their co-worker. Trevor hit the floor, and they descended on him with a flurry of kicks, punches, and savage whacks from their coshes. Trevor continued to fight back, but was overwhelmed. He screamed profanities and insults until, eventually, he was beaten unconscious, lying in a pool of his own blood. Two orderlies grabbed Trevor and dragged his limp body away, as others helped their still-screaming colleague, who now had a chunk missing from his face, the teeth beneath visible through the ruined, bloodied flesh.

The other orderlies went to work on the inmates who had gathered, unleashing random attacks to push back the crowd. Whatever trepidation these men had been feeling earlier was now gone, washed away by this chance to unleash their frustrations.

Adrian took an elbow to the face during the melee, and it was powerful enough to snap his jaw shut and send him sprawling.

When he looked up, a brawl had broken out.

Well, maybe *brawl* was the wrong word. It was a one-sided beating, dished out by the men in white uniforms who overpowered anyone daring to stand against them.

Adrian got to his feet and stepped back, feeling himself bump into someone. He turned around to see Seymour.

'Watch where you're going, boy,' Seymour said. Adrian sensed an opportunity, hoping his actions would just get lost in the chaos.

Without thinking, he lashed out and swung his right fist, connecting with Seymour's jaw, which gave a satisfying crack. Seymour's eyes opened wide in surprise, and he took a few steps back.

That should have been enough. Adrian had paid Seymour back for the things he'd said earlier, for the way he'd made Adrian feel, but that one punch felt good.

Too good.

So, it was not the last. He swung again, lefts and rights, battering the staggering man about the head.

'You fucker,' Adrian said through gritted teeth. Seymour wailed like a pig.

'Stop,' he begged in a pathetic, high-pitched voice. 'Please.'

His begging only made things sweeter for Adrian, and he pushed Seymour to the ground. The fat man flailed on his back like a stuck pig.

Adrian dropped down on top of the other man and began striking him again as Seymour tried to cover his face. Each blow was further release of the pent-up rage and misery that had been building inside.

It was a purging.

And it felt exquisite.

The idea that this was wrong, and that Adrian was descending into the kind of behaviour that had defined his father, soon registered in his mind. Upon realising what he was doing, and *who* he was becoming, Adrian stopped. Just as he did, he felt himself pulled away and thrown to the hard, tiled floor. He looked up to see three orderlies surround him and instinctively prepared himself for a beating.

He was not disappointed.

Like Trevor before him, Adrian was kicked, punched, and struck with the brutal coshes. Pain bloomed in his ribs and the side of his head as the blows continued.

Adrian did not fight back—knowing that path would only lead to more pain.

The chaos continued until, eventually, all the patients in the room were subdued, and they huddled together in fear of more retribution.

Adrian was hoisted up, barely conscious, and dragged from the room. Just as he reached the door, the two orderlies that were carrying him stopped. Adrian lifted his head, painful though it was, and saw someone blocking the way.

Jones.

'I'll take him,' Jones said, curling his top lip. 'The rest of you restore some fucking order in here.'

'Yes, sir,' one orderly said.

Jones leant in closer to Adrian. 'Take it you've been causing a bit of trouble, have you? Gonna make sure you learn never to do that again.' He then crouched down farther and, in one swift, powerful motion, hoisted Adrian up on to his shoulder with such ease it made Adrian feel like a child.

He then left the room, Adrian slung over his shoulder like a sack of meat.

'You're in for a world of trouble, now,' Jones said, with no small amount of glee in his voice.

11

ADRIAN WAS CARRIED from Ward B, through the Main Hall, and into a place he had heard of but was unfamiliar with— all the while draped over the shoulder of the large orderly. His view was obstructed by the form of Jones as Adrian hung upside down, dangling behind the man's back. Adrian had to turn his head to the side to see anything of the passing scenery.

He knew he was heading to isolation. Like so many other areas of the building, the walls here were tiled up to head height, this time a dull-white, before bare plaster took over up to the high, arched ceilings. The floor added a little more flavour to the decor with interlocking, diamond-shaped, cream and burgundy tiles. Adrian's head already spinning from the beating he'd taken, and the pattern of the floor only served to increase his nausea, so he closed his eyes until Jones stopped walking.

They had reached their destination.

Jones opened a blank door with a closed viewing hatch and tossed Adrian inside like a sack of discarded meat. Thankfully, the floor was soft, and as he fell into it, Adrian realised it was padded, as were the walls. A single bright bulb overhead illuminated the area with a sharp light that spilled down the white padding to the walls that were streaked with yellow and dark brown stains. Adrian also noted that the room had a foul, sour smell to it.

Jones entered and pulled the door closed, sealing them both inside.

'Your friend is next door,' he said, nodding his head to the left-hand wall of the room. 'The one that thinks he's a woman. He ain't awake yet, but when he comes to, I'll take pleasure in giving him a good going over. But, until then...'

Jones then took a heavy step forward and grabbed Adrian by the throat, heaving him to his feet. Adrian again braced himself for whatever pain was about to come and, even though Jones was only one man, the power and ferocity of his first punch was a shock. As the punch crashed against his cheek, Adrian felt a split form in his gum as a tooth dislodged. A sharp pain spread through his jawbone, and Adrian let out a cry as his vision spun.

Another punch, this one to his gut, winded Adrian, and he bent double and coughed as he struggled to regain his breath. Jones released his hold on Adrian's throat and allowed him to drop to his knees.

'Now, I need you to remember the pain you are feeling,' Jones said in his deep, gravelly voice. 'See, I can't have people acting up in here. We need to maintain order so that the masses fall in line. And do you know the best way to maintain order?'

Adrian let out another cry as Jones stepped down atop his left hand, which was splayed flat on the floor. The bone of Adrian's knuckle was pinned in an agonising position beneath the heavy boot of the orderly.

'By making sure people like you know what the punishment is for stepping out of line. I want you to tell your friends about what is happening to you here today. I want you to tell them every detail. Then, maybe, little outbreaks like the one we had today will not happen.'

Jones reached down and pulled Adrian to his feet, bringing them both face to face. Adrian swayed unsteady in the man's grip.

'But if not, then I'm still happy. And I'll let you in on a little secret as to why...'

He pulled Adrian in close, and Adrian felt Jones' breath on his ear as the orderly whispered to him.

'Because I really, really enjoy doing this.'

Two large hands suddenly gripped the sides of Adrian's head as Jones unleashed a savage headbutt to the bridge of Adrian's nose.

He heard an audible crack and agony erupted all over his face.

'Stop,' Adrian pleaded, feeling blood flow from his nostrils and over his lips. The pain continued to grow and throb. 'Please.'

Jones just laughed. 'Oh, I don't think that is going to happen, inmate. We just started, and I'm just getting warmed up. Feel free to fight back if you think it will help.'

Jones then threw Adrian to the floor and swung a hard kick into his ribs. Arian screamed out again before the sole of Jones' boot found its way down onto Adrian's throat, pushing down and cutting off his air.

Yet again, Adrian was beaten down and belittled.

When Seymour had done it earlier, Adrian had managed to get some measure of revenge. But here, with Jones, that just wasn't going to happen. He was forced to take whatever was coming to him.

Just like he did as a child whenever his father came home—sometimes drunk, sometimes sober.

Always violent.

Adrian hated it—the feeling of helplessness, of not being able to stand up for himself and fight back. Of being forced to accept what was thrust upon him.

'I...' Adrian wheezed, 'want to speak with—'

But then Jones pressed his foot down harder, cutting Adrian off.

'Speak to who?' Jones asked with a sneer. 'Sorry, I can't make out what you're saying. Make yourself clear, inmate. Enunciate.'

He laughed at himself and kept the pressure up. Adrian's throat felt like it was about to collapse beneath the weight, and the sides and ridges of the boot sole scratched and scraped at his skin.

'Director,' Adrian forced out. 'Speak... with... Director... Templeton.'

Jones laughed again. 'Afraid you don't get to make orders like that. You don't get to decide when the director will listen to you. Understand?'

Adrian then croaked out one more word, hoping it would be enough.

'Monster.'

The weight eased ever so slightly as Jones' expression changed. His eyes narrowed, and his brow furrowed.

'What did you say?'

'Monster,' Adrian choked out, finding it a little easier to speak now that Jones' foot had lifted a little. 'Last night.'

The foot removed itself completely, and Jones squatted down over him.

'And what do you think you know?'

Adrian took deep, painful breaths between his words as he replied. 'In the corridor. A monster.'

'Monster?' Jones sneered. 'I think your faculties are slipping, inmate. Fortunately, you are in the best place for that.'

Adrian shook his head. 'No. I know what happened. And I want to talk to the director.'

Jones also shook his head. 'Ain't going to happen,' he said. 'No reason for it. You've nothing of any importance to say.'

Adrian narrowed his eyes and lifted his head, trying to sound as serious and assertive as he could, given his position on the floor. 'I saw it,' he said. 'I saw that monster, and I saw what it did to those men. And... I know who it was before it changed. Now get the director, otherwise, I tell everyone in here what I saw. Think you can keep order if the patients believe vicious creatures are roaming the halls?'

Jones bent down and grabbed hold of Adrian's throat. 'You pathetic fuck,' he said with a snarl and genuine anger in his voice. 'You don't issue the orders here.'

Adrian shrugged. 'Then you have a choice to make. Keep me in here for good. Kill me. Or get the director. If not, I go back and shout about what I know.'

Jones punched Adrian again, driving his massive fist down into Adrian's chest, almost cracking the chest bone. But, while Adrian rolled around in agony, Jones left the room.

It seemed Adrian would get his audience with Director Templeton after all.

Not that that he had any idea what he was going to say.

12

REID SAT IN HIS OFFICE, pretending to work on reports in solitude, but instead paying close attention to the corridor outside. The wooden door to his room had a pane of glass across the top half, allowing a clear view into the hallway. If he stood close to the door, he would be able to see Templeton's office farther down the hall. But right now, he knew that Templeton was in his office, so he had to wait for his opportunity to act.

Reid heard footsteps outside again and saw the large brute Jones come storming past his door.

The man looked angry, more so than usual. Reid got to his feet and approached one of his bookcases, angling himself so that he could see through the pane of glass in the door. From this position, he watched as Jones walked up to Templeton's office and banged on the door. Templeton appeared, and the two spoke. Jones seemed to be agitated, gesturing animatedly with his hands. However, they were too far away for Reid to hear anything of what was said.

Not that it mattered.

Reid just wanted Templeton out of his office for a while.

He had studied the director's movements that morning, trying to find any pattern to his behaviour that would leave his office abandoned for a period of time. If no opportunity presented itself today, that meant waiting until the following morning when the director spent time in the Chapel.

The man had left his office a few times over the course of the day, but locked it each time, so Reid was also trying to formulate a way to get his key.

Or a spare.

But one way or another, he was going to get inside of that office, and he would find the answers that Templeton was so reluctant to give.

Reid continued to watch as Templeton finally stepped from his office and pulled the door closed behind him, then followed Jones back down the hallway.

However, Reid noted that Templeton did not lock the door behind him. Reid buried his head in a book, making a show of studying the words within as the two men passed his office. As Reid glanced up, Templeton gave him an unreadable look as he went by, and Reid found himself nodding in acknowledgement. It seemed the natural thing to do.

Soon, both Jones and Templeton turned a corner up ahead and were out of sight. Reid had no idea how much time he had to work with, but he knew it wouldn't be long.

He knew he had to act quickly.

Reid jogged from his room, not bothering to lock his door, either, and ran down the empty corridor to Templeton's office. He quickly glanced around, to make absolutely sure no one was present, then opened the door and stepped inside.

Director Templeton's office was much different than his own. For one, it was larger, which did not surprise Reid too much. But the other significant difference was just how tidy and ordered everything was.

His sleek oak desk had on it only an open ledger and a selection of pens, all lined up neatly. A stained oak chair with leather padding was tucked under the desk, and the books in the cases around the room were all organised in alphabetical order, rather than jammed into any spare space as most of the paraphernalia on Reid's shelves were. Oak dominated the room—not only the desk and chair, but also the full-height wood panelling on the walls. Even the bookcases were built from good, sturdy timber.

The office also smelled of incense, reminding Reid of the Chapel, and he saw a single, wall-mounted candle on the far side of the room, beside a tall window that was positioned centrally. Outside, Reid could see the grounds run up to a high stone wall that closed the facility off from the outside world. A thick rug lay beneath the desk and chair, plush red, leaving the rest of the wooden floorboards beyond it exposed.

But Reid did not have time to dwell on the details—he was here for a reason.

He ran around to the other side of the desk, to the ledger that was practically begging to be read.

It was filled with reports on the facility's day-to-day activities. Quickly flicking through the pages, Reid searched for something of note—anything out of the ordinary, or some reference to the mysterious substance Templeton was administering to the patients of the asylum. However, other than a few brief notes about how much of it was to be administered, he could see nothing that gave him anything to go on. Perhaps if he had time to study the ledger in more detail, he could find more.

But time was short.

Reid next looked at the desk drawers, but found them locked, much to his frustration. However, surely that meant there was something inside worth seeing?

He continued looking and realised that many of the books that lined the shelves were not medical but, strangely, tomes on the occult and strange practices. Not the sort of thing one would expect to find in the office of a religious man who ran a mental facility.

Then again, it was not the sort of place one would expect to find an actual monster, either.

As Reid took a step toward the bookshelves, he felt a floorboard beneath the thick rug sink a little under his weight. It might have been nothing but a loose board, or it could be something more.

He quickly pulled the carpet back and saw that one of the boards beneath was a slightly different colour than the others. And, where the others were nailed down, this one was loose. Digging his fingers around the edges of the cold wood, Reid soon managed to tilt the board up, revealing a small, dark hole beneath.

And there, sitting in the hole, was a small, shiny key.

Secrets upon secrets.

Reid grabbed the key, already having an idea as to what it opened. He put it into the lock on the desk drawers and, as expected, it released.

With no small measure of excitement and nervous energy, Reid dug through the drawers. He found many folders, and in one Reid saw records of written correspondence between Director Templeton and someone named Kane Ainsworth. There was also, in the shallow top drawer, a thick black pocketbook. Reid flicked through it, noticing the dates and neat handwriting within, and realised it was a diary.

The private diary of Director Templeton.

He knew he had something to go on here and weighed up his next move. Did he stay here and look through as much as he could? That came with the very real risk of Templeton walking in on him, especially as Reid had no idea how long the director would be. The other option was to take something with him—steal it to review later when he had more time and privacy.

That seemed the most sensible idea, so he stuffed the diary into his jacket's hidden pocket that was cut into the lining.

He considered taking some of the folders as well, but they were larger and more difficult to conceal. If he ran into anyone on his way back to his office, he would not be able to hide what he was carrying.

So he shut the drawers, leaving the folders where they were.

For now.

Hopefully, the diary would shed a little more light on things for him. Working quickly, Reid locked the drawers and placed the key back beneath the floorboard where he had found it. He flattened out the rug and made sure the chair was back in its correct place, the legs finding the corresponding indentations in the carpet fibres, and quickly strode to the door and looked out.

Much to his relief, there was no one around.

Reid then slipped from the room and pulled the door closed behind him. A brisk, uninterrupted walk back down the corridor saw him reach the safety of his own office without discovery. Once inside, and with the door securely locked, he allowed himself a moment to bring his nerves under control. Thieving and sneaking around in the shadows was not his forte—he was a doctor, after all—

though he could not help but feel a little delight at his success.

Reid then walked over to his chair and let himself fall into it. He pulled the diary free and looked at the cracked leather of its cover.

'Now, Director Templeton,' Reid said to himself, 'let's find those answers you were talking about, shall we?'

13

WHILE WAITING for Director Templeton to show, Adrian took stock of his injuries; he ached everywhere, and suffered acute pain in his chest, ribs, and even his jaw. He dug a finger into his mouth and touched his teeth, feeling that one rear molar had come loose. When he brought the digit back out again, it glistened red, coated in blood.

Not long after his arrival, Adrian had resigned himself to seeing out his days in Arlington Asylum—suffering in this hell. Existing here was not a pleasant experience, as days seemed to mix in with each other, becoming one long, monotonous cycle of stupefying misery. But he was, in a macabre kind of way, comfortable with that.

He deserved it.

But now, given what had happened recently, he had to consider if that sentiment still rang true.

He was, after all, here of his own volition, and he wondered what the director would say if he decided that he wanted to be set free.

Adrian cast his mind back to his first meeting with

Director Templeton—a moment when Adrian was about to do something rather drastic.

AFTER FILLING his belly with booze, using the last of his money, Adrian took himself down a dark alley in the bustling, uncaring city. The public house he had come from was a place for the lower echelons of society to gather, but with its roaring fire and friendly chatter it was at least a warm place. What he needed now, however, was somewhere cold and forgotten. Somewhere he could bleed out from this world, unnoticed. With a blade tucked into his hand, he found a suitable narrow alleyway, which was dark and secluded—perfect for his needs. His body would probably remain there for a few days, unfound, but this dirty, cobbled corner of the earth was as good a resting place as any for him.

Adrian walked far enough into the alley that no one passing by the main street would be able to see him. He leaned against the cold brick wall, slid down to his rear, and pulled free the blade from the shaving knife—dull and rusty as it was. He put it to his wrist and took a breath as he prepared to slice.

'Things really that bad?' a voice said.

Adrian pulled the blade away and spun his head, instantly embarrassed at getting caught in the act. He was confused as to exactly why it embarrassed him, but he quickly folded the blade away and tucked it into the pocket of his old, worn coat.

'Who's there?' Adrian asked, struggling not to slur his words with the amount of alcohol that swam in his system. He squinted into the darkness to see the silhouette of an approaching figure coming towards him from the main street.

'Don't be alarmed,' the well-spoken man said. 'But I see a chap disappear into a dark alley, holding an ill-concealed blade in his hand, and I have to worry about what his intentions are. I

didn't see you follow anyone down here, so I assume you plan to do something rather foolish to yourself. Am I correct?'

'Leave me alone,' Adrian replied, in no mood for discussion. He just wanted to be left in peace to slice his wrists open and bleed out on the ground.

'Oh, come now,' the mystery person said. 'What sort of man would I be if I did that? I have a feeling you are in need of help. Let me guess, down on your luck?'

Adrian just shook his head as the man came closer, stepping out of the shadows. He was advanced in years, with grey hair and a friendly face. He wore a thick coat, and Adrian could make out dark robes beneath. 'What would you know?' Adrian asked.

'More than you think, actually,' the man said. His voice was friendly, almost chipper. 'You could say I'm an expert in this field.'

'An expert in misery?' Adrian asked, not bothering to hide the sarcastic tone in his voice.

'You could say that, yes.' The man walked up to Adrian and squatted down before him. He gave Adrian a smile, one that attempted to be warm, friendly, and understanding. However, Adrian sensed the kind expression was rather rehearsed and not quite genuine. 'I work with people who are suffering, people with nowhere else to turn. People like you.'

'You don't know me,' Adrian said. 'You don't know anything about me.'

'Well, that is only partly true. But I know you are suffering. A man tries to take his life in an isolated, miserable place like this alley? That tells me you are also alone in life. It tells me you have no one to turn to. Hence, you feel this is the only way out.'

'It is the only way out,' Adrian said. 'It's what I deserve.'

'No,' the man said, firmly. 'It isn't. You only think it is. And you only think that because you can't see any other options. But there are options, my friend. There are people out there who can and will help you.'

'People like you, I assume?' Adrian asked, and then he looked closer at the strange man and saw a white collar beneath his coat.

'Indeed,' the man replied. 'I appreciate that you will be skeptical of what I'm about to tell you, but I would ask you to hear me out. In my work I deal with misery and mental disorders on a daily basis. I help people who are suffering from... how should I put this... non-physical ailments? And I have developed a medicine that is, if I may say so, ahead of its time. It is showing results that many doctors around the world have only dreamed of achieving. And it is actually making people better, I tell you.'

'Wait, aren't you a priest or something?' Adrian asked, pointing to the collar. 'I've never heard of priests developing medicines.'

'Well, now you have,' the man said. 'And this medicine can work for you. It can make you better.'

'I don't want to be made better,' Adrian insisted. 'I want to be left alone.'

'I don't believe that,' the man said. 'I don't believe you've done anything so bad that you don't deserve a second chance.'

'You don't know what I've done.'

'Not yet, but I will soon enough, I'd wager. And I guarantee that no matter what it is that you think is so heinous, I will have heard worse. And I promise you, I have cured people who have done worse. You don't have to suffer with this guilt.'

Adrian studied the man's face, looking for some hint that would give him away, reveal the lie, but he seemed serious and genuine.

'Come on,' the man pressed. 'Considering what you were about to do, what do you have to lose?'

That struck a chord with Adrian. After a long moment of silence, he answered. 'Nothing, I suppose.'

'Indeed,' the man replied. 'You come with me and you have a chance at a better life. If I fail in what I'm offering, then you are *free to walk away and, should you still want to, end things as you wish. In fact, I could probably offer something that would not hurt as much as what you were planning. It would be like dropping off into a deep sleep.'*

Adrian shook his head, confused. 'Just what kind of priest are you?'

The man held out his hand. 'One offering you help,' he said.

Adrian didn't shake, not straight away; instead he rolled the offer over in his mind.

Could it be possible? A way out from his misery?

Did he even deserve that?

Eventually, Adrian took the hand.

'You won't regret this,' the man said with a grin. 'And allow me to introduce myself. My name is Isaac Templeton.'

'Adrian James,' Adrian told him as they shook.

Mr. Templeton widened his smile.

After that, Adrian left the alleyway with his new acquaintance and was taken to a facility—an asylum—just outside of the city, tucked away in a large, wooded area.

And so began his stay.

During his first consultation with Templeton—in the facility's Chapel, rather than the director's office—Adrian learned that Templeton was the director of the asylum and that everyone here reported to him. Of all the people who could have found him in that alleyway, it just so happened to be this man.

Was that luck, or something more? Could it be that fate had handed Adrian a second chance?

However, it didn't take Adrian long to detect that there was something very wrong with the people in the asylum. That was obvious of the other patients, but it also held true of the staff.

After his first few days it became clear that all was not as it seemed, and he seriously doubted that Director Templeton's promises would come to fruition.

But then again, it did not concern him too much. This place would offer him a miserable existence, which was exactly what he deserved.

'MY ASSOCIATE here tells me that you wish to speak to me, Adrian?' Director Templeton asked.

With Jones behind him, the director looked down at Adrian from the doorway of the isolation room, but without the normal expression of warmth that he had held in past meetings between the two. Nor did he look shocked at the bloody and beaten state Adrian was in.

'Yes,' Adrian said, still nursing his jaw.

'He tells me you have something to say about last night?' the director went on, then cocked his head to one side. 'What could you possibly have to tell me that is so interesting, I wonder?'

'I'm sure you already have an idea,' Adrian said. 'There was an attack in my ward last night. Happened right outside of my room.'

'Is that so?' the director asked, clearly acting coy.

'It is. And during that attack, the hatch on my door was knocked open. And do you know what I saw when I looked out?'

'Enlighten me,' the director said, taking a step inside the room. Jones grabbed his arm.

'Director, I'd rather you—'

'It's quite all right, Mr. Jones,' Director Templeton said, giving a nonchalant wave of his hand. 'I do not think Adrian here intends to try anything stupid.' He then turned back to Adrian. 'Do you?'

Adrian shook his head. 'No. I don't want to cause any trouble.'

'You are here for a reason, inmate,' Jones said. 'Attacking another patient is not something we tolerate.'

'Is that right?' the director asked with a smile. 'Is that what happened?'

Adrian looked away. 'I guess so.'

'Interesting. I don't recall you being violent in here before. Did something happen?'

'It doesn't matter,' Adrian said.

'I think it does,' the director replied. 'It matters very much. I wonder what caused you to regress. To become the monster that you are trying so hard to outrun.'

'I think you are focusing on the wrong thing,' Adrian said. 'I saw exactly what was loose in the halls last night. And I saw it pull the head from the body of one of your men.'

Director Templeton chuckled. 'I'm sorry, Adrian, but it sounds like the medication has been giving you some rather vivid dreams. But you were aware that this could be a side effect. Quite frankly, I'm surprised you have let it confuse you so.'

Adrian shook his head. 'This wasn't a dream. I was as awake as I am now. And I know what I saw.'

'I'm afraid you are mistaken. I can say for certain that there are no monsters running around our asylum, Adrian. If there were, would today just carry on as normal around here? Come on, my friend, just think about what you are saying.'

'Where's Malcolm?' Adrian asked. 'I haven't seen him today.'

'He has been moved,' Director Templeton said, without skipping a beat. 'Unfortunately, his condition was worsening, so we needed to relocate him to a ward where we could pay closer attention to him.

'I don't believe you,' Adrian said.

Director Templeton simply shrugged. 'Whether you do or do not is of no consequence. But I am telling you the truth. Now, are we finished here? I have a lot to do today.'

Adrian paused for a moment before asking the question that was playing on his mind. 'I came here of my own free will. What if I said I wanted to leave?'

'Leave? The facility?'

Adrian nodded. 'Yes.'

'Is this a hypothetical question, or do you actually want to throw away the progress you have made?'

'I'm not certain,' Adrian said, honestly.

'Either way, the answer remains the same. Given your recent, violent outburst, I do not believe I could release you in good conscience. I believe you would be a danger to others. So, your request would be declined.'

Adrian had expected that answer. 'You would keep me here against my will?'

'Until you are better, yes,' the director said. 'Speaking of which, I think it would be a good idea to step up our efforts with you. We will administer more medicine tomorrow, and at a much higher dosage.' He paused, before adding, 'And I expect to see great results. But for now, I must be on my way. You can spend a little more time in here thinking on your actions, Mr. James.'

With that, Director Templeton turned and left the room. He stopped next to Jones and addressed the man while looking back at Adrian.

'Come along, Mr. Jones,' the director said. 'I wish to discuss something with you.'

The door to the isolation room was closed and locked, leaving Adrian alone.

In truth, ever since he had first set foot into Arlington Asylum, Adrian had suspected that he would never be allowed to leave. There was something off here, but at the time he honestly hadn't cared.

But now, after what he witnessed the previous night, and hearing Director Templeton actually confirm his suspicions, Adrian was conflicted.

Any illusion of free will that he had been subconsciously holding onto was now shattered. He was a prisoner here.

And he would die here.

14

DIRECTOR TEMPLETON'S diary was a find indeed.

It started at the turn of that year, 1954, on the eighth of February, and from the way it was written Reid guessed that earlier records were in previous diaries. In the first entry, the asylum was in full operation, and it made mention of a head physician—one Christopher Vine.

8TH FEBRUARY 1954

Things are progressing well here. My one concern is Mr. Vine. Whilst his knowledge in his field seems second to none, he is a somewhat ethical man, which means pushing our patients to their limits is difficult with his involvement. Still, he is proving useful in helping us develop our methods, and it is thanks to him that we will soon be able to administer the substance to patients in a more efficient manner than ingestion. Of course, he would not have divulged the information needed if he knew our intentions, but I was able to coerce out of him the best way to efficiently administer a foreign liquid into a person's bloodstream without causing unforeseen complications.

He is also training my brothers who accompany me on my mission here at Arlington Asylum on this method, thinking it would be used for blood transfusions. Though perhaps that isn't too far from the truth.

As helpful as he has been, I fear his moral compass may provide a problem in the near future if we are not able to make him see and believe in what we are trying to achieve.

That would be no small feat, as I remember my own reluctance in accepting the truth—such was my ingrained and short-sighted way of thinking. I thought I knew for certain how the world, and beyond, should exist.

Still, for the short term, we shall carry on as we are.

REID CONTINUED to thumb through the diary, looking for passages in the immaculate hand-writing that could be of interest. It was not an easy task, as time was against him— given it was still the middle of the day—and he had work to be getting on with. Not only that, Templeton would likely be returning to his office shortly and, while Reid had no intention of returning the diary any time soon, if the director discovered it was gone, Reid imagined he would be one of the first people questioned about its disappearance.

He was prepared to lie his way through this, of course, and planned to keep the diary with him and read more tonight, hopefully undisturbed; but for now, he felt an urge to discover as much as he could in the short space of time he had.

A number of names popped up throughout the various passages, and the former head physician was a constant presence. However, there was another that was mentioned a number of times.

Robert Wilson.

15TH FEBRUARY 1954

I paid a visit to my old friend Robert today.

Sharing the same space as him is always a sombre, wondrous, and even frightening experience. To be in the presence of such a being, in whatever incarnation this could be classified, never fails to instill in me a sense of awe and a feeling of insignificance when compared to the entities and intelligences we now know to exist somewhere beyond our understanding.

Oh, what it must be like to exist as such a being, to know what they know. Secrets and truths about the order of things that we, lowly creatures as we are, can scarcely comprehend.

One even wonders if perhaps, just perhaps, ascension is possible for us. My initial thoughts were that the notion was nothing more than fanciful hopes and dreams, but recently I have not been as convinced of that.

There may yet be a way. Not to worship a god, but to exist as one.

And I often wonder what happened to my good friend Robert Wilson. Where is his soul now? And what wonders does he behold?

TO REID, the diary entries sounded like the ravings of a madman—or a religious zealot, which to him was the same thing.

During his conversation with Templeton, he had guessed that the director's motives were in some way related to God, but after reading the entries, he no longer believed that to be the case. Templeton spoke of things—beings, he called them—that could perhaps be conceived as gods, but not the God that a Catholic or Christian priest would worship. Regardless, it was all nonsense, but Reid was concerned that such fanciful notions were the very reason this facility seemed to be in operation.

There was also mention of a church—and again, this church was not one that Reid was familiar with. It seemed to be the organisation behind the asylum.

This facility was the church's operation, and Templeton was the one heading it up.

04TH MARCH 1954

The Church has given me instructions to progress things, as demanded by the Great Ailing One. We are to administer more doses of what we have collected to the inmates here.

The results should be... interesting.

Dr. Vine is also becoming more of a problem. I had hoped to bring him into the fold, into our family, but I fear his mind is not open to new possibilities. And he would, no doubt, strongly object to the real work we need to carry out here. Things will come to a head soon.

For his own sake, I hope he can see the potential before him.

REID THUMBED through further and eventually found the entry he was looking for.

29TH MARCH 1954

It is done.

Unfortunately, Dr. Vine could not accept the truth and would not be swayed, as I feared, so we had no choice but to act. Still, his expertise will be missed, and we will need to consider replacing him as soon as possible. While we will be able to cover up his death relatively easily, I think the next successful applicant would need to be someone with fewer connections to the outside world. And someone who is a little more willing to push the boundaries in the treatments they develop.

I shall begin my search. In the meantime, we will continue administering the medicine to selected patients.

The discoveries we have made in such a short amount of time have been remarkable.

REID WOULD HAVE CONTINUED READING MORE if he had not heard approaching voices outside of his office. He quickly slipped the diary into his desk drawer and picked up a file from his desk. He opened it up and looked at the scrawled notes on the page, feigning interest.

In his peripheral vision, he saw Jones and Director Templeton pass by his door, stopping just outside. As the two talked, the director cast a look inside at Reid.

Templeton seemed a different person to him now.

Before, he was merely an old fool. A man who followed a make-believe god and had found himself in a position that was beyond him. Someone Reid was using as a stepping stone to move on to greater things. He had been a man Reid could simply manipulate and deal with until he was ready to leave Arlington Asylum behind.

But now?

Now Reid knew that Templeton was something else entirely. True, he still believed in the fantastic and the impossible—though the creature from the night before was testing Reid's conviction on that—but Templeton was also backed by this strange group, or organisation, which held the same beliefs. Also, it would seem that most, if not all, of the staff here were members of the same... cult.

And to top it all off, this diary strongly implied that Reid's predecessor had met an untimely end, and that Templeton was responsible.

Whether he had carried out the act himself or not, Templeton had the power to decide who lived and died here —patients and staff alike. And that was a terrifying thought.

Jones and Templeton finished their conversation, and Jones strode away, leaving Templeton alone. He looked inside Reid's office again and gave Reid a smile and a wave.

Reid felt a knot form in his stomach.

He gave a quick courtesy wave in return, and the director headed back to his office.

Suddenly, Dr. Thomas Reid felt like he was living on borrowed time.

15

A LOUD KNOCK on the door of the isolation room pulled Adrian from his thoughts.

'Stand away from the door,' a voice yelled, though it was muffled by the thick iron. An audible click sounded before the heavy door swung open. Three orderlies stood outside, one of them Adrian recognised as Duckworth.

Thankfully, Jones was not among them.

'Get up,' Duckworth said, brandishing his cosh.

Adrian did as instructed, though his movements were laboured and lethargic due to the pain that radiated throughout his body. His jaw still ached with every slight movement, and a sharp, stabbing pain continued in his ribs.

When he got to his feet, two of the orderlies swooped into the room, and each took hold of an arm. As they restrained him and jostled his body, another jolt of searing agony erupted in his sides. Duckworth remained at the door, overseeing proceedings.

'Don't try anything, understand?' he said. Adrian just nodded in response, feeling beaten and broken. 'Good, now let's go.'

The other two orderlies pulled him forward, and he followed without resistance. Adrian barely registered the trip back to Ward B, instead lost in his thoughts, struggling with his internal conflict.

Did he really want to remain here at the asylum any longer? Was his need for punishment that great?

Adrian had no idea how it was possible, but he knew in his gut that what he had seen was real, despite Templeton's assertions to the contrary. And, if Adrian remained here, he knew that he, too, would eventually end up like Malcolm, which was an irony in itself.

He was desperate not to become his father—a monster —and he had come here in the hope of avoiding that fate. And yet that was literally what he could soon become—a monster.

He remembered the sound the creature had made.

That laugh.

Maybe becoming something like that was fitting for him, but he dreaded to think of what his poor mother would have made of that.

Not that she wouldn't have hated him already, of course.

After Adrian was dragged through the Main Hall, where the workers at their desks barely looked up at him, Adrian was then pushed through into the corridor of his ward and released.

'Keep your nose clean, inmate,' Duckworth said to him before the secure door was closed in his face.

With nothing else to do, Adrian ambled back towards his room.

16

'TRY TO RELAX,' Reid said to David Readman, who lay on a stainless-steel table that came up to Reid's midsection. He was standing at its head so that he could look down at the face of his young patient.

David solemnly nodded, knowing something was going to happen that would change things forever. Reid hadn't outlined to David what he was planning to do, feeling there was little need in worrying the patient unnecessarily. David had been strapped down with leather restraints across his chest, waist, and legs to ensure he did not try to lash out and make things more difficult than they needed to be.

Reid had postponed the procedure once already and, truth be told, wasn't exactly feeling like himself today, either, so had considered delaying it again. After all, his plan of using Arlington Asylum as a stepping stone to propel him on to greater things now looked like a miscalculation. He didn't think he would be allowed to leave this place. Not alive, anyway.

But then again, he had to keep himself occupied, and

finally succeeding with this procedure was as good a use of his time as anything.

Two orderlies were present with him in the room, watching Reid as he prepped himself. Normally, he would have paid their presence no mind, but now that he knew they were all wrapped up in the same cult—if that's what it was—it made them more difficult to ignore.

The small room was barely big enough to fit them all in, especially with the table that held David Readman. The walls were bare, and there was a single, barred window on the back wall. Fortunately, the light given by the fitting in the ceiling was generous, and that was important for the procedure Reid was about to carry out.

Come on, concentrate, Reid said to himself. This was important to him, a chance at redemption. Whatever trouble lay ahead with Templeton could wait. He needed to be in the *here* and *now*.

Reid turned to the instrument table at his side; it contained only two objects, a mallet and a pick, both made from lightweight metal. He took them both in his hands and turned back to David.

The young boy's eyes were wide with fear and, for a moment, Reid could have sworn he was looking into the eyes of Elton Breyer, the person he'd tried this on before.

The boy who had died.

'Everything will be all right,' Reid said in as comforting a tone as he could muster. He then lifted the pick and brought it slowly down towards the inside corner of David's eye. For his part, young Mr. Readman was able to hold himself together quite well, despite his obvious worry. And especially considering he had no choice but to watch the sharp point of the spear-like object as it dropped towards his eyeball.

Reid heard the young man give out a whimper, and he felt the pick make contact. Reid then raised the mallet and braced himself.

This was it.

'Please,' David begged. 'Don't.'

Reid dropped the hammer and felt the pick slide into the socket with a faint *squelch*. Another tap and it dropped down farther. He noticed the eyeball bulge slightly in its pit, the same as had happened with Elton.

Tap, tap, tap.

The pick burrowed in deeper, and David began to convulse, but the restraints held firm. The pick was buried in too deep to be dislodged by the boy's movements.

Another tap and Reid felt it—the sharp point had found and penetrated the brain.

He just prayed it hadn't speared its way in too far. David began to moan as Reid set the hammer down and took a firmer hold of the pick. He gently moved the instrument from side to side, feeling resistance as the point scraped away at the matter it was buried into.

Reid was working blind, but he proceeded carefully.

David began to buck wildly now, and a string of saliva rolled from the corner of his mouth. He uttered a sound, but it was incomprehensible—like the babbling of a child.

Reid wanted to continue, to scrape away more of the matter, and to know for certain that the connections to the prefrontal cortex and frontal lobes were severed. But that was precisely how he'd felt when doing this to Elton, and then he had wound up killing his patient. This time he would show restraint. If the procedure was not successful, then he would just try again.

So, instead of scraping further, he eased the pick from

David's eye socket. A *squelch* sounded as it released, like the sound of a boot pulling free from mud.

The patient continued to buck and writhe for a good ten minutes, and Reid studied him the whole time.

Slowly, the convulsions ended.

'David?' Reid asked. The young man turned his gaze to Reid, and the doctor noticed a bruise already forming on the inside of his left eye. 'Can you hear me?'

David did not respond.

'Do you understand what I'm saying?'

Still nothing, just a blank stare.

'I think you broke him,' one of the orderlies said from behind. Reid spun his head and shot the man an angry scowl. Whether they were part of the cult or not, Reid was still in charge in this room.

'Shut your mouth, you stupid fool,' Reid snapped. 'You are here to assist, not make comments. Understand?'

The man clenched his jaw, but nodded his consent.

Reid then got to work undoing the restraints that held his patient. Reid knew that David had been prone to bouts of violence, so he would need to be monitored just to be sure those episodes did not continue. However, Reid was confident in his work, and pleased at his success.

'Come on,' Reid said, 'get up.' He pulled at David's shoulder and was encouraged when the young man obediently followed Reid's lead. He then swung the man's legs from the table and pulled him up completely, praying David could stand and hold his own weight.

He could.

David stood, swaying gently and waiting, like a zombie without a purpose.

Reid clicked his fingers in front of the man's eyes, and they moved towards the noise, following Reid's digits.

David's motor skills seemed to be functioning, but the man simply would not—or could not—speak.

'Take him back to his room,' Reid instructed the orderlies. 'I want him under constant observation. If anything changes, I want to know about it. Especially if he becomes agitated or excited.'

The two orderlies grunted in confirmation, but that was all they said before grabbing David by the arms and pulling him from the room. Again, David was completely submissive and stumbled along with them from the room.

Reid was then left alone to consider how the procedure had gone. David indeed seemed more docile, but there was a danger he was now too docile. Just a husk of a person, with no personality to speak of.

The man he used to be, scraped away and erased.

Still, better that than the way he was before.

And at least he was still breathing... for now.

Reid felt a small surge of pride at his work. Things were still inconclusive, but so far the signs were good. And it was a massive improvement on his last effort.

All in all, a success.

And the distraction had been a welcome one. If Reid continued to concentrate on his work, then he perhaps could keep his mind occupied a little longer until he had the time and privacy to get more acquainted with Templeton's diary.

He wanted to know as much as he could about what was going on here, because one thing was for certain—he did not plan to stick around to see much more for himself. He would escape this place, and not look back.

17

As ADRIAN GHOSTED his way back to his room, he passed his neighbour's cell and saw Tom lying on his side with his knees pulled up to his chest. The old man was shaking and sweating profusely. If it was possible, Tom seemed even worse than the last time Adrian had seen him, and the skin around his face had sunken further, making him look deathly ill. His eyes were bloodshot, and the skin beneath them was a dark purple colour.

'You don't look so good, Tom,' Adrian said through the open door. He stepped inside, and Tom turned his head. The man forced a friendly smile, but he looked pained, and his skin was horribly pale.

'Don't look too hot yourself, son,' Tom replied with a strained voice. 'You been done over?'

Adrian nodded. 'Yeah, apparently I was a little unruly. Took a beating and got thrown in isolation.'

Tom forced out a chuckle. 'Always thought you were one to keep your head down.'

Adrian shrugged. 'Me too.' He walked over and squatted

down next to the old man. 'Is there anything I can do for you? Should I call for help?'

'No,' Tom said. 'No point. I know what's ailing me. It's that cursed poison they keep pumping into me. And they'll be back tonight, I'm told. It'll probably finish the job.'

'Refuse it,' Adrian said.

'Won't do any good, friend,' the old man replied. 'You know that as well as I do. We're prisoners in here. Things to be played with at the whims of those above us, until we are too bent, broken, and buckled to be useful anymore. Then we are cast out. Ignored, forgotten, and left to die.'

Adrian went to respond, but quickly realised he couldn't think of anything to say. There was a moment's silence between them.

'You been getting this medicine too?' Tom asked.

Adrian nodded. 'Just started the treatment.'

'Treatment?' Tom replied, forcing out a chuckle at the word. 'It ain't treatment, lad. Like I say, it's poison. You know, I remember seeing the Krauts use poison gas a few times in the Great War. Our own men used it a few times as well, to be fair. I was out in Belgium and saw what that gas did to people. Not just soldiers, townsfolk as well. People just trying to avoid death, but it got them all the same. Ruined their insides and burnt them away. I reckon I'm just going through the same kind of death as those poor people, only slower and more drawn out.'

'Jesus,' Adrian said. 'I had no idea it was that bad.'

'It wasn't, at first. I barely noticed it. In fact, I felt a little better. Brighter. Almost had a spring in my step. But it changed me, changed the way I think. Even now, part of me is wondering if I could reach out and grab your throat.'

'Are you serious?' Adrian asked, instinctively leaning back.

'Don't worry, I don't have the strength even if I wanted to. Guess this is what you've got to look forward to, lad.'

That struck a chord with Adrian.

'Let me ask you something,' Tom said. 'Since they gave you that poison, do you dream?'

Adrian nodded. 'Yeah.'

'They'll get worse. Everything you've ever done that you've regretted is going to be replayed to you, night after night, like a stage play of shame. But behind that stage is... a place; somewhere horrible, like hell, only worse. And you know what's scary? I think that place is real.'

'They're just dreams, Tom,' Adrian said, but couldn't deny how much the other man's words resonated with him.

'See, that's the thing. I don't think they are. And I swear to the Lord above that there is something inside me, in my head, and when things are quiet, I can hear it talking to me.'

'Sounds like a fever,' Adrian said.

'Fevers don't talk, lad,' Tom replied. 'Fevers don't tell you things about the people you share this place with, and what torments them.'

'What do you mean?'

'It told me a little about you today. Told me what wracks you with guilt. How the life that you took eats you up inside.'

Adrian was stunned. How could Tom possibly know about his past?

'My father? Yes, I regret what I did, but—'

'Not him, lad. That isn't what I'm talking about. That isn't what tortures you, is it?'

Adrian said nothing in response. He couldn't explain how Tom knew that and, furthermore, he had no desire to continue the conversation. He rose to his feet.

'I think you should sleep,' he said, then walked back towards the door.

'Only more dreams waiting for me there, lad,' Tom said.

'Bye, Tom,' Adrian said. He was about to leave the old man alone when Tom stopped him.

'It's coming for you, Adrian,' he said. 'It knows you, inside and out, and wants you as well. If you have the strength, maybe do something about it before it's too late. Lord knows I wish I was strong enough to do what I need to, but to be honest I just don't have the guts for it.'

Adrian didn't need to ask for clarification; he knew exactly what Tom was talking about.

Adrian said no more and left Tom alone. He walked to his room next door and dropped down onto his bed. His stomach ached for food, but he had no desire to face anyone else today. He felt drained and utterly confused.

Adrian lay back and rolled on to his side, trying to quiet the frantic, confused voices in his mind.

But they would not be silenced.

Was the thing Tom spoke about now talking to him as well?

18

DIRECTOR ISAAC TEMPLETON sat in the Chapel, enjoying the quiet. It afforded him the chance to think things through in an orderly manner. He was pleased with how things had progressed with Adrian James—an excellent candidate who was starting to show a reaction to the treatment already, indulging in violent tendencies even after only a single dose.

By chance, the man had witnessed more than he should have, but that would not be a problem. The situation concerned Brother Jones, however, as he thought Adrian James' story would create tension and agitation within the ranks of the afflicted, especially in Ward B. But Templeton was confident that another crazy tale floating about between the patients would not create any complications. Still, better to deal with the issue, just in case.

Ending the life of Adrian James was not an option, of course, not after the treatment had already started. It was a waste, and besides, Mr. James was marked now, and promised to... it. Templeton dared not take away that which was owed.

Dealing with the thing in the basement was a privilege,

he knew that, but one that had to be handled carefully. Everyone answered to someone, and his superior in the Church—one Kane Ainsworth—was growing concerned at the speed with which things were moving. Because of that, Templeton had to check in with the man by telephone each and every day. Failure to do so would mean a visit from a clean-up crew, who would put an end to what they were doing at this asylum. For the greater good, of course. It was an annoyance, to be sure, as Mr. Ainsworth was far too cautious, but it was one that Templeton had to bear. And he did not doubt that if, and when, things stepped up, his check-ins would need to be more frequent.

The other issue that played on his mind was that of their new physician: Dr. Reid.

After speaking with Adrian James earlier, Templeton had returned to his office and immediately felt that something was off.

It did not take him long to discover that the position of his chair was ever-so-slightly different than he always left it —rotated to the left by a fraction.

Someone had been in the office in his absence, just as he had expected they might.

Templeton had then moved his chair and pulled back the rug beneath, retrieving the key and opening his desk drawers. He then checked to make sure everything was in place.

It wasn't.

His diary was gone.

And he knew who was responsible—the good doctor had taken the bait.

Hopefully, it would be enough to push Dr. Reid to follow the trail Templeton left for him. If the man came to discover the truth at his own pace, rather than having it forced upon him, he might come to accept it more easily.

And what had happened poor Dr. Vine could be avoided.

Templeton felt that Dr. Vine had found out too much, too quickly, and his scientific mind could not accept what was in front of him.

It was just too unbelievable.

And so, measures had been taken to protect the facility.

Now Dr. Vine existed in the basement below the asylum, in the dark, surrounded by horrors.

Templeton just hoped Dr. Reid would be different. Having him join them, as a true believer, would be a valuable thing.

However, if that proved not to be possible, Reid would have to be dealt with as well.

And now was the time to take another step. Dr. Reid would again see the medicine in action, only this time he would witness its full effects.

Templeton stood up. He used to make the sign of the cross over his body when leaving a place of worship.

No longer.

In truth, he now just liked the familiarity the Chapel offered him. Places like this always instilled in him a sense of wonder, where he worshipped a being much greater than he.

It still fulfilled the same purpose, only he no longer worshipped a false god. The cause he now devoted himself to was very real.

19

THE HOUR WAS GROWING LATE, and Reid was in his office, engrossed in Director Templeton's diary.

He had learned a little more about the mysterious Church, and Templeton's devotion to it. It was not an organisation Reid had heard of before, but it would seem that they somehow had a great deal of reach and resources. And it was also apparent that this facility was only one of many operations the Church had in place, all of which seemed to study what they called *the other place*.

Movement from beyond his door caught his attention, and Reid looked up to see the director outside, raising his hand to knock on the glass.

In a panic, Reid dropped the diary and buried it beneath some loose papers that cluttered his desk.

Reid waved Templeton in, trying not to appear as flustered as he felt.

Templeton was smiling as he entered and wore an expression that simply said *caught you*. Reid felt a tightening in his chest and knew precisely what the director was here for—he'd realised the diary was missing, and Reid was his suspect.

Caught red-handed.

'I hope I haven't disturbed you?' Templeton asked.

'Not at all,' Reid replied, exerting every ounce of composure he could summon. 'How can I help you?'

'I need to ask you something,' Templeton went on. He then took the small chair that rested against the far wall and placed it opposite Reid. He sat down, uninvited.

'Go ahead,' Reid said.

Here it comes.

'I want you to accompany me later, if you would be so kind?'

That was not what Reid was expecting.

'Accompany you where?' he asked.

'We are administering more of the medicine to a patient tonight in Ward B. One that has been receiving the treatment for a while.'

'Of course,' Reid said. 'I'd be happy to.'

'Excellent,' Templeton said, clapping his hands together. 'I know the medicine we are testing here is something that interests you, and I think it only fair that you get to see the full effects.'

Again, Reid was taken aback, as Templeton had previously withheld all information about the medicine.

'I'd like that very much,' Reid said. 'But can I ask, what has changed?'

'What do you mean?'

'When I asked you about it did previously, you always avoided giving me an answer.'

'True,' Templeton said, 'but you've seen it administered to Adrian James, and also you were present when he came around.'

'That didn't exactly give me a lot of answers, though.'

'No, but it gave you information. A taste. Tonight, I think you will learn a lot more.'

Reid nodded. 'Okay. When should I be ready?'

Templeton shrugged. 'No time like the present. Are you busy now?'

'I guess not,' Reid said, hoping Templeton had not seen him hide the diary and, more importantly, could not see it now. Reid had hastily thrown papers and a file over it, but couldn't be sure it was completely hidden to Templeton from his vantage point.

'Excellent. Then let us make haste. We will be going to see a patient named Tom Cunningham. He has been taking the medicine for a while now, but I think tonight's dosage will be his last.'

'Will he be cured of his ailments, then?' Reid asked.

Templeton smiled. 'Oh yes. After tonight, I guarantee he will be a different person completely.'

The older man rose to his feet, his knees popping as he did.

'That sounded painful,' Reid said, but Templeton just shook his head.

'Just a symptom of my age,' he said. 'Creaking old bones. If one lives long enough, it is unavoidable, I'm afraid. Something you have to look forward to.'

Templeton then opened the door and turned back to Reid. 'Let's go. You can finish my diary when we are done.'

With that, he disappeared from view, leaving Reid standing alone, open-mouthed.

So Templeton *had* known he had taken the diary, and perhaps even seen him reading it.

And what's more, he didn't seem to care.

'Whenever you're ready,' Templeton called back from

down the corridor. Reid slowly got to his feet, suddenly feeling very apprehensive.

20

ADRIAN HAD KILLED AGAIN——RE-LIVED *the moment when he had taken a life.*

And not just any life.

He felt the same sense of horror, shame, and crippling guilt. And he knew that his own life was now forfeit, no longer worth living.

He did not deserve to exist anymore.

He had just proven that he was exactly like his father.

Adrian raised the pillow and looked at the lifeless husk on the bed below him. A frozen expression of panic was etched on the face of the corpse. That look would stay with Adrian forever.

Then, everything changed.

The room he was in——one that he recognised from his past—— disintegrated. It pulled itself apart like torn-up paper and blew away on a breeze that Adrian could not feel.

And the landscape he was now left standing in could be summed up in a single word——Hell.

That word perfectly captured the nightmarish surroundings.

And this hell was familiar to him.

Behind him was the same boiling expanse of water that he

had seen before. The landscape was as he expected—vast plains of black rock with towers and mountains in the distance. Large ravines sunk down in places, and there were pockets of moving, vein-like trees, some denser than others, scattered about.

And up above was an alien sky.

And that eye.

It both amazed him and filled him with wonder, but also instilled in him a profound sense of dread that shook him to his core. Never had he felt as insignificant as he did under the gaze of that unknowable thing.

Then he heard the voice.

Not from the cosmic entity above, but from somewhere else.

From the boiling sea.

'Adriaaaaan.'

ADRIAN AWOKE with the sound of that terrifying, inhuman voice still playing in his mind.

As inexplicable as it was, it sounded both evil and ancient at the same time. Even though he knew it was something that had only been conjured up by his sub-conscious, it still scared him.

He looked around and realised he was still in his room, but his door was now closed. It was dark outside and, again, his stomach cried out in hungry protest. But it was too late to feed now.

He must have dozed off after lying on his bed, though for how long he had no idea. All he knew was that it was now the dead of night.

And people were approaching outside.

He heard muffled voices, but could not make out what

was being said. He did recognise some of them, however—
Director Templeton and Dr. Reid.

'I JUST THINK I owe you an explanation,' Reid said, as they
approached the door to Tom Cunningham's room. 'About
the diary.'

Templeton gave a dismissive wave of his hand. 'Not
necessary. We've more important matters at hand.'

The two of them were accompanied by Jones and three
other orderlies, one of whom had with him an intravenous
drip connected to a plastic bag. He was carrying it very carefully, and a black substance swam within the bag.

The medicine.

Another orderly had some heavy-looking leather
restraints with him, while Duckworth was wheeling another
bed down the corridor. Its rusty wheels squeaked with
every turn.

Lastly, Jones was carrying with him the same weapon
Reid had seen him use only the night before. When Reid
had first laid eyes on the weapon strapped on Jones' back,
Reid had raised an inquisitive eyebrow at Templeton. The
director had merely shrugged.

'All will become clear,' he'd said. 'But I hope it won't be
needed.'

Templeton unlocked the door, and they entered to see the
patient curled up in bed on top of his covers, his thin clothing
soaking with sweat. A potent, sour odour permeated the air.

'Good evening, Tom,' Templeton said to the man, who
seemed to be rousing from sleep.

'Huh?' the disoriented patient croaked in reply,

squinting through reddened eyes that narrowed further when Jones flicked on the single light above.

'What's happening?' Tom asked, still groggy.

'I think you know,' Templeton said. 'Time for more of your medication.'

Tom curled his top lip, and Reid was a little taken aback at how ill the man looked. No medication in the world would save him.

'Don't want it,' the patient said, but Templeton only chuckled.

'We will decide what is best for you.' He then turned to the orderlies. 'Prepare him.'

'No!' Tom managed to yell out, but it sounded weak and feeble.

Jones and the others descended on him.

ADRIAN COULD HEAR something happening in the room next door.

Tom's room.

He could hear the old man yelling out in protest. Adrian knew what was taking place and, after last night, had an idea of what would become of Tom.

He considered screaming for them to stop, to try to prevent what was happening, though he knew it wouldn't do much good.

So why waste the energy?

Every single soul in this asylum was doomed.

He knew that.

Might as well accept what was deserved.

REID WAS NEVER one for showing much in the way of emotion, certainly not towards his patients, but seeing the old man—desperate and weak—so easily overpowered and strapped down to the mobile bed they'd brought with them, made Reid feel sorry for Tom.

'Please,' Tom begged, and Reid could see tears roll from the sides of his eyes, following the wrinkles and contours of the man's cracked skin. 'I can't bear any more.'

Templeton bent down and brought his face close to Tom's ear. In a gentle voice, he whispered to the old man, 'Try not to resist. I promise you, Mr. Cunningham, this will be the last time you will ever have to take this medicine. And afterward you will be relieved of all your misery, torture, and torment.' He raised a finger and placed it to the centre of Tom's forehead. 'You will be free.'

'I'll die,' Tom argued, his voice cracking as he started to sob.

Templeton did not confirm or deny the statement. 'Be brave,' was all he said. Then he turned to the orderlies again. 'Insert the drip. Let's begin.'

Tom could only cry, helplessly, as the men got to work. A sharp needle penetrated the skin to the inside of his arm and found a vein. A cannula was then inserted, connected to a drip bag that was held on a thin metal stand.

Reid watched on as the black liquid oozed down the length of the transparent pipe and into Tom's veins.

'Please,' Tom begged again, but his voice was not one of importance or consequence. He simply did not matter.

ADRIAN CONTINUED to try and ignore what was taking place next door. After being put into isolation and beaten by

Jones, he did not want to give them a reason to punish him any further. And he certainly didn't want to give them cause to up his treatment.

But Tom's pitiful moans and pleading were getting to be too much. The poor old man had suffered far too much, and now he just needed some care and compassion.

Adrian sprung to his feet and thumped the wall with the meaty side of his fist. However, the wall was so thick that the strikes only gave off a pitiful, muffled thud, one he doubted would be heard by anyone but himself.

'Leave him alone,' Adrian yelled. 'For the love of God, just leave us all alone!'

REID COULD HEAR SHOUTING COMING from the cell next door, but, like everyone else in the room, he paid it no mind.

Instead, he was transfixed on Tom Cunningham, as the black ooze continued to enter his bloodstream.

'How much are you putting in?' Reid asked. 'The last one I saw was only a few milligrams. Won't this kill him?'

'Just show patience, Dr. Reid,' Templeton said. 'As you can see for yourself, Tom is not in the best of health, so I want to be sure that we are on top of what is happening.'

'What do you mean?'

'Remember what you told me, about what you witnessed last night?'

Reid nodded. 'Yes.'

'Well, that was unfortunate. And unforeseen. It was the first time we hadn't been prepared for such an event. It took us unaware.'

'So what the hell was it?' Reid asked.

But Templeton just went on with what he was saying,

dismissing the question.

'I'm not sure how much more time Tom here would have, so we need to speed up the process while we are in a position to handle it.'

The man on the bed stopped his groaning and fell silent after giving out a prolonged wheeze. Templeton went on.

'I am aware that you have read at least some of my diary, Doctor. And, as you said, you saw something last night that you could not explain. Tell me, how hard was it for you to believe what you were seeing?'

'What do you mean?'

'I mean, did you accept what your own eyes were showing you?'

'Of course.'

'That's good, Dr. Reid. Many in your line of work would not. Now, let me ask you this. What was it, exactly, that you saw?'

Reid paused for a moment, considering the question. Tom gave a brief moan, then settled again into silence.

'I don't know,' Reid said.

'Try. How would your scientific brain rationalise something that couldn't be rationalised?'

'I'm guessing that this medicine has something to do with it,' Reid said.

'Indeed,' Templeton replied.

'So it does something to the human body? Mutates it somehow? I'm not a chemist or biologist, so I cannot even begin to explain how that happens.'

'That may be partly true,' Templeton said. 'But in actuality, there is a kind of transference taking place. The medicine you see entering Tom Cunningham's veins is the catalyst for that change.'

'A transference of what?' Reid asked. 'Cells?'

'You are still thinking in terms of science, Thomas—of things we understand. Just how much of my diary did you read? I would like you to consider possibilities more... eldritch in nature.'

'Eldritch?'

'Something a little more outside of your belief system, Doctor.'

'These gods you spoke about?'

Templeton nodded.

'I don't know what else to say, Isaac,' Reid snapped. 'You are asking me to use fantasies and fairytales to replace actual science.'

'Something that *you* cannot explain, I remind you.'

'There is a lot in this world that I can't explain. It doesn't mean I attribute it to make-believe gods.'

Templeton just smiled. 'You still cling to redundant notions of how things are, Dr. Reid. I sympathise. I've been there myself. But I have seen the truth, as you soon will.' He then pointed to Tom. 'Watch.'

It did not take long for things to happen. Tom's eyes flicked wide open, and his jaw dropped. Then he let out a horrifying scream.

His eyes rolled back in his head, but he was not dead.

An unnatural growl emitted from his throat.

And then the change began.

His jaw cracked and dislocated, and the mouth pulled itself open farther to an unnatural length. His teeth were pushed out from the gums, along with small pools of blood. Some of the teeth fell back into his mouth, others to the bed beneath him. Longer, sharper teeth now emerged, pushing their way through as the mouth continued to contort, taking in more of a vertical, elliptical shape. Both eyes dropped and engorged, the whites and irises flooded by a pool of black.

At the same time, Tom's thrashing body transformed, too. His arms and legs elongated, becoming spindly things, and Reid could hear bones crack and splinter as they changed shape. The knees buckled inwards with a nasty pop, and a webbing formed between the long fingers and toes. All the while, skin that was turning a dirty green, tightened around bones. The chest cavity pushed itself out so far that the flesh split around it, revealing bone beneath.

Lastly, Tom's tongue thinned and stretched as well, dangling from the mouth like a sore, loose nerve ending.

The abomination that Tom had now become—bearing qualities of both amphibian and insect—let out a screech.

Reid moved back to the far side of the room, pressing himself into the wall, and put a hand over his mouth in horror.

'Steel yourself, Dr. Reid!' Templeton yelled above the horrifying noise. The director did not look at Reid as he spoke; instead his gaze was fixed on this creature in awe and wonder. 'This is exactly what you wanted to see. This is the truth of how things really are, so bear witness to it.'

'This is insane,' Reid yelled back, terrified. The creature writhed and squealed on the bed, fighting against its bonds. The leather straps creaked and groaned in protest. Eventually, Reid knew, this monster would break free. 'Kill it,' he shouted to Jones, trying to make it sound like an order. Jones just ignored him, but did, Reid noticed, keep the weapon he was carrying trained on the monster.

'Remember this moment, Dr. Reid,' Templeton said. 'For when you look back, you will know it was now that you started to believe.'

'I want nothing to do with this,' Reid snapped, and Templeton eventually looked over at him. The creature on the bed continued to fight.

'Yes,' Templeton said, 'you do. The night is not yet over.' He now turned to Jones and the others. 'We must move this child. Follow me.'

Templeton then walked to the door and pulled it open as the orderlies gathered around the bed. They carefully wheeled it out to the corridor as the monster kicked, bucked, and roared.

Reid pressed himself further into the wall as they passed him. His breathing was fast and erratic.

Templeton yelled from the corridor outside.

'Dr. Reid, I suggest you accompany us. You still do not know everything there is to know. You wanted answers? You wanted the truth? Well, tonight is a night for revelations.'

Reid remained in place, terrified and conflicted. He *did* want answers, but now feared what those might be.

'Well?' Templeton called back over the sound of the creature.

Reid took a breath. 'I'm coming,' he said. He then pushed himself off the wall and left the small room.

THE TERRIBLE SOUNDS of whatever ungodly thing poor Tom had become eventually died down, leaving only the frightened cries of Adrian's fellow inmates. God knows what they made of the nightmarish noises.

But Adrian knew exactly what had happened.

He had seen firsthand the thing Malcolm had become, and now the same fate had befallen Tom. He knew it.

And he remembered the poor old man's words from earlier.

Guess this is what you've got to look forward to, lad.

21

REID HESITANTLY FOLLOWED as Templeton led the way; the group of orderlies gathered around the bed they pushed along. The creature tied to the bed did not relent for a moment, struggling and thrashing against its restraints, which seemed to give more and more. Reid was concerned that they would not hold much longer and he prayed they would reach their destination quickly, as he did not want to get caught up in the kind of carnage he had seen the previous night.

Jones walked beside the bed as it moved, flame-spewing weapon in hand. The end was lit, and the small blue flame was ignited, ready to burst forth with a stream of red-hot flame.

They moved from Ward B and into the Main Hall, then from there continued to the very back of the large open space. Given the late hour, the room was empty and would have been deathly quiet if not for the noise the thing they were transporting created.

They finally stopped before the old service elevator, the

one that Reid had not yet used, though he had a feeling that was about to change.

A mesh gate protected the dark red steel door to the lift. Templeton unlocked the gate, and it swung open with a creak. He then slid up the inner door to reveal a bare, spacious internal area.

Templeton moved aside, allowing the bed to be wheeled into the elevator. Templeton then joined his group inside and turned to Reid, who had still not crossed the threshold.

'Well?' he asked, but Reid hesitated. If that thing got loose in such an enclosed space, then they were done for, and Jones' weapon would be useful only to incinerate them all.

'I...' Reid began, but trailed off.

'Mr. Jones, could you please help the good doctor along?'

Reid looked up to see Jones stomp back out towards him, and the large man grabbed him. 'Come along, Dr. Reid,' Jones said and dragged Reid into the elevator.

'What the hell are you doing?' Reid snapped as he fought uselessly against the bigger man, but Jones seemed to have no trouble manhandling him with his one free hand.

'It is too late to back out now,' Templeton said as he slid the door closed. Reid was then released, and he felt the sway of the elevator as it started to drop. The mechanics of the machine worked noisily, partially drowning out the screeching of the impossible thing that still fought on the bed.

The feeling of nervousness in Reid increased, and even though the inside of the lift was far from cramped, he still felt as if the walls were closing in on him. Claustrophobia was never an affliction that had troubled him before, but now he had a desperate need to be out of the space.

The elevator rumbled down farther, eventually coming

to a stop with more force than Reid was expecting, causing all inside to rock on their feet. Templeton pulled open the door to reveal a subterranean level. From his vantage point within the elevator, Reid could make out a long, wide passageway with a high, curved ceiling above.

The walls and ceiling were both constructed from wet stone, but the ground that the group walked on was little more than dirt and dust. And whereas ceiling-fixed electric lights illuminated the facility above, there was no such luxury down here. Instead, the flickering light was cast by lit torches mounted on the walls, giving off circles of light not quite powerful enough to reach the other side of the passageway and leaving pockets of darkness between.

They did cast enough light, however, to illuminate doors cut into the thick stone walls, formed from rusted iron grates on hinges and showing only darkness behind.

But from that darkness, horrible noises could be heard. Inhuman moans echoed, and they became more agitated— or excited—when the creature the group had with them on the bed cried out as well.

'What's down here?' Reid asked. His throat was dry and his palms damp.

'Allow me to show you,' Templeton said. He turned and walked out first. The orderlies wheeled the bed after him... and then it happened.

One of the orderlies, who had taken a position at the head of the bed, bent his body double as he pushed forward —it was at this moment that the creature opened its dripping mouth, and that thin tongue burst forward with frightening accuracy. The flimsy-looking muscle penetrated the orderly's right eye with force, and as it did, it straightened out to its full length. The orderly let out a sharp shriek and instinctively pulled his head back, but it snapped to a stop as the tongue buried into his eye socket held him in place. Greasy water spilled down his cheek as the orderly started to scream.

There was a frantic buzz of activity as the other orderlies —sans Jones—tried to pull their colleague free. Jones, instead, turned his weapon on the creature on the bed, but Templeton calmly placed a hand on the long nozzle and pushed the aim down.

Reid himself had backpedaled farther into the lift, removing himself from any immediate danger as best he could.

But the chaos and panic continued and, eventually, the orderlies managed to pull their struggling colleague free. The tongue of the monster, upon losing its hold, quickly slithered back into its mouth, but not before Reid noticed a few drops of black liquid pump out from its end. Reid then looked to the wailing orderly, who was thrashing in pain as the others helped him down to his back. He had a hand clamped over his ruined eye, and dark fluid ran from between his fingers.

It was quite clear to Reid that something had been excreted into the man's eye socket from that vile tongue. Jones and Templeton, who were now more animated, were clearly thinking the same thing, and it seemed to concern them more than the injury caused to the orderly.

'Sir,' Jones said, 'the liquid. Is that...?' He trailed off, but Templeton answered anyway.

'I believe it is.'

'That hasn't happened before.'

'It has not. I think things are progressing, the transformations evolving.'

Reid had no idea what the hell was going on, but he wanted to be away from this madness.

'Will he turn?' Jones asked.

'I don't know,' Templeton said as the man continued to scream. 'But we must take precaution. We can't let a change take place while we are unprepared.'

'We keep him here, then?'

Templeton nodded.

And that was it. Jones walked forward, pushed away the other orderlies, and took hold of the squirming man, dragging him across the ground with one hand. The orderly kicked and writhed as Jones pulled him over to one of the grated doors, where Jones peered inside, checking the space. He then retrieved his ring of keys and, in short order, unlocked the door and pulled it open.

The orderly had begun to crawl away. 'No,' he yelled out, seemingly aware of what was going to happen. 'You can't.'

'Be calm, brother,' Jones said. 'This is for the best. Embrace what will happen.'

Jones then stepped towards the pleading man and grabbed him. The man tried to fight back, but Jones quickly overpowered him and thrust him through the now open door. He then pushed it closed and locked it, trapping the orderly inside. He quickly reappeared from the darkness, his face pressed up against the iron bars.

'Please,' he begged again. 'Please don't do this.'

Jones ignored him and walked back over to the others.

'Now,' Templeton said, looking down to the thing that used to be Tom Cunningham, 'our new friend here grows angry. We must move quickly.'

Jones took the lead, grabbing the bed—from the bottom this time, aware of what had happened before—and pulled it farther into the open corridor. The bed wobbled on the uneven ground, but he still maintained a steady pace, pulling the bed over to a door adjacent to the recently imprisoned orderly. That man continued to plead for release and continued to be ignored. The other door was opened, and Jones wheeled the bed inside.

He reemerged and locked the door.

'Thank you, brother,' Templeton said to him, giving him a warm pat on the shoulder. The director then looked back to Reid, who still stood in the elevator, terrified for his life. The noises that reverberated from the cells, and through this subterranean ward-from-hell, were maddening.

'Doctor?' Templeton said. 'Would you care to join us?'

Reid didn't move. 'I want to go back upstairs. I've seen enough, now let me go.'

Templeton shook his head. 'I'm sorry, but you have *not* seen enough. Not even close. There is more to see, good doctor, and I did not bring you down here merely to show off these cells. Now come along before I order Mr. Jones to collect you. I can't promise he will be gentle.'

Even at this distance and in the dim light, Reid could make out the cruel smile that spread across the face of Jones.

Reid took a breath and forced himself out of the elevator.

'Fine,' he said, but when he crossed the threshold out into the open space of this area, he suddenly felt horribly exposed. The air was cold and stale, and as he walked forward he swore he could feel eyes on him.

He peered into some of the dark cells he passed, trying to see as much as the dull light would let him. Some of the cells appeared to be empty—or if they were inhabited, then the things inside were content not to show themselves—but the residents of others stood in full view behind the iron doors, revealing their forms through the metal.

Monsters, creatures, and nightmarish abominations.

Seeing such horrors caused Reid to pause and draw in a sharp breath. The first monstrosity that he saw had a vaguely humanoid shape to the top of its body and walked like an ape, supporting itself on two long, trunk-like arms that ended in sore-looking stumps, devoid of hands or fingers. It had broad shoulders, but its body withered away at the waist, curling to nothing so that its bulk hung between the massive arms. Its head, once human, was bald and the cranium was lined with small, white eyes that all gelled together like fish eggs. Instead of a mouth, the skin seemed to have sealed over, gagging it, however the thing was still able to make animalistic noises from the strange opening across its stomach: a circular wound with spiralling flesh behind it that kissed and puckered at the air.

Suddenly, the thing lifted a great arm and slammed it forward into the door, causing a deafening, metallic crash to ring out. Reid jumped back and let out an involuntary shriek. The thing punched again, and the metal door shook violently against its frame. The sounds from the other cells grew more frantic and more... excited.

In another cell, Reid saw a creature with a stick-thin body lined with sharp spines. It had a grotesquely engorged head that looked like little more than a sack of fat, hiding whatever face it had beneath. Strained moans could be heard from within the folds of the sagging, pulsating flesh.

Reid pushed himself on, trying not to look at the surrounding horrors, but a morbid curiosity worked against him. The next thing he saw at first seemed human—normal height, standard build, and naked. However, when it moved forward—with odd, jerky movements—Reid saw that its face had sunk so much that the eyes bulged from the sockets, ready to pop out, and its arms were buried inside its own stomach, fused into the flesh and lost within. It smiled and giggled, then opened its mouth wide, allowing Reid to see rows of small, stubby teeth running to the back of its throat.

Another creature, smaller than the rest, clung to the door of its cell, gripping on it like an underwater mollusc on a rock. Its once human shape had flattened out, its skin gelatinous, slimy, and transparent, revealing stringy insides. The creature's face, now only spirals of small eyes around a large suckling mouth, was central to the mass of its body.

Reid saw more twisted visions—a thing with multiple legs that was more spider than man, a creature with no skin and pulsating innards that opened into separate mouths—in each and every cell he looked into. Templeton and his congregation waited for him at the end of the passage before a tall, imposing double door made of sturdy metal. It was rusted and aged, but Reid had no doubt that it would hold firm.

When Reid reached them, Templeton spoke. 'Are you ready, Dr. Reid?'

'What's in here?' Reid replied.

'An old friend.'

The door was unlocked and then heaved open, each of the two leaves scraping against the dirt floor as they were pulled apart.

Reid looked inside.

'What is this?' he asked, his voice barely more than a whisper.

'This,' Templeton said, 'is Robert Wilson. At least, it used to be.'

The room inside was a large one, of similar construction as the passageway outside—stone walls and ceiling—but the flooring within was cast with uneven concrete.

In the centre was a bed, and on it was the form of a man.

His skin was pale and sunken, revealing the outline of

bones beneath, and he had long, thin hair with a scraggly beard to match—both the colour of ash. His eyes were shut, and Reid could detect no signs of breathing.

'You brought me down here to see a corpse?' Reid asked.

'Not quite,' Templeton said. 'Robert has been lying here, like this, for a long time. However, you will notice that there is no pooling of the blood in lower portions of the body, no purple patches on the skin, and rigor mortis has not set in. Please, examine him and see for yourself.'

'I'll take your word for it.'

Templeton chuckled. 'Very well. What I'm telling you is that the body you see before you is alive, technically. And blood pumps through its veins.'

'So he's in a coma?'

'Robert? Truth be told, I don't know where my old friend is anymore. *If* he exists anywhere at all, that is. But this body is still a host to life, that much I can promise you.'

'What kind of life?'

'The kind beyond our understanding,' Templeton answered with a wide smile. 'There is something using this body as a vessel. Using it to reside, at least in part, in our world. In our reality.'

'That is ridiculous,' Reid said, raising his voice. 'For sanity's sake, Isaac, will you please just give me a straight and honest answer?'

'This is your answer,' Templeton said, gesturing towards the man on the table before them. As Reid focused more on the details of the room, he noticed that fine growths lined the body—thin tendrils of a pinkish-purple colour that were almost as fine as hair. These tendrils fell from the body to the floor, some wrapping around the legs of the bed as they pushed farther out into the room.

The director went on. 'This being is something that

exists in a place beyond our own.'

'What kind of place?'

'We do not know, exactly. A realm of purity. The beings that dwell there know secrets to the cosmos that we can scarcely comprehend. They are many orders of magnitude above us. And this is one such being.'

'A god?'

Templeton chuckled. 'For so long I had an erroneous comprehension of what that word meant. But now I know.'

'I hate to derail your speech, Director, but this doesn't look like a god to me. It's a bag of meat, like the rest of us.'

'The body is exactly that, you are correct. But the body is only a puppet, one the Great Ailing One uses to form a connection to this world, allowing it to exert its will here.'

'Great Ailing One?' Reid asked, now even more confused.

'This is what we have come to call it.'

'Ailing? As in it's ill? Dying?'

'In a sense. Its time of existence in its own realm is eroding.'

'A dying god? Am I supposed to believe this? Isaac, if something can die, then it is very much mortal, like you and I.'

'No,' Templeton said. '*Nothing* like you and I. We do not know much, only that something happened in its own existence, and now it is decaying.'

'And you know all of this how? You talk to it?'

The director nodded. 'That's right.'

'This is ridiculous,' Reid snapped. 'I cannot believe what I'm hearing. You people and whatever cult you are part of have lost touch with reality.'

'Then explain what you have seen with your own eyes, Dr. Reid. Explain to me how those things out there came to be?' He pointed back to the area behind them where the abominations were imprisoned.

'I can't,' Reid conceded. 'But it is not attributed to a god. Just think about what you are saying. I won't fall victim to the same hysteria that has gripped the rest of you weak-minded fools,' Reid said, raising his voice even higher now, letting the anger that was building run free. 'Enough is enough.'

Templeton shook his head. 'I'm disappointed, Doctor. I expected more from you.'

'Then I'm glad to have let you down,' Reid said defiantly. He knew that by rebuking what they were saying, he was putting himself in danger, but it was all too much.

'*Bring him... to me.*'

Reid spun his head around at hearing those words. No one present had uttered them, yet he had heard the voice clear as day. Then he saw that the body on the table had its eyes wide open, revealing black orbs.

'What was that?' Reid asked, unable to hide the fear in his voice.

'It seems someone, or something, would like to speak with you,' Templeton said, with a sinister smile.

Then Jones and the other orderlies made their way over to the doctor.

Everything else was a blur to Reid—flashes of them taking hold of him, moving him over to the body of Robert Wilson, and seeing the mouth open to reveal the blackness within. An inhuman tongue slithered out and forced its way into his own mouth.

He tasted the foul, slimy thing as it spit something inside of him.

Then he dreamed.

Oh, how he dreamed.

22

'OUT OF ISOLATION ALREADY?' Seymour asked, his lip curled into a cruel smile. 'Thought they would have kept you in there all week.'

Adrian took a seat, ignoring Seymour completely. Regardless of what had happened yesterday, and what he had suffered, he still couldn't say he regretted attacking the obnoxious man.

He had considered staying in his room all morning, just so that Seymour would not see the bruises and wounds now displayed on his face, but his hunger was just too great.

'Give you a beating, did they?' Seymour went on, pressing the issue and looking for a rise. Adrian did not give him the satisfaction. Instead, he turned to Jack and greeted the giant with a friendly smile. Jack smiled back and patted Adrian on the shoulder with a large paw.

'How are you today, Jack?' Adrian asked. He didn't expect a verbal answer, but Jack instead gave him a thumbs up. Adrian looked to the others in the group, Sean and Trevor. Poor Trevor looked as beaten as Adrian was, with a large lump on his forehead and dark, purple bruises to the left side of his face.

'They let you out, too?' Adrian asked. Trevor nodded, seemingly his usual self at the moment.

'Yes,' he said. 'This morning.'

'Seems like you had a rough night.'

Again, Trevor nodded. 'I guess.'

'Makes two of us.'

'Well,' Seymour cut in, 'can't say you both didn't deserve it.'

'Not today, Seymour,' Adrian said. 'Just drop it.'

Seymour just laughed. 'Don't tell me what to do, boy.' He was still trying to exert his authority over Adrian, who gritted his teeth together but kept himself in check.

'Anyone hear that last night?' Sean asked, thankfully changing the subject, though not to one Adrian necessarily wanted to discuss.

'Hear what?' Trevor asked, seemingly not aware of the disturbance.

'Same as the night before,' Seymour said. 'More trouble. Think someone else got free.'

'It wasn't someone getting free,' Adrian said, then stopped himself.

'What would you know?' Seymour asked, challenging him. Adrian still didn't want to divulge anything, fearing he would just upset Jack and Trevor. Seymour and Sean he was less concerned about.

'Whatever it was,' Sean said, 'something's going on. It isn't safe here anymore.'

'When was it ever safe?' Seymour asked. 'In here there is no such thing as safe.'

'Well, there's nothing we can do about it,' Adrian said, looking past the group he sat with, impatiently waiting for breakfast to arrive. It would be more slop, but right now that sounded downright appealing.

'Speak for yourself,' Seymour said. 'You may be happy enough staying here like a good little puppet for your masters, but I'm not.'

'This again,' Adrian said, shaking his head.

'Yes, this again,' Seymour answered. 'And you might want to listen, boy. If you had any sense about you, you'd be begging me to come along when I get out.'

'Have a plan of action, do you?'

'Not yet,' Seymour conceded. 'But that doesn't mean I won't make it happen. I'll get out of this prison, I promise you that.'

'Of course you will,' Adrian said, then got to his feet.

'Where are you going?'

Adrian nodded to the food that was now being wheeled into the room in large, silver vats. 'Breakfast,' he replied, tired of listening to the fat man. 'Anyone else coming?'

Jack smiled and got up with him. Seymour remained seated, and Sean seemed in two minds, clearly wanting food, but looking to Seymour for approval.

'What about you, Trevor?' Adrian asked. 'I'm guessing you're as hungry as I am.'

Trevor did not answer.

Someone else did.

'Oh, I'm hungry all right,' an effeminate voice said.

Trevor then turned and flashed Adrian a sinister smile.

Shit.

It appeared Mother was back.

23

'THOMAS, HELP US!'

The flames in the room were absolute and the heat unbearable.

Thomas Reid stood in the doorway to the bedroom while the fire spread through the house—but this room was worst of all.

It was an inferno.

And inside were his wife and his young son.

The blonde boy hugged his mother tightly, tears streaking his blackened face. The smoke was suffocating, and Reid struggled not to vomit as he coughed and heaved.

The flames crept closer to his family.

'Please,' his wife begged.

He knew he should be helping them. As the husband, wasn't it his job to burst in there, face down any danger, and carry them to safety?

But the fire and heat grew stronger.

And Thomas Reid stepped away.

He fled from the house, listening to the screams of terror from his wife and child.

He made it safely from the house as they were burnt alive.

In an instant, time seemed to have passed, hours gone by, and he was standing close to the scorched, blackened shell that used to be his home. The authorities, having successfully put out the fire, were wading through the fragile structure. Grief and shame over-came Reid. He broke away from the officer he was speaking with and bolted into the house and up to the bedroom.

There, he saw what was left of his family. Woman and child, black and charred, fused together from the ungodly heat.

He fell to his knees and screamed.

And when he looked up, Thomas Reid was not in his house anymore. He was somewhere else.

A terrible hellscape that defied belief.

And a voice came to him, from a raging, bubbling sea.

'GOOD MORNING.'

Reid opened his eyes. His heart was racing, his breathing quick, and he could feel perspiration line his body. He saw a familiar, smiling face looking down at him.

Templeton.

Reid scanned the room he was in, one that was alien to him at first, but his mind soon started to catch up and calm his panicking body.

He was in his sleeping quarters. A small room, like the others in this wing, containing just enough space for a single bed, a writing desk, and two wardrobes. There was a window above his head that let in daylight, and the entire room was decorated in light colours—from the white plaster on the walls, to the cream carpet, and even the white bedsheets.

Reid let himself take a deep, soothing breath.

The springs beneath the mattress squeaked as Director

Templeton shifted his weight from the seated position he had taken on the foot of the bed.

'How are we feeling?' he asked in a kind, gentle manner.

'Fine,' Reid said, still confused. He sat up and rubbed his eyes. 'What are you doing here?' he asked, then he remembered what had happened the previous night.

Tom Cunningham's mutation. The ward-from-hell beneath the asylum. The creatures that lurked down there in the shadows.

And the room beyond that housed Robert Wilson.

Reid gagged as he remembered that sickening tongue worming its way into his mouth and throat.

'You,' Reid snapped and jabbed a finger at Templeton. 'You let that thing at me. Forced me to it. What the hell did it do to me?'

Reid pushed himself up to a sitting position, fists clenched. Templeton just chuckled. 'Please stay calm, Dr. Reid,' he said. 'There is no need for anger or overreaction.'

'Overreaction? I ingested the same filth that mutated the patient last night.'

'And you will be fine for it,' Templeton said. 'I promise you that.'

'You call turning into one of those abominations *fine*?'

'You will not turn, as you didn't take enough.'

'Then why do it? Is this just the start? Do you plan on keeping me prisoner here and turning me gradually, like you did with those patients? Is that what you did to my predecessor?'

'What happens to you will be your decision, Dr. Reid. Now, indulge me. Did you dream?'

'What difference does that make?'

'Please, just answer me.'

'Yes,' Reid snapped. 'I dreamt. What of it?'

'Of something from your past, am I correct? A painful memory or regret. And then you saw a place, didn't you? Somewhere not of this world?'

Templeton was indeed correct, of course, but even so, Reid had heard this before—from the patient Adrian James. He guessed Templeton had heard it countless times from other patients on this so-called treatment as well. 'That's right. I sense that is a common occurrence after taking that... fluid.'

'Indeed. Amazing, is it not?'

'Not really,' Reid answered. 'A hallucinogenic property?'

'Oh no, that was no hallucination.'

'You should try for yourself and see.'

'I have,' Templeton said, still smiling.

Reid paused. 'You have?'

'Of course. And the experience was exhilarating. I know I called it a dream, but since you have experienced it you can appreciate that it is so much more.'

'And what would you call it?' Reid asked.

'A vision,' Templeton replied. 'The place that you saw really exists. Our world, our reality, is not the only one—far from it. What is inside of you now, swimming through your veins, is the blood of a Great Being.'

'A god?'

'Yes, but not as we understand the term. You see, with its blood in our veins, even a small amount, we are imparted with some of its wisdom. However, it seems the more we administer, the less we can take it. And, well, you have seen what happens when it goes too far. But I am certain that we can somehow overcome this temporary barrier and learn more secrets from the Ancient Ones. You see, I have discovered that when we die, we do not simply rot in the ground. The soul is a very real thing, though maybe not as we had envisioned it. And if that is true, it is perfectly possible that the dead actually exist out there in the ether somewhere.'

'Nonsense,' Reid said, letting his anger show. From gods to spirits and now to the afterlife—what rubbish would the director throw at him next?

Templeton laughed. 'Even after all you have seen, you still don't believe?'

'I believe there is something strange going on here, and this substance is somehow responsible for patients mutating in ways I never thought possible, but I do not believe that some great being in the sky is responsible.'

Templeton stood to his feet and shook his head. 'Well, I hope you come around soon, Dr. Reid. For your sake.'

'Is that a threat?'

'A warning. At least consider that what I'm saying could be true. Also, consider the possibilities of what could come from that, and what kind of rewards would be presented to you, being at the forefront of this discovery.'

'What do you mean?'

'Well, I know about your family. And as I say, I firmly believe that there is a chance you could one day meet with them again. Is the possibility of that truth not worth having an open mind?'

Reid looked away and shook his head. Fairytales and magic stories—he was growing tired of it all. Moreover, if that *were* true, he did not think he could ever face his wife or son again. 'I'll not hear it,' Reid said.

'Then hear this,' Templeton went on. 'What we discover here will one day soon be made known to the world. Our beliefs will be the one true way, because no one will be able to refute it. And then, imagine where we will be. Those of us that want to could become rulers of this reality. And if you were among our ranks, there would be a seat at the table for you. Imagine that—all the renown and respect you've ever wanted would be yours. No one would ever look at you as a failure again. Does that not sound appealing?'

Reid clenched his teeth, but did not reply, because, as much as it shamed him to admit it, the notion was indeed appealing.

Fairytales and magic stories or not.

Perhaps the substance in his veins was making him more susceptible to this nonsense, or maybe it was his own hubris, but a small part of him found the director's suggestions tempting.

'Is that what you are hoping to get out of all of this, Isaac?' Reid asked. 'Power and fame? Is that worth all the death and misery you have caused?'

'Power and fame are not my goals,' Templeton said as he got to his feet. 'I look to something beyond that. But consider what I've said, Dr. Reid. I think you would be a great addition to our Church, but only the devout can be accepted. However, you now have a special link with the Great Being, so the next time I take you down there, I am hoping your experience will be a little more... enlightening.'

'I have to go and see that thing again?'

'Yes. Tonight.'

'And do I get a say in this?'

Templeton shook his head. 'Unfortunately not. Feel free to take the day off today. Finish my diary if you like. You can wander the upper level of the asylum, as always, but you understand that you cannot leave.'

'So either I join your religion or I die here? Not exactly a good way to turn me into a true believer, is it?'

Templeton shrugged. 'On the contrary, fearing for one's life is often the best way to keep people in line. At least until their minds can finally accept the truth.'

Templeton turned and walked over to the door. 'You're insane, you know that?' Reid told him.

'Insanity is just perspective, Dr. Reid,' the director replied. 'You will see things my way soon enough. Good day.'

And with that, the director left the room.

Reid lay back down in his bed, unable to believe what had happened to him these last few days. His head spun at the madness of it all, and now he was left with two choices: stick to his beliefs and die here, or join a delusional cult and pledge his life to them.

Neither option sounded appealing.

Unless what the director is saying is true?

24

ADRIAN, like the others, pushed his chair back away from Trevor. If Mother was here, then that meant trouble was not far behind. Adrian looked over to an orderly in the hopes of catching his attention.

'Seeing you quite a lot lately, boys,' Trevor said, and Adrian realised that was true. Mother making an appearance two days in a row was unheard of, at least to him. No one answered Trevor, but thankfully one of the orderlies happened to look over, and Adrian, in turn, gave the man a wide-eyed, pleading look, hoping it would be enough to get noticed.

'I'm feeling a little achy,' Trevor went on. 'Something happen to me while I was asleep? One of you boys get a little rough with me?'

Adrian did not want to get caught up in whatever chaos Mother brought with her—not again—so he pushed himself further away. The orderly seemed to take an interest in what was going on and started to walk over. Adrian hoped that he could summon help and be able to restrain Trevor without needing to hurt him, and that the whole thing could be handled with without any violence or injury.

Of course, that was asking too much.

'Something going on here?' the orderly asked.

Trevor turned to him and smiled. 'Oh, you'll do. Come over here and play with me, boy.'

'Sit down,' the orderly snapped. Adrian shook his head. Hadn't the fool witnessed what had happened the day before? Threats just wouldn't work.

And they didn't.

Trevor screamed like a demon and launched himself at the orderly, again kicking and biting in an effort to cause as much damage as possible. They both tumbled to the floor, and Adrian noticed the orderly's ring of keys spill from his belt as the pair fell. An impulse quickly gripped him—to dash over and grab the keys, hoping he would not be seen. He could potentially use them to escape and get free of this place. But almost as soon as the notion came to him, he quashed it.

There was too much risk.

And, regardless of everything he had witnessed recently, he still didn't think he deserved his freedom.

Other orderlies ran over to break up the scuffle, and this time Adrian removed himself from the situation as they piled in with their fists and feet, punching and kicking at Trevor, who was hauled from his prey. A ring was formed around the two as the man Trevor had attacked seemed dazed and confused, but—other than some cuts and scratches—not as badly hurt as his last victim.

'Everyone back!' one of the orderlies yelled, and everyone in the room dutifully complied, with no repeat of the brawl that had erupted yesterday. Trevor was dragged, kicking, screaming and cursing from the room without further incident.

'Bunch of cunts,' he screeched as he was taken from the room. 'Not a strong dick between the lot of you.' His voice faded out as he was pulled farther down the corridor outside.

'Don't any get any ideas,' an orderly barked. 'Keep calm and get back to what you were doing. Anyone tries anything, you'll follow that madman into isolation. Understand?'

A silence followed and Adrian saw one of the orderlies push Seymour out of the way, retrieving the ring of keys that had been discarded on the floor. After that, it didn't take long for everyone to disperse, and Adrian and his group retook their seating positions.

He breathed a sigh of relief. That could have been much worse.

'That fucker is a liability,' Seymour said, 'but he does have his uses.'

'Uses?' Sean asked.

'A good distraction,' Seymour replied with a big, self-satisfied grin.

'What do you mean?'

'Remember what I said before, about finding a way to get out of here? Well, I think I have a plan.'

'What?' Adrian asked.

Seymour leaned in close to them and held up his hand. There, in his chubby palm, sat an iron key.

'How did you get that?' Sean asked, but Adrian had already pieced it together.

'Swiped it from the ring the guard dropped,' he said.

'If someone finds out you took that—' Adrian started, but was cut off.

'But they won't find out, will they?' Seymour snapped. 'Now, guess what this will unlock?'

Adrian knew exactly what it would open, as it looked like the same ones the orderlies used to lock them in their rooms every night.

'But then what?' Adrian questioned. 'So you get free of your room? Where do you go then? You won't get far.'

'I'll get far enough,' Seymour said. 'Because I'm willing to do whatever it takes. We all have a chance here.'

'We?'

'Are you telling me you just want to stay here when you actually have a chance to escape?' Seymour turned to Sean. 'What about you, worm-boy? Fancy getting free of this place and getting some more of that opium you crave so much?'

Sean didn't seem to consider the proposal for very long before he nodded.

'I do,' he said.

'And you, big fella?' Seymour asked, looking over at Jack, but the large man quickly shook his head and brought his arms up to hug himself protectively.

'Come on,' Seymour pressed, 'stand up for yourself. Come with us and have a chance at a half-normal life. I'm sure there is a girl as big and dumb as you out there that can make a man out of you.'

'Leave him alone,' Adrian said. 'He isn't going anywhere.'

'Keeping him here to die with you, then?'

Adrian didn't get a chance to reply because an orderly yelled out to them all.

'Everyone make your way over and get your food, and be quick about it.'

People started to rise obediently, and the hunger Adrian

had briefly forgotten about during the fight quickly returned.

'Well?' Seymour pressed with an urgent whisper. 'What about it? You were handy enough with me yesterday. Figure you might be of some use.'

'I don't want anything to do with it,' Adrian said, getting to his feet.

'Stop being so fucking placid,' Seymour spat. 'Whatever self-loathing you need to do, do it outside of this prison. Show some backbone.'

'Just drop it,' Adrian said.

'No,' Seymour replied. 'Now think hard about this, boy. Tonight, Sean and I are getting out of here. Are you coming with us?'

Adrian didn't know how to answer that. He didn't know if he deserved freedom, but he also didn't fully trust what was going on in this asylum. 'I'm... I'm not sure.'

'Well hurry up and make up your mind,' Seymour hissed. 'When we're out, we'll come to your room. But you'll only have one chance, so choose wisely. I won't hang around.'

Adrian spent the rest of the day in the Communal Area, debating the choice in his head. Every so often Seymour would push him on the subject, but Adrian ducked the questions because he genuinely didn't know how to answer them.

Could he really allow himself to believe that he deserved redemption and a second chance outside of the asylum?

Eventually, night fell, and the patients were all ordered back to their rooms and locked in.

Adrian sat on his bed and continued his internal struggle. In a few hours, he might have the chance to escape this place. He knew the odds were against Seymour and Sean, and the consequences of their actions would be harsh. But what if they made it?

Adrian couldn't decide if it was a risk worth taking, or if he even wanted his freedom.

The hours rolled on, and Adrian lay on his bed... waiting.

25

REID'S DAY had been a slow one, without direction or purpose. The idea of going to work seemed futile considering the position he was now in—any strides he made would be pointless if he wasn't around to collect the plaudits from the medical community at large.

Instead, he spent the day in his office, sometimes paging through Templeton's diary—which outlined more of what he now knew about Arlington Asylum and its workings—but mostly daydreaming and staring at the blank walls, weighing up his options.

Surely there was only one answer to give to Templeton. To agree to the offer and live.

But that would mean accepting that he was a prisoner here for the time being, until an opportunity presented itself to escape.

He also considered the substance that was now flowing through his veins—the black liquid that had excreted from the tongue of Robert Wilson. While he didn't feel ill, exactly —he actually felt healthier and more alert than he had for a long time—Reid did wonder if the substance was poisonous, and if even a small amount would lead to a slow, prolonged death. Still, if Templeton was telling the truth, then the director had the same substance in his blood as well, and he seemed to be suffering no ill effects.

Other than his mental state, perhaps.

As much as Reid was certain that the beliefs Templeton and his followers clung to were fallacies, he still couldn't explain the things he had seen here, which was maddening to him.

And that was how he spent his day—driving himself crazy and mentally going round and round in circles, waiting for Templeton to show as he promised he would.

Eventually, when night fell, Templeton arrived at Reid's office and entered without knocking.

'Have you left this room at all today, Dr. Reid?'

Reid shook his head. 'Not really.'

'Well, let us remedy that,' Templeton said, clapping his hands together. 'It is time.'

'To see your old friend again?'

'That's right. And I promise it will be a little more enlightening for you this time.'

Reid chuckled. 'And by that, do you mean I will be violated again?'

Templeton shook his head. 'That won't happen. Now, if you will, we should go.'

'You come alone?' Reid asked. 'Thought you would have brought your bodyguard.'

'Mr. Jones is out in the hallway, along with some other believers who have requested the privilege to go down to the basement.'

'Privilege? Wow, you people really have your perceptions messed up.'

'If you don't mind,' Templeton said, tapping his foot,

'there is nothing more to talk about. Now please, let's go. Otherwise I will have to call in Mr. Jones.'

Reid sighed, but got to his feet. He hated that he was being bullied into this, though he knew he had no choice. Jones was perfectly capable of incapacitating him and carrying him down there if Templeton wished it.

Reid figured he may as well walk under his own volition and prolong an illusion of choice for as long as he could.

'Fine,' he said, 'let's go.'

'Excellent,' Templeton said and, as Reid passed, took hold of his arm. Reid turned to face him as Templeton spoke, making strong eye contact. 'Keep an open mind tonight,' he said, 'because what you will experience will determine your future.'

It was a clear threat.

Reid shrugged Templeton off and stepped out into the hallway, in no way ready for what was to come.

26

ADRIAN WASN'T sure of the exact hour that Seymour showed up at his door, only that it was the dead of night.

And Adrian had made up his mind.

His hatch dropped open, slowly, as to not make too much noise.

'Adrian,' the voice of Seymour whispered through the void.

'I'm not going,' Adrian told him, hoping it would be enough to drive Seymour away. He didn't want an orderly to wander by and associate Adrian with the escape attempt.

'Why?' Seymour asked, incredulous.

'Because it won't work.'

'Idiot,' Seymour seethed in an angry whisper. 'Fine, stay here and rot. No more than you deserve.'

The hatch slowly closed with a squeak, and Adrian let himself breathe a sigh of relief.

Though that turned out to be premature.

'Hey,' a voice called. It wasn't Seymour, however, but someone farther away. Adrian heard Seymour frantically whisper to someone else—Sean, he assumed—before he heard his door unlock. Seymour and Sean came hurrying into the room, shutting the door behind them.

'Shit,' Seymour whispered, looking panicked.

No, no, no.

This couldn't be happening. Adrian would inevitably get drawn into this and apportioned some of the blame.

'Get out,' he said through gritted teeth.

'Shut up,' Seymour snapped back. They could all hear quick footsteps approach from farther down the hallway. 'Shit,' Seymour said. There was no way to lock the door from the inside and, therefore, no way to stop whoever was approaching from gaining access.

Adrian felt anxiety begin to rise, and his palms began to sweat.

Okay, he thought to himself, *no need to panic. Just explain what happened. Get them to believe that you aren't part of this.*

The door swung open, and a large, overweight orderly stood on the other side, cosh in hand, ready to attack.

'How the hell did you get out?' he said and stepped inside. Even though there were three of them, he showed no fear of being outnumbered. But then, why would he? Patients were beaten and ground down into submission here. And neither Sean nor Seymour seemed like they had it in them to overpower the orderly. They looked terrified.

'Please,' Adrian said, 'I have nothing to do with this.'

'Shut up,' the orderly said. 'You're all in trouble. Gonna get taken off to a more secure ward, I reckon. The director has things in place to deal with people like you. And believe me, you'll be sorry when you see the... therapies... he'll put you through.'

The orderly sneered as he spoke, relishing the fear he was instilling in them. He walked over, and Seymour and Sean pressed themselves onto the bed, next to Adrian.

'I didn't have anything to do with it,' Adrian repeated.

The only response he got this time was a club from the cosh across the side of his head. The blow hit him so hard it knocked him from the bed to the ground below, and his vision spun.

He heard the sound of a scuffle above, but was too disoriented to know exactly what was happening. He managed to push himself up to his knees, hoping things would soon come back into focus. Another blow hit him, this one to the back of the head, and again he went down. Then another—a kick this time—then punches rained down as the orderly beat him mercilessly. Adrian tried to croak out an explanation, and an apology, in an attempt to make this stop, but nothing would work.

A familiar feeling of helplessness washed over him as the ferocious attack continued. It was as if he were young again, back home, at the hands of his father.

But he had stood up to his father. And upon realising that, another familiar feeling emerged.

Rage.

Anger at the injustice of it all. It bubbled and boiled, coursing through him until it claimed him completely.

'No!' he screamed, loud enough to momentarily shock the orderly. Adrian then used this brief pause in the attack to jump to his feet and, with a roar, wrap his hands around the orderly's throat. The two wrestled and fell to the floor, with Adrian able to position himself on top of the bigger man. He kept his hold on the orderly's neck and squeezed as hard as he could.

The man fought back and struck Adrian, punching him in the head, but Adrian was overcome with blind fury and barely registered the blows. He tightened his grip, and the guard began to gag.

'Let... me... go,' the man wheezed with tears starting to form in his eyes. It started as an order, but Adrian didn't let up. 'Please,' the man added, now begging with Adrian to stop. It felt good to hear the man's pleas, so Adrian didn't let up; instead, he pushed the tips of his thumbs down onto the man's Adam's apple. The orderly gagged and coughed as Adrian continued to press down as hard as he could.

The cartilage beneath the tips of his thumbs resisted for a moment before he felt a crunch, but still he did not let up, pushing with even more force. The skin gave way, and his thumbs pierced through while the orderly made a horrible, gargling sound. Blood pooled, then ran freely from the wound that opened in his throat. The orderly made a weak attempt to fight back, but it was futile, and Adrian indulged himself further, digging his fingers into the hole he had created.

Then he ripped.

The orderly's throat pulled open, forming a gaping red gash as the man's wet gargles continued to sound. The stringy insides of the gullet were exposed and blood gushed freely. The orderly kicked and fought as his life slipped away.

Adrian continued to rip the ruined throat apart until the guard stopped moving completely and his eyes became glassy and blank.

It took a while, but slowly Adrian's rapid breathing eased, and he once again started to regain his composure. He pulled his hands from the open wound and lifted them before his eyes. The sight of the murderous weapons—dripping with blood and chunks of claret—brought him fully back to his senses.

'What did you do?'

It was Sean. Adrian turned to see both him and

Seymour standing in the corner of the room, huddled together, having witnessed his barbaric act.

And it was a good question—*just what the hell had he done*? There was no way he could go back to how things had been after this.

He was in trouble. Serious, serious trouble.

He began to panic.

'I didn't mean to,' Adrian said. 'I just... I just...'

'You just made up your mind,' Seymour said, with a hint of a smile breaking through his obvious shock. 'And now, we need to move.'

27

'WE NEED TO GO,' Seymour repeated as he bent down to the dead orderly and relieved him of his set of keys. The one he had stolen earlier was on its own, whereas this appeared to be a full set, all attached to a black metal loop. One in particular stood out as being longer and chunkier than the others.

He got back to his feet and saw that Adrian looked like he was teetering on the edge, ready to lose it, but Seymour didn't want that to happen. He needed Adrian with him, as the man had proven he could be an asset—the body of the orderly with the yawning throat confirmed that—but Seymour also knew that the more people he had with him, the more potential there was for others to take the fall should something go wrong.

And considering what Adrian had done to one of the guards already, it wouldn't take much to divert all blame his way.

Seymour also knew he couldn't give Adrian—who was now just staring at his bloodied hands—the chance to dwell on what he had done, so grabbed the younger man by the arm. 'Move,' he commanded and heaved Adrian up. Thankfully, the confused man complied.

'I... I... I just...' he stammered, but Seymour didn't want to listen to it.

'It's done,' Seymour said, 'no going back now.'

He didn't wait for an answer, and instead pulled Adrian from the room, ushering Sean out ahead as well. Only when they were in the hallway did he realise it would have been wise to check to make sure no one else was around first. The oversight annoyed him, and he knew he would have to be more careful. This time, they had gotten lucky.

'Sean,' he hissed, 'go and check up ahead, make sure no one else is around.'

'Me?' Sean asked, looking genuinely shocked. Seymour felt a pang of anger bubble in his gut. Sean was a liability, a pathetic soul who drifted along with no drive and no initiative of his own. Seymour didn't know if it was the drugs that made him this way, turning his mind to mush, or if it was his natural personality, but he didn't care.

He wouldn't let anyone stop him from getting out of here.

He kicked Sean in the back and sent the thin man sprawling to the floor. 'Just fucking go,' he said, pointing up ahead into the darkness of the corridor.

At first, Sean looked like he was going to protest, but he soon saw sense and scuttled ahead, as light-footed as he could.

'Useless,' Seymour said under his breath. He then tried to focus on what the next move would be. While this was not a well-thought-out escape attempt by any stretch of the imagination—the opportunity itself having come about by pure chance—he still knew that some form of plan would be needed.

The first step was easy—they had to head forward to the ward entrance in the Main Hall, which was in the opposite direction from the Communal Area. Sean was up ahead already, and peeked around the corner before turning back and giving a thumbs up.

All was clear.

Seymour set off, pulling Adrian behind him. Seymour hoped one of the keys they were now in possession of would unlock the door from Ward B and bring them out into the central area of the facility.

Seymour had no idea how many orderlies or other staff would be present at this time of night, so they would need to tread carefully and, if at all possible, stick to the shadows.

He caught up to Sean and looked around the corner as well, seeing a thick metal door at the end of the corridor. This was the exit from the ward.

There were no vision panels or viewing hatches, so they would have no idea if someone was on the other side until they opened it.

If they could open it.

As he set off towards the door, Seymour noticed his heart-rate rise; the nerves and adrenaline that were already present after watching Adrian work now ramped up further. He clenched his fists and felt sweat on his palms and prayed the way ahead was clear.

They reached the door, and Seymour pressed his ear to the cold metal, hoping to pick up any sounds from the other side. There were none, which meant that no one was present, or the door was blocking out any noise. If it were the latter, then it would be a problem.

'Now what?' Sean whispered, already out of breath.

Seymour brought out the set of keys and knelt down in front of the lock. The first key that drew his attention was the longest one, but this didn't fit, so he moved on to the next.

'This is taking too long,' Sean said. Seymour reached up and grabbed a handful of the man's scraggly, greasy hair.

'I'm going as fast as I can,' he said through gritted teeth. 'So just shut up and keep a lookout. Understand?'

Sean nodded, and Seymour released him. He didn't want to—he wanted to beat him, to kick him up and down the hallway, and the urge to hurt this man who dared question him was difficult to control—but he couldn't give in to it. Not just yet.

So he turned again to the job at hand and worked his way through the keys.

'I'm going back,' Adrian said. Seymour looked up at him, wide-eyed.

'What do you mean?'

'I can't do this. I need to go back.'

Seymour got to his feet. 'For God's sake,' he said, 'you need to stop this and open your eyes. Look at the position you are in. Look at your hands, for God's sake. They're covered in blood. If you go back, then you take the punishment for what you've done. With us, at least you have a chance to get out of here. And why on earth would you want to stay in this hell-hole? Don't you have any respect for yourself? What they do to us here isn't right. They don't want to help, you know that. And you also know that nobody ever leaves here. Not alive, anyway. So make up your mind, because I'm not going to keep having this argument. Do you want to stay here and die, or take a chance at having a life?'

'I don't deserve to get out of here,' Adrian said, his voice quiet. More rage bubbled inside of Seymour, and he struggled to keep it under control. It had only been a few minutes ago that Adrian himself had unleashed such rage—which impressed Seymour—but now he was acting more like Sean, more like a husk of a real person.

Submissive and pathetic.

'No one deserves to be stuck here, Adrian,' Seymour said, going against his instincts and trying a more friendly approach. 'I don't care what you've done. So stop wallowing and pull yourself together. Sean and I need your help, because we sure as hell don't deserve to be trapped in here.'

Seymour then turned away from Adrian and again bent down, working on the lock, trying key after key. Thankfully, Adrian didn't go anywhere and just loomed over him, looking lost, but still present. That would do for now.

Eventually, a key fit, sliding smoothly into place and taking hold. Seymour held his breath, slowly turned it, and was rewarded with an audible click.

The three of them looked at each other, knowing the time was at hand.

'Well,' Seymour said. 'All or nothing now. Are we all in this together?'

The truth was that he certainly wasn't in this with them, and would gladly throw them to the wolves if needed, but he wanted them to think that he could be trusted.

'I'm in,' Sean said.

'Good,' Seymour answered as he got to his feet. He looked to Adrian. 'And you?'

There was a frustrating pause, and Seymour half-expected him to go crawling back to his room and wait for his master's punishment, like a disobedient dog. But the answer surprised him.

'Okay,' Adrian said. 'Let's get out of here.'

'Excellent,' Seymour said.

The door gave out a slow creak as he pushed it open.

28

THE DOOR from Ward B led them through a shorter hallway, one lined with wood panelling. On the walls above the panelling were pictures and paintings of men in suits. Adrian only recognised the person in the last photograph, the one nearest a wooden door at the end of the corridor. It was a black and white photo of Director Templeton, who stood poised for the camera.

But Adrian ignored the pictures and instead focused on escaping, something that would have seemed absurd to him less than an hour ago. And now he didn't have a choice as he, quite literally, had blood on his hands. The wet, sticky substance was already starting to dry and flake, darkening in colour.

Fuck.

How had things spiralled out of control so much?

Seymour led them to the door, which they quietly opened, looking through to see a large, dark, open space. The Main Hall was cluttered with ill-matching desks and bookcases, and loose papers and books were strewn everywhere, stacked on desktops and crammed into the over-flowing shelving.

Whenever Adrian had been brought through here previously, it had always been during daytime hours. Now, however, in the dead of night, the vacant office seemed eerie.

They stepped into the space to see other doors, like the one they stood in front of, cut into the walls of the hall, both on the same side and opposite. And to the back of the room, Adrian saw a large, metal elevator door, painted a dull red. It seemed out of place with the decor of the rest of the room, as did the smaller, single door of the same colour farther to its right.

But it was the other end of the Main Hall where everyone's attention was drawn.

Towards the exit.

A double door set with long, full-height, glazed panels. Beyond the glass, like every other possible point of escape in this place, Adrian could make out the familiar sight of those restrictive bars. There would be no breaking through, so they had to hope one of the keys they had would unlock it.

They quickly ran up to the large entrance door, and Adrian could feel his heart pounding.

Would escape really be this easy? And where the hell was everyone?

Granted, the office staff probably wouldn't work through the night, but the route from their ward—save for the orderly Adrian had killed—was too straightforward.

Something didn't seem right with all of this.

Seymour didn't wait to be asked, however, and started trying every key he had on the front door, working through systematically.

Adrian and Sean looked around, nervously. It was quieter here than on their ward, the background sounds of the damned drowned out by the thick metal doors and walls that separated the place from the individual wards.

'No,' Seymour said, frantically trying to jam the last key into the lock.

But it was no use.

'What?' Sean asked, though it was apparent what the problem was.

'None of them fit,' Seymour said, a hint of panic now creeping into his voice.

'How can that be?' Sean asked.

Seymour answered, but not verbally. He dropped the keys and let loose with a punch, catching Sean on the jaw and sending him flailing to the floor.

'Because none of them fit, you cretin!' he shouted.

'Quiet,' Adrian snapped, 'someone will hear us.'

Seymour suddenly turned on him, grabbing a handful of Adrian's clothing. 'Don't tell me what to do,' he said through gritted teeth. Thankfully, however, he lowered the volume in his voice a little. Sean slowly got to his feet, nursing his jaw.

'If you keep shouting,' Adrian said, keeping his own anger in check, 'then you'll draw people to us. We've been lucky so far.'

Seymour let go of Adrian, but did not step away. 'Well, now what? If we don't have the keys to get out, then we're in trouble.'

'What do you mean, *now what*?' Adrian asked. 'This whole thing was *your* idea.'

'Well, we're out of options. We need to go back.'

'Go back?' Adrian asked, grabbing Seymour's arm. 'We can't go back. There is a dead guard in my room with his throat ripped open. Did you forget about that?'

'I didn't forget,' Seymour said with a sneer. 'But it's your problem. I can go back to my cell, and you can take the fall for all of this. Nothing to do with me or Sean. Isn't that right, Sean?'

Seymour turned to look at Sean, a self-satisfied grin on his face. Adrian was raging—there was no way he was going to allow Seymour to lay the blame for all of this at his feet, or let the fat man carry on like nothing had happened.

He would make the bloated fucker pay.

Visions of tearing open his throat surged through Adrian's mind, and he clenched his fists, ready to indulge.

'Quick,' Sean suddenly said, 'people are coming.'

Adrian listened, then heard it too. As much as he wanted to hurt Seymour, there wasn't time right now.

'What do we do?' Sean asked, his voice trembling.

'Shit,' Seymour said. 'We can't just stay here.'

'But we can't go back,' Sean said. 'They'll see what *he* did.' He pointed to Adrian. 'And they will know it was us.'

Adrian knew there was no way out now. By killing that guard, then following Seymour blindly, he had doomed himself.

He had nothing left but time, and likely only a small amount of it. Still, maybe there was a way to avoid detection for a little while longer.

That meant picking a door and finding somewhere to hide to regroup. Ideally, a door that would not lead to a heavily populated area.

'There,' Adrian said, pointing to the other side of the room to a door next to the elevator.

'Why would we go through there?' Seymour asked, but Adrian didn't feel the need to answer. Instead, he just snatched the ring of keys from Seymour's hand and ran over. 'Hey!' Adrian heard Seymour yell, but he didn't stop.

He didn't care if they followed him or stayed where they were—the hell with them.

If Adrian couldn't avoid whatever repercussions lay ahead, then he could at least postpone them for as long as possible. As it turned out, he wasn't going to be alone—he heard Seymour's and Sean's rapid footsteps as they followed behind.

When he reached the door, Adrian noticed further details—the dark red paint had blistered and flaked, revealing rusted metal beneath, and there were also what appeared to be gouges, or deep scratch marks, cut into its surface. Adrian lifted the ring of keys he had taken from Seymour and took hold of the longest one, somehow knowing that it—distinguished from the others —would work.

The key slid easily into the lock, and when Adrian twisted it, the lock clicked open.

'What's the point of going through here?' Seymour asked. 'It doesn't help us get out.'

'If we stay here we get caught, simple as that,' Adrian explained, though he still wanted to strangle Seymour. Adrian then pushed the door open to reveal a stone stair-case running down below, twisting back on itself. The walls had small electric lamps on them that burned a dull yellow, but were too weak to give off any meaningful light.

'What's down there?' Sean asked.

'Don't know,' Adrian said, 'but you can stay here if you want.'

'I'm not going,' Seymour said, crossing his arms defi-antly. That was actually music to Adrian's ears, but then they heard something that changed everything—a door in the Main Hall opening, from Ward B, and frantic, approaching voices.

'Get the director. We need to find whoever did this,' someone yelled.

Clearly there had been orderlies patrolling the group's ward, but had been behind them as they made their escape. Now, however, it seemed that they had found Adrian's handiwork, and they were furious.

'Shit,' Seymour said.

Adrian, Seymour, and Sean quickly slipped through the door, and Adrian pulled it closed behind them, locking it as soon as it was shut.

'They're going to find us,' Sean said, his voice quivering.

Adrian turned and looked down the spiral staircase, seeing it twist into darkness. And from that dark, strange moans and cries drifted upwards to meet them. Not the usual shrieks of the patients who resided here, but something entirely different.

And it came from the only way forward.

'Let's go,' Adrian said, and they began their descent.

29

REID DID NOT WANT to be back in this room.

Even being surrounded by Templeton and his selection of *privileged* orderlies did not make him feel safe here.

None of them were safe in the presence of that thing.

Templeton and his group all looked upon this husk of a person in awe, some seeming positively excited to be in attendance.

First timers, he guessed.

'I cannot believe I am here,' one of the orderlies said.

'You have done well, Brother Andrew,' Templeton said, like a teacher praising a young pupil. 'But remember we are here for a reason. I would like you all to be steadfast and resolute.'

'Understood,' Brother Andrew replied, straightening up his body—all that was missing was a salute.

Reid looked back to the body of Robert Wilson on the steel bed and saw that things had changed in here since his last visit. The body had bloated somewhat, but that wasn't all—those thread-like tendrils that ran from its skin had grown in girth as well as number, no longer resembling fine hairs, and now more like string. Their reach was increasing as well, some even running up the walls to the ceiling above. Whatever mutation was taking place in the room, it was growing stronger, and was clearly far from finished.

'So why are we here?' Reid asked.

But it was not Templeton who answered.

Robert Wilson's eyelids slowly parted, revealing dark eyes below—orbs that swam in black. His mouth opened, and he spoke with a breathless voice. *'I... see... your... wife... and... child.'*

Reid looked to Templeton, who raised his eyebrows and smiled.

The thing that seemed to be speaking through Robert Wilson went on.

'They... still... burn.'

'What do you mean?' Reid asked Templeton. 'Is this some kind of trick?'

'It is no trick,' Templeton said in response. 'You may want to listen to what is being said.'

'They... still... suffer. Outside... of... your... world. And... in... mine.'

'Lies,' Reid snapped.

'They... blame... you. You... abandoned... them.'

'Tell it to stop!' Reid shouted at Templeton. 'Enough of this nonsense.'

Templeton just shook his head.

'It... is... time,' Wilson said, and Reid was unsure as to whom he was referring. *'I... grow... stronger. More... of... my... blood... must... flow.'*

'Increase the administration?' Templeton asked. 'We will need to draw more from you.'

'Take... it. Bestow... my... knowledge... unto... others. Increase... my... flock. It... must... be... done... now.'

'It will be,' Templeton said, and he turned to Jones. 'Do it.'

Jones nodded and retrieved a large case from the corner of the room. He placed it on the floor and opened it, revealing an assortment of needles, tubing, clear plastic containers, and plastic drip bags inside.

'What's happening?' Reid asked, feeling utterly confused.

Templeton smiled. 'It's time to step things up.'

30

THE STEEP, dark stairwell had taken them down to a subterranean level and brought them out into a long, wide passageway that, to Adrian, had more than a passing resemblance to a dungeon.

The walls were stone, as was the curved ceiling, but the ground they walked on was dirt. Torches were fixed to the walls, and there were grated doors at regular intervals along both walls all the way to the end of the long passageway.

Ominous grunts, moans, and some decidedly inhuman sounds could be heard from whatever lay beyond the metal doors.

'It isn't safe down here,' Sean said, and Adrian had to agree. While he'd never felt particularly safe in the asylum, the fear in him now spiked, and his thoughts turned back to the abomination he had seen outside of his room a couple of nights ago. Were the things inside these cells down here similar creatures? If so, that meant the group were in real danger.

'I say we go back,' Seymour said.

The idea was appealing, but going back meant certain

capture, so instead, Adrian studied the thick metal bars on the doors—they looked strong and sturdy, and evidently had been sufficient to hold back whatever was inside. As long as that remained the case, were they really in any immediate danger?

'Go, then,' Adrian told him.

'And you're just going to stay down here, are you?' Seymour asked.

'What else am I supposed to do, Seymour? You made it perfectly clear what my situation is. If I go back, then I get blamed for what happened to that orderly—'

'Well, you did kill him,' Seymour snapped.

'Only because you brought him to me. I was happy being left alone,' Adrian said and pushed Seymour, who backpedaled a few steps.

'Stop,' Sean said meekly. 'This won't help.'

But Seymour—never one to keep his anger in check or to think things through—ignored him and shoved Adrian in return. 'Don't you dare lay your hands on me,' he said. 'Typical of someone like you, always blaming others for your mess.'

'Typical of someone like you,' Adrian countered, 'to always use others for your own benefit.' He lunged forward, thrusting his palms into Seymour's chest again, pushing him as hard as he could and this time sending Seymour toppling to the floor. 'I'm warning you,' Adrian said, 'don't push me any further.'

Seymour looked enraged and slowly got back up to his feet. Adrian braced himself for an attack. 'Or what?' Seymour asked. 'You'll tear my throat open too? Like you did to that orderly?'

'I might,' Adrian said.

'I'd like to see you try.'

Seymour then ran at Adrian, and the two wrestled with each other, each trying to gain the upper hand. As they fought, they stumbled over to one of the side walls of the corridor. There, Seymour managed to get the upper-hand and forced Adrian back until Adrian was pushed into the cold metal of one of the doors.

Seymour then wrapped his meaty hands around Adrian's throat and squeezed. Adrian struggled for breath, and he heard Sean's feeble pleas for them to stop, but he had no intention of listening. Instead, he gave in to his anger and brought up a hand. He then pushed a thumb into Seymour's eye, and the larger man screamed out in pain. Using the momentary relief, Adrian grabbed Seymour and spun them both, now pushing him against the grated metal door, face first. He took a handful of the man's greasy hair, pulled his head back, and then slammed it into the hard metal.

Seymour cried out again, but this only served to drive Adrian on. Again and again, he slammed Seymour's face into the unyielding iron of the door.

And then he stopped, with his breath caught in his throat.

Something was moving within the cell before them, and through the flickering of a nearby torch, Adrian caught a brief glimpse of it.

And from Seymour's whimpering, it seemed he had seen the same thing. 'Let me go,' he said, his voice a scared whisper. 'Please, let me go.'

Adrian realised that he still had the man's head pushed hard into the metal door, his face pressed into a space between the bars.

The thing inside stepped farther forward, and Adrian backed up as it emerged from the shadows. Seymour, now released, quickly backed away the door as well. 'What the hell is that?' he asked.

Not that anyone could give him an answer.

Something large, with no lower half, stepped forward on two massive arms. The thing looked like a creature born from hell, and its head was covered in small, jelly-like eyes that flicked about in all directions. A thick, guttural sound came from the round mouth that opened within its stomach, parting the dark grey skin.

'It can't be real,' Sean said. 'This can't be real.'

Adrian knew that it was. This wasn't a dream or hallucination—something very wrong, and very unnatural, was going on at this asylum.

They stepped back from the door, away from the monster inside, but Adrian needed to see more. He crept to another cell and cautiously peeked inside. There, he saw another one of those things, though he was confident the one he was looking at was dead. And, though it was now little more than a burned and charred husk, it looked familiar to Adrian, with its wide, snake-like mouth, twisted features, and tall, spindly body.

It was the thing he had seen outside of his cell.

Malcolm.

'What the hell is going on here?' Sean asked, looking over Adrian's shoulder.

'I have no idea,' Adrian said. He then walked to the other cells, getting as close as he dared to look inside. Within some cells there were only smouldering remains, but in most there were demonic things that were very much alive.

Most retained a semblance of the humans they once were, but whatever transformations they had gone through had changed them into nightmarish beings that defied belief.

'Hello,' a voice called from one of the cells, catching them off guard. Adrian looked over at the cell close to where the sound had originated. He slowly walked towards it and peered inside.

To his surprise, he did not see another monster, as expected, but a human. An orderly, to be precise, one he had seen in the facility before, though he looked a lot different now. The man's face had swollen horribly, and his rubbery-looking skin was uneven and had turned various shades of greys and greens, reminding Adrian of mould. 'You have to help me,' the trapped orderly begged in a raspy voice.

Adrian felt like he had stepped out of reality and into a nightmare.

'We need to get out of here,' Seymour insisted. 'Now.'

Adrian didn't like Seymour, but after seeing this place, he could not argue with the man. There was nothing they could do for this orderly even if they wanted to. Coming down here suddenly seemed like a bad idea.

'I agree,' Adrian said, then turned back to face the stairwell they had descended, ready to flee this place, but a voice from behind stopped them.

'Well, well, how did you all get out?'

Adrian's heart dropped. He recognised that voice. He slowly turned around to see Director Templeton at the far end of the ward, emerging from a large door. He was accompanied by Dr. Reid, Jones, Duckworth, and three another orderlies.

'Shit,' Adrian said.

'Shit, indeed,' Jones agreed. 'Shit, indeed.'

'Please wait,' Sean said, holding his hands up in supplication. 'We're sorry.'

But Adrian could see the look in the director's eyes; there would be no mercy here.

No forgiveness.

The group, led by Jones, started to walk over to them.

'I'm afraid it is too late for apologies,' Director Templeton said. 'And you, Mr. James,' he added, pointing to Adrian. 'I'm especially disappointed in you. I thought we had made real progress.'

'Rubbish,' Adrian said. 'Whatever it is you're doing here, it certainly isn't helping people.'

The director shrugged. 'Believe what you will. I have little time for this.' He turned to Jones. 'Handle the situation, will you?'

Jones nodded, then commanded the rest of his men, 'Restrain them.'

'Fuck,' Seymour said from beside Adrian. 'What have you gotten us into?'

Adrian ignored the insinuation, focusing instead on the advancing men. He felt his heart begin to race again as his adrenaline spiked.

Tonight had not turned out as expected. He had gone from being resigned to a continued existence in this miserable place, to an unwilling participant in an escape attempt, and now it appeared he would be fighting for his life.

And it was a fight he would probably lose.

Still, he clenched his fists and raised them up.

'We can't win this,' Sean said.

'I know,' Adrian replied.

Seymour let out a growl of frustration. 'This can't be happening,' he said. 'I was so close. I refuse to be trapped in here any longer.'

'You don't have any choice, fat man,' Jones said.

Adrian heard Seymour's breathing deepen. 'Fuck you,' he spat back.

Instinctively Adrian, Seymour, and Sean huddled together as the group of orderlies started to surround them.

'This isn't going to go well,' Sean said. Adrian knew he was right, but there was nothing they could do to change that. It was going to happen, regardless.

Once the group was fully surrounded, Jones gave the order.

'Get them.'

And the assault began.

The orderlies rushed in, all armed with their coshes. Adrian swung a punch, connecting with the cheek of the first guard to reach them. It was enough to knock the man back, but Adrian felt pain shoot through his hand. Through his peripheral vision, he saw two orderlies tackle Sean and easily wrestle him to the floor. Unfortunately for Seymour, he had Jones to deal with, and the large orderly beat him down quickly with vicious blows to the head.

The remaining orderly dove into Adrian and tried to restrain his arms, but Adrian managed to pull them free and gouged at the man's eyes. He then grabbed the orderly by his uniform and, remembering how he'd pinned Seymour up against the door earlier, attempted to do this same again. He pushed the orderly back, managing to overpower him, and slammed the man into one of the gates in the wall.

His plan was an absurd one, but Adrian was hoping that the thing within would perhaps take care of the orderly he was struggling with. But as crazy as the plan may have been, when the orderly started to scream in pain, Adrian knew it had worked.

He backed off the guard, who remained stuck in place at the metal door. Looking past the orderly, Adrian saw why.

A thin, purple stalk had penetrated the man's torso, and it snaked its way down his form, wrapping around his leg and holding him in place. Adrian took another step back as the orderly continued to cry out in pain, his screams growing higher in pitch as blood oozed from the wound in his gut. Adrian moved to the side, and could now see the creature from which the tentacle originated—a gelatinous thing that clung to the metal door. The spindly vine had emerged from a puckering mouth, but the open maw had stretched in size, and Adrian saw it had clamped around a portion of the man's back that had protruded through a gap in the bars and was pulling him inside as much as it could.

The orderly's screaming drew the brawl behind Adrian to a temporary close as everyone watched the gruesome, macabre scene unfold.

After another scream, Adrian could make out a powerful sucking sound coming from the creature's gulping mouth. It took Adrian a moment to realise what was happening, but the situation made a terrible kind of sense as the jelly-like body of the monster began to expand.

At the same time, the orderly began to wither.

Blood spluttered from the man's mouth as he continued to flail.

He was being pulled inside out, the contents of his body —blood, guts, and organs—now slurping through and pooling in the transparent mass of the feeding entity.

'Andrew!' one of the guards cried out, shocked to see what was happening to his friend, who continued to squirm in vain. The writhing stalk had a firm hold of the orderly, and the mouth proceeded to pull his innards from his body. It continued to feed even as Andrew's movements slowed.

When it had eventually taken its fill, the vine worked its way back through Andrew and back into the mouth, which closed with a slurping sound. There was a large hole in the man's stomach, showing a hollow, red pit behind, and his body sagged and drooped unnaturally. He tried to take a step, somehow still alive, but his knees buckled, and he tumbled to his side, sliding along the wall and falling motionlessly to the floor before an adjacent door.

Adrian was sickened by what he'd just witnessed—the way that thing had fed was so bestial, so inhuman. Not evil, just instinctual, like the way a spider would feast on a fly—uncaring and impartial. The blob slowly worked its way down the door; its sticky skin, which now gave off a red hue, rolled down the metal bars before it pulled itself along the floor and disappeared into the darkness of its cell.

So caught up in the vile sight was Adrian that he didn't hear Jones approach from behind. The first he knew of it was when the orderly had knocked him to the floor with a mighty blow to the side of the head. His vision spun, pin-pricked with white dots.

Adrian barely had time to roll onto his back before Jones started to kick him viciously, every swing connecting to the head, side and stomach. Adrian begged him to stop, but Jones would not let up.

'I'll kill you,' the orderly said, gritting his teeth. 'I will fucking kill you, you pathetic piece of shit.'

Adrian had no opportunity to fight back, the attack overwhelming him completely. He felt his consciousness begin to slip away, and the last thing he heard before blacking out entirely was the voice of Director Templeton.

'Be calm, Mr. Jones. He is more useful to us alive.'

Another kick to the head, and darkness claimed Adrian completely.

31

'ADRIAN, WHY?'

The voice rang out all around him, coming from everywhere and nowhere at the same time.

It was sad, full of hurt.

And all around him was that nightmarish hellscape.

Demons as small as bugs, and others taller than the smooth black mountains, roamed across the land.

Up above, in a sky speckled with stars that moved and pulsed, many swirled together and formed that great eye in the cosmos. An eye that seemed to look down directly at him.

'Why?' the voice cried out again, sobbing. It seemed to echo from somewhere. He turned. Was it coming from that vast expanse of bubbling black liquid?

Then he heard a different sound.

Mocking laughter that boomed loud enough to fill the sky around him.

∾

AS ADRIAN CAME BACK to consciousness, he immediately

sensed movement—a forward momentum—before he opened his eyes. His head hurt, badly, and a throbbing pain jack-hammered around inside his skull, strong enough to make him nauseous. Adrian had no idea as to the extent of his injuries—a concussion, or maybe even a cracked skull.

He could make out a constant squeaking sound among the loud moans and cries of the damned. He was apparently in some area of the asylum, but the screams here seemed louder and more intense than his own ward.

Adrian slowly opened his eyes.

The squeaking sound was coming from the thin wheels of the uncomfortable wheelchair he was restrained to.

A corridor, different from the one he had grown used to in his own ward, moved by as he was pushed forward. The walls here were a dull grey plaster and the floor a combination of mismatched tiles streaked with filth and even... blood.

As well as doors, the walls were punctuated by large viewing windows filled with wire-mesh glass. Some rooms here looked much larger than Adrian's own, but it soon became clear that these were used for more than just accommodation.

He saw what they were doing to people inside—therapies that seemed more like torture. Multiple examples of mistreatment could be seen through the various windows that did nothing to drown out the agonising screams of pains.

One man was strapped down to a table, his head facing the window. Instead of a scalp or hair, Adrian could see the exposed brain, the top of the man's head cut away cleanly. A group of orderlies stood close, taking great interest as one of them pushed needles into the creases of the unprotected matter. The poor man enduring the torture did not kick or scream or fight, he merely stared up to the ceiling, evidently catatonic.

In the next cell, darker than the last, a screaming patient was strapped to a wooden chair in the centre of the room—only the chair was upside down, secured to a thick pole. It slowly rotated, again and again, with the man begging for it to stop—his face purple from the blood that had rushed to his head. Adrian could only guess at how long he had been left alone like that.

In another room, a poor man was tied to a chair and had a large, metallic contraption secured to his head. The device held two oversized screws on each side that were being turned and tightened by orderlies who turned the lengths of metal, twisting them in, so that the thick ends exerted pressure to the temples of the patient's head. He, like so many others, was crying out in desperate pain. Blood ran from his nose as the orderlies continued to increase the pressure, and another stood by, taking notes.

A larger room contained multiple patients, these all wearing plain uniforms with arms that wrapped around each other, fastened together at the back. The men in here looked painfully thin, almost skeletal, and their eyes were blank, lost, and dejected.

Absolutely hopeless.

One man lay motionless in the centre of the room, his eyes a glassy, blank stare. He was clearly dead.

Adrian quickly realised where he now was—Ward A. He knew nothing good would come of his stay here.

Adrian was wheeled into a room that was bare, save for a single chair in its centre, one that tilted backwards and had a foot and headrest, so that the user could lie back. A thin metal stand was next to the chair.

The room stunk of stale sweat and urine.

Adrian was turned around and now saw the orderly who had been pushing him through the hallway—and he recognised the man immediately. There was a dark purple lump on his cheek from where Adrian had punched him down in the underground ward.

The orderly touched a finger to the cheek. 'You're gonna pay for this, boy.' Adrian didn't answer. The orderly then walked from the room and called out to someone unknown. 'We're ready.'

It didn't take long for more of his colleagues to join him and, with no further fanfare, the group freed Adrian and wrestled him from the wheelchair and into the tilted seat. Adrian tried to fight back, but was struggling against too many people and was quickly overpowered. Thick straps were fastened around his ankles, wrists, throat, and waist, securing him to the chair.

'Now what?' one of them asked.

'We wait,' another said. 'The director will be here soon to guide us in the required treatment.'

The orderly with the lump on his cheek chuckled and leaned in to Adrian, bringing his face close enough so that Adrian could smell his rancid breath.

'Oh yes,' he said, 'you really are going to pay. Believe me, this is not going to be pleasant.'

32

BROTHER JONATHAN STEVENS felt a coiling in his gut. Something was changing inside of him.

He could feel it.

Ever since that creature had punctured his eye with its tongue and emitted its blood into him, he had been aware of the continuous change. His body felt—and looked—swollen and bloated, with sores developing over his greying, rubbery skin.

He knew what he would soon become.

And it terrified him.

Jonathan believed in the cause, always had, but could now see how unimportant his devotion truly was. The director had ordered him imprisoned down here, and Brother Jones had been all too eager to comply.

Then Jonathan had been thrown in this cell, like one of those monsters he could now hear around him, and was left alone in this dark, hellish dungeon.

But now he had an opportunity—for escape and revenge.

Brother Andrew Ellis, a good friend of his, had been

killed by one of the creatures in the cell next to Jonathan's own. Andrew's ruined body had fallen directly outside of Jonathan's door, close enough to reach. And, while a melee had broken out between his brothers and some escaping patients, Jonathan had used the distraction as an opportunity—he had reached his hand through the grated door and retrieved his brother's keys from his belt before sinking back into the darkness.

He would no longer be a prisoner down here, to the Church he once gave his life to. He would not be cast aside as something to be locked-up and experimented on.

He would get his revenge.

33

DR. REID and Director Templeton made their way to Ward A, where Adrian James and his fellow would-be escapees had been taken. And, per Templeton's orders, they would be increasing the administration of the medicine in this ward as well.

Dr. Reid walked at Templeton's side, completely silent. The encounter with the entity below weighed on him. Even if he was not wholly devoted to the cause of this Church—which he wasn't—he was now questioning himself.

And that was a start, he supposed.

'Penny for your thoughts, dear Doctor?' Templeton asked.

Reid was slow in responding. 'I'm not sure I can make sense of my thoughts.'

'Understandable,' Templeton said. 'I know how over-whelming it all is. And believe me, I wish things could have been different. But, as you can appreciate, there is no easy way to reveal this kind of truth to people.'

'Why even reveal it at all?' Reid asked. 'Why couldn't you

have just left me in the dark? Why did you have to bring me here in the first place?'

'Because we need someone like you, someone with your expertise.'

'But why? If you believe in what you say you do, then what good is my knowledge to you? Isn't it primitive and useless to you and these... gods?'

'In all honesty, when we know more, I expect it will be. But so far, our greatest findings have come through study and experimentation. It has always been that way. In fact, it was your predecessor who helped in our breakthroughs here at this facility. But as you can imagine, getting people with the requisite knowledge to join our cause is somewhat difficult. They usually find it hard to accept when we show them.'

'So why me? What made you think I'd be any different?'

'Frankly, desperation,' Templeton said. 'You were in a position where you had few options, if any. And that was to our advantage.'

'So you preyed on me.'

'If you want to be that dramatic about it, then yes. But let us not pretend that you are a victim here, Dr. Reid. You were cast out from medicine through your own actions, and I offered you a path to redemption. But now surely you realise that the things you can achieve with us here are orders of magnitude beyond anything you ever expected? Never lose sight of that.'

'And if what you are saying is true, then what do you hope to get from that thing in the basement? If it is as powerful as you say, what use are you to it?'

'It needs our help to continue in what it is trying to do,' Templeton said.

'And then what? You think you will survive it? You can't trust that thing.'

'We don't need to. We just need to learn from it... for now.'

'For now? What happens when you lose control?'

'We won't. This is a breakthrough the likes of which my organisation has never known: constant communication with one of these Great Beings, carried out through the vessel it inhabits. I am well aware there will be a time when things perhaps go too far, in which case there is a fail-safe.'

'Which is?'

'We burn the vessel. Scorch the link.'

'That will work?'

'It will.'

'But then your connection with this Great Being will be no more.'

'Which is why we need to learn as much as we can in the time we have.'

'By turning patients into monsters?'

'By learning how much the human body, and more importantly the human mind, can withstand. And then we wish to discover how to push beyond that barrier. To ascend.'

Reid stopped in his tracks. 'Ascend? You mean to become one of those things?'

Templeton smiled and drew to a halt as well. 'Possibly. I wish to gain their power and knowledge. Why restrict ourselves to these mortal coils? I believe that there is a way for us to evolve into one of these beings.'

'You want to be a god?'

Templeton chuckled. 'And you don't? Regardless, I feel we are on the edge of something great. Increasing the distribution of the Great Being's blood should lead to some interesting results. Time to pick a side, Dr. Reid. You can either stand with those who turned their backs on you, or join us in forging a new future for mankind. But choose quickly; this offer is not indefinite.'

The two walked on in silence until they reached their destination. Reid could hear the cries of the tortured and tormented in the ward around him. It was this torment, he knew, that the Great Being fed on, and drew strength from, thanks to the spread of its blood. The director felt a tingling in his body.

He had some of the sacred blood in his own veins, as all the believers here did. Not as much as was administered to the patients, but a sample nonetheless. Enough to give them a glimpse of the truth and power the entity possessed.

It was clear that Templeton's orders were being carried out, and the medicine was administered with greater frequency and enthusiasm than ever before. He saw many drips—filled with that black liquid—connected to the patents as they walked down the corridor. The sight made him remember a term he had heard during his studies in school: that blood is life.

That may be true, but now he knew there was more to it than that, at least concerning the substance that was so coveted in this place.

The blood was the truth.

They reached the cell where Adrian James was being kept, and even though the man was restrained to the chair, a group of orderlies stood by to make sure there would be no repeat of his attempted escape.

'Mr. James,' Templeton said as they entered the room. 'I want to say that things didn't have to be this way. I was prepared to take things slowly with you, but you brought this on yourself. I guess I was wrong about you—I think you are very much a man like your father. More animal than human.'

Adrian glared at him, but did not respond.

'What do we do with him?' one of the orderlies asked.

'First, what of the others who were with him?'

'They are currently being treated,' another orderly answered.

'Excellent,' Templeton said, clapping his hands together. He took a step closer to Adrian. 'You know, I'm well aware that you did not tell me everything there was to know about you during our sessions. Killing your father was only the start of your misery, and there is more that you haven't shared—that you are desperate to keep secret. Well, know this, when the blood is in your veins, as it already is, there are no secrets from the Great Ailing One. It already knows everything about you... about what you've done. I have a feeling that you are going to face that unpleasant truth very soon, in ways you can't imagine. It will likely destroy you. I want you to remember that as you lose consciousness, Mr. James. I want it to be the last thing you think of while you leave this world and arrive... somewhere else. All because you dared to cross me.'

With that, Templeton swung his hand and struck Adrian across the cheek. He then turned to one of his colleagues.

'I think it is high time we make use of the device we recently received, don't you?'

One of the orderlies smiled and nodded before running from the room, taking another two with him. Templeton turned back to Adrian. 'I have not had the chance to use this as yet, you see. Bit of an experimental method where volts of electricity are pumped into your body. The power of the surges can vary, I'm told, depending on the condition one is treating, and I think that yours is most serious. So, let us see just how high the device will go, shall we?'

The director smiled as fear crossed the face of Adrian James. Soon the orderlies returned, wheeling in a control board filled with switches and dials. From this board, multiple wires ran out, with electrodes at the ends. The orderlies took their time taping these electrodes to the patient's head, chest, fingers, and even his groin. Reid knew what this would do, and also assisted in the placements of the electrodes after seeing the haphazard way the other orderlies were applying them. This drew a smile from Templeton, and Reid felt a momentary sense of pride.

Then he admonished himself—was he really trying to please this man?

'No, don't do this,' Adrian James pleaded. 'I'm sorry, I really am.'

'Too late for that,' Templeton replied and stood at the controls. Each electrode could be activated individually, so he chose the one connected to Adrian's left temple and turned it up, not all the way, but enough for a good shock. Adrian convulsed, his body jerking up and down, and veins formed on the man's face as he tried, and failed, to push out a scream.

'Oh, I like this toy very much,' Templeton said, and flashed a smile over to Dr. Reid. 'Shame I don't have time to utilise it. There is too much to be getting on with. But I will leave it to my colleague.' He waved over one of the orderlies to take over. 'I have work to do,' he said. 'And so does everyone else. Get to it.'

There was a buzz of activity as those not needed left the room, with only two orderlies remaining. Reid and Templeton left as well, as Mr. James screamed in agony—

the sounds of pain accompanied by the crackling buzz of electricity.

Reid looked up to Templeton, who was smiling, as some orderlies gathered around, making Reid feel distinctly threatened and uncomfortable.

'Well then, Dr. Reid,' Templeton said, 'what is it to be? Are you with us, or are you against us?'

34

ADRIAN WAS IN AGONY.

Seething, white-hot pain stabbed through his skull and threatened to burst it open.

He was faintly aware that he had been left in the company of a single orderly now, and that the man was controlling the device that sent waves of agony coursing through Adrian's body. So absolute was the torture, that it was hard to focus on anything other than the pain.

Eventually, however, the suffering subsided, and Adrian was allowed the opportunity to scream. He felt drool running down his chin.

'Please,' he mumbled, but he could tell that his speech wasn't clear. The orderly laughed—a spiteful, mocking chuckle.

'Sorry, friend,' the man replied, 'under strict orders here. Can't say I'm not enjoying it, though. But I'll vary things a little bit for you, how does that sound?'

Adrian didn't answer.

Instead, he tried to ready himself for the pain that was coming; but no matter how much he braced, when it came it overwhelmed him completely. And this time the relentless, pulsating shocks did not explode into his skull—instead they centred on his groin, causing excruciating spasms, as if a thousand stinging needles were penetrating his testicles. Adrian bucked and writhed involuntarily before vomiting down himself.

No pain that he'd ever previously experienced could have prepared him for this.

And then it increased.

The orderly sent volts coursing through Adrian's arms and chest, but did not let up on the pain centred on his groin. Adrian wanted to call out and beg for this to end, to kill him if need be, but to just stop the torture. Yet speech was impossible, as he could barely control a single muscle in his body.

The orderly then turned down the electric current, but the effects remained with Adrian, and he continued to convulse. His vision slowly came back into focus, and he saw another orderly staring over him, fixing a clear bag of black liquid into the drip stand. Somewhere in his tormented mind, Adrian knew what that was.

The medicine.

A large needle was lifted to Adrian's arm, ready to penetrate his skin to fix the cannula and administer the poison into his bloodstream.

But the orderly stopped.

'What the hell was that?' he asked.

Adrian had heard it too. It was an almighty roar, coming from somewhere outside the room. Then other voices could be heard, panicked shouts and screams, as well as other inhuman noises, reminiscent of what Adrian had heard in the underground ward.

'Go and see what's happening,' the orderly at the controls ordered. 'I'll stay here with him.'

The second orderly seemed to hesitate, but did as instructed and walked out to the hallway.

'Don't think you are getting out of this so easily,' the remaining orderly said. 'I'm still under orders.'

He switched on the electricity, and Adrian's pain began again, this time throughout his whole body.

The pressure and pain that built up inside him penetrated to his very core, to his bones, and he was sure he would die.

To add to his humiliation, Adrian felt his bladder release.

Thankfully, this round of torture, while the most extreme yet, did not last as long. When he was able to refocus, finally, Adrian saw that the other orderly was back, and he looked terrified. He was speaking to his colleague in frantic tones.

'What do you mean?' the first man asked.

'I don't know how else to describe it, but I'm telling you it's true. We've lost control. It's hell out there.'

'It can't be.'

'I'm telling you, it is,' the second orderly insisted. 'We have to go. If we don't, we'll die.'

The other man seemed to consider the words as the nightmarish noises outside increased in volume. 'Fine,' he finally said; then he turned to Adrian. 'What about him?'

'Forget him,' the other man said. 'Leave him here.'

The first orderly nodded. 'Let's go,' he said, and the two of them ran out of the door, leaving it ajar and Adrian alone.

Adrian took the time he had available to him to try to compose himself. Slowly his spasming body began to calm, and the pain, though still throbbing, started to ease and become somewhat bearable. He could now concentrate fully on the noises outside.

Something was indeed happening out there. Something serious.

Screams, cries, and monstrous bellowing sounded out. Some noises closer than others.

Then he heard panting and approaching footsteps, the slapping of bare skin on the tiled floor coming closer and closer.

Adrian held his breath. He knew that whoever—or whatever—was approaching would not be friendly, and to make matters worse, he was completely immobile.

Then he saw the shadow on the floor of the hallway outside, one that approached with uneven movements. The silhouette looked human, but swayed on unsteady legs. Eventually, the form appeared in the open doorway and looked inside.

Adrian breathed a sigh of relief.

It was a patient. Not one Adrian knew, but he looked terrible. His skin was grey and covered with welts and lumps.

'Hey!' Adrian called, alerting the man to his presence.

'What... happened?' the man replied, but his voice was strained, and he was clearly in pain.

'I don't know. What's going on out there?' Adrian asked him in return, as the man staggered into the room.

'I don't know,' he said. 'They tortured me and put that... stuff into me. Lots of it. Then... something happened. Everybody ran. And now people are changing. Everything is changing.'

The lights in the room, and in the corridor beyond, began to flicker.

'Okay, listen,' Adrian said, 'I need you to free me. Understand? I need you to get me out of these restraints.' The patient didn't seem to be listening, instead lost in a faraway gaze. 'Hey!' Adrian yelled, startling the man back into focus. 'Let me out of here!'

Eventually, the man gave a slow nod, and he began to undo the straps on Adrian's arms. When those were free, he started work on Adrian's legs, but stopped as he began to cough. It was light at first, but quickly rose in intensity until the patient could barely control himself.

'Are you okay?' Adrian asked, but the man stumbled to the floor, hacking up spit and bile. He began to convulse, and a stream of blood erupted from his mouth, even running from his nose and seeping from his eyes.

'Help... me,' the man croaked, reaching up from the floor.

His skin began to change. It twisted and melted, pulling itself into a different form as he started to scream.

Adrian quickly began to undo the rest of his bonds, all the while keeping his eyes on the transforming patient. The lights continued to flicker, leaving Adrian with flashes of the painful change that the man was now going through.

His sores grew more substantial and opened at their heads, taking on a more distinctive form: small, puckering mouths. Tiny, needle-like lengths of pink flesh wriggled free from these mouths, and rolled around their edges, licking the skin, before disappearing back inside.

Tongues.

The patient's skin turned a sickly yellow, and his limbs began to stretch out as he continued to scream—elongating as his fingers melted together. Eventually, his arms and legs extended to form long, sharp appendages.

'Help!' the patient screamed, looking desperately to

Adrian as his eyes expanded, pooling wider like the yolk of a cracked egg.

Adrian knew that he could do nothing for the man, and he had seen enough in that ward-from-hell underground to know that the patient was becoming something else: an ungodly creature that would act in only one way.

Adrian finally freed himself and jumped down from the chair. His legs were still unsteady, and strength evaded him, nearly causing him to fall into whatever the struggling man was now becoming; but he managed to grab the chair and steady himself. He then moved as quickly as he could and ambled from the room, leaving the screams of his fellow patient behind as the transformation continued.

Once out in the hallway, Adrian pulled the door shut and secured it with the thick deadbolt that was fixed to its outside face. He allowed himself a moment to lean against the wall and gather what little strength he could.

Then he looked up and saw how everything had changed. It was no longer the same asylum.

It was hell.

35

THINGS HAD BEEN quiet for a while. The body of his former colleague still lay outside of Jonathan Stevens' cell, and it didn't look like anyone was going to be coming down anytime soon to clean it up.

Which meant that this was as good a time as any.

He knew had to act before he lost his mind entirely to whatever was taking over his body and soul.

Jonathan drew out the keys that he had taken and approached the door. He pushed his arm through the space in the iron grating and carefully angled the keys in his hand back on themselves, working to find the lock. It was difficult, but eventually he was successful and he heard the *click* that signalled his release. He pushed the door and it swung open.

Jonathan was free.

But he did not intend to free only himself. He walked to another cell and peered at the creature inside. It looked back with insect eyes, studying him. Curious, but in no way aggressive.

Perhaps it knew what Jonathan was—or what he would soon become.

And so, Jonathan walked to the cell and released the unholy abomination. Then another. And another.

None that walked from their cages attacked him, though a few did turn on each other, and once all the cells doors were open, the dungeon quickly turned into a pit of chaos and violence. Many of the smaller, weaker monsters were torn limb from limb.

Which would not do at all.

Jonathan quickly ran to the exit from this level—the smaller, single door next to the elevator. He opened it and turned to look back.

Many of the creatures were watching him... and following.

He hoped they would continue to do so as he made his ascent.

And thankfully, they did.

He allowed himself a smile as he continued up, bringing hell with him.

36

THE SIGHT of the hallway before Adrian shocked him. The lights above still flickered, threatening to cut out at any time. The corridor itself, however—the materials and construction—seemed to have changed somewhat. Organic matter and flesh had begun to seep through the cracks of the tiling, streaking out in vein-like patterns. The floor beneath his bare feet felt slippery and squishy to walk on, and there was a rancid smell that permeated the air.

Then there were the nightmarish sounds—wails and roars, coupled with terrified and pained screaming.

Through the screens and windows that punctuated the walls, Adrian could again see acts of cruelty and torture being committed, though now they were much worse—and things had reversed as the orderlies were no longer the tormentors.

In one room he saw an orderly stripped naked and secured to a bed—a horrific monstrosity with an exposed brain and hanging mouth stood over him. The creature had already torn off the skin from the orderly's head and face and was now stripping lengths of flesh from his body with long, thin fingers, revealing the red, glistening muscle beneath. Adrian ducked down below the window and crept farther down the hallway that was, so far, thankfully clear.

In the next cell, Adrian saw another role that had been reversed; an orderly now sat in the upside-down chair, and he was being rotated by a tall, gangly thing with no face, though it did have a long, slit-like mouth along the length of its boney chest. The unfortunate man's intestines had been pulled free from his gut, and the thing held a length of it in one hand as it operated a wheel to rotate the orderly with the other. With each and every turn, more of his insides spilled free and wrapped around him as he screamed and screamed.

Adrian kept going as quickly as he could, trying desperately to stay out of sight of these horrific creatures—not that he didn't find some justice in the acts of depravity they were acting out on the staff of the asylum.

In the larger room where Adrian had seen multiple malnourished patients, he caught sight of the monstrosities within actually feeding on each other, two unfortunates chosen as prey as the others violently ripped and tore at their bodies. An orderly had also been caught up in the chaos, but was long since dead, and there was very little left of his body save for a fleshy husk.

Adrian continued to the ward exit, moving as quickly and quietly as he could until he heard a loud banging sound coming from one of the rooms behind.

Turning around and looking down the corridor, he could see that the noise was coming from the room he had just escaped.

The door was forced open as the savage creature he had left locked inside fought its way out and into the hall. It walked on needle-like arms and legs, scuttling like a spider, and even from this distance Adrian could see that the man's head was now at the rear of the insect-like thing, and a new face, complete with mandibles and multiple eyes, had formed where his groin used to be. The once human face at the back seemed to be locked in an eternal scream, the mouth opening and closing with no sound emitting from it. From the other end, however, a terrible screech sounded out as the thing laid its many eyes on Adrian.

It scuttled forward with scary speed, and Adrian was forced to forgo stealth and just get the hell out of there. He leapt up and ran as the monster crawled after him, making a hissing sound as it did. He sprinted around an upcoming corner and spotted the exit to the ward up ahead. The other monstrosities in the ward became aware of his presence, alerted by the noise he was making as he ran, and fierce growls rose all around as Adrian pushed and gave an extra burst of speed.

Then two people stepped out from one of the rooms up ahead, close to the exit. However, they were not one like the other demonic things in this ward; they were people Adrian recognised. The large, round man in the lead looked panicked and appeared to be running for his life, escaping from... something.

Another man, this one more slender, ran behind him— also terrified and looking very, very ill.

Seymour and Sean.

Seymour's hands and arms were coated in blood, and in his right hand he held a set of keys.

Adrian had no idea where Seymour had gotten them, but he didn't care—he was just thankful that he now had a chance to get out of here.

Seymour and Sean reached the exit from the ward and freed themselves, stepping over the threshold. Adrian then pushed himself harder, running for the door. Seymour turned to close it, and as he did, he locked eyes on Adrian, who was sprinting for all he was worth.

'Seymour,' Adrian screamed, now agonisingly close, 'let me through.'

Seymour paused, then a snarl formed on his face.

He started to close the door.

'No!' Adrian cried out. He was so close and could feel the scuttling creature behind him gaining ground. If Seymour trapped him in here, then Adrian was doomed to a violent, agonising death. In desperation, he launched himself forward into the door, just as it was about to slam shut. He thrust his arm through the gap, and the heavy door pressed into it, trapping the appendage. He let out a cry of pain, but knew he had to ignore it. He pushed as hard as he could against Seymour, who was keeping him from entering.

Normally Seymour, with his weight advantage, may have been the stronger man, but Adrian had adrenaline and desperation on his side. With that horrible, crawling nightmare almost upon him, he found additional reserves and managed to force the door open—overpowering Seymour and creating a large enough gap for him to squeeze through.

Adrian fell to the floor on the other side and spun his head to see Seymour slam the door shut, just as the creature leapt towards it. Before it closed completely, he saw that other abominations were pouring out from the various rooms off the main corridor. Adrian then heard great bangs against the door that Seymour was fighting to keep shut.

'Help,' Seymour yelled, desperately. Sean was frozen with fear, and part of Adrian wanted to run and leave Seymour to it —to let him meet his fate. But if he did that, then the creatures would swarm out and no doubt finish him off as well. So

Adrian jumped up, his arm screaming in pain, and heaved the strong metal bolt across into its latch. Angry, frantic pounding could be heard from beyond the door, growing stronger as more bodies joined in the attempt to force it open. And as sturdy as the door looked, he knew it wouldn't hold forever.

Seymour took a few steps back and turned to say something, but Adrian didn't want to hear it, instead unleashing a furious punch with his good arm, connecting with Seymour's chin. The fat man stumbled backwards, and Adrian kept up his assault, hitting him again and again, forcing him to the floor. Seymour tried to bring his hands up to protect his face, so Adrian unleashed a flurry of kicks to his stomach.

'You tried to leave me for dead!' Adrian shouted. Seymour pulled his knees up and tucked his head down, arms around himself in a protective foetal position.

'Stop!' he shouted, but Adrian was in no mood to listen —he was in a mood to fight. So he continued, feeding his anger.

'I'll kill you,' he said, truly believing every word. The selfish, fat bastard had it coming.

'We need to go,' Seymour managed to get out between blows. 'The exit. It's right there.'

Adrian paused his attacks and looked down the length of the Main Hall. There, beyond the reception area, was the exit, precisely as Seymour had said.

However, it made little difference, as neither of them had a key.

'Doesn't matter,' Adrian said, preparing to attack again, 'we can't get out.'

And then the room was swarmed.

Not by creatures, but by orderlies, led by Jones, who was

armed with a fire-spewing weapon. They poured in from other wards that connected to the Main Hall.

Even Director Templeton and Dr. Reid appeared as well, and everyone looked concerned.

'What happened?' the director demanded.

'Not sure,' Jones said. 'Ward A seems to be compromised.'

'Not compromised,' another argued. 'Lost.'

Adrian looked around, frantic, trying to figure out his next move. But he did not get far.

'Grab them,' Templeton said, pointing over to Adrian and the others. Knowing it was useless, Adrian did not fight back. 'Everyone calm down,' Templeton ordered, trying to quash the growing sense of panic in the room, made even worse by the sounds coming from Ward A.

But then Adrian heard it. Similar sounds as those monstrous nightmares, but not those from Ward A.

These were coming from somewhere else.

He turned to look at the back of the hall, towards the door to the spiral staircase. Inhuman shrieks sounded beyond.

And they were getting closer.

'What the hell is that?' one of the orderlies asked.

Then the door slowly creaked open and out stepped an orderly. But he looked... different, somehow. Riddled with sores, and his body had swollen with tumour-like growths.

'Brother Stevens,' Templeton said. 'How did you get free?'

But Brother Stevens did not answer.

He just smiled.

And from behind him, a legion of those nightmarish creatures poured into the room.

37

REID'S HEART was in his mouth as he saw those things burst through the doorway—a variety of monstrosities and nightmarish visions that had once been imprisoned down below, were now free and here to cause destruction.

The men that were gathered, armed as they were, stood no chance.

It was a slaughter.

The closest orderly to the advancing creatures was quickly attacked and pulled to the ground by that ape-like thing with no lower half. As the orderly screamed and flailed, it started to thrust its monstrous arms down onto him, one after the other. The orderly's body crumpled beneath the heavy blows as red, glistening insides burst free. Adrian could hear his bones snapping, cracking, and crumbling. The rapid, vicious assault did not let up, and soon the body became unrecognisable, a disgusting mash of red meat and pink skin.

Limbs were torn free from another screaming victim who was caught by a group of those horrors, until a jet of fire was spewed towards them in an attempt to push them back. Jones stepped forward, spraying a stream of flame, arcing it left and right. Some of the creatures, and even the dying orderly, were set alight. They all screamed and screeched as the flames stripped them of skin and flesh. The other nightmares were wary and moved back as a brief standoff took place.

'Director, I need you to get out of here,' Jones said.

Reid thought that was a good idea, and he noted the director moving away from the conflict, backpedaling. Obviously, he was a coward when it came down to it, but Reid did not want to die either, so he joined Templeton and headed the same direction. The thunderous crashing and banging sounds still emitted from Ward A as a horde within fought to get through.

'I think it may be time for those measures you mentioned, Director,' Reid whispered to him, but Templeton did not answer—he simply stared at the prowling monsters that were temporarily held back by Jones.

'Get into Ward B,' someone yelled. Reid turned to see the three patients that had been apprehended. It was Adrian James who had spoken. 'It's safer in there,' he went on. That made sense to Reid, not that there was anywhere particularly safe here anymore—but it seemed as good a place as any to retreat to.

But then a more obvious solution came to Reid, and he kicked himself for not realising it sooner.

'No,' he said. 'We get out of here. Out of the asylum.' Reid then grabbed Templeton and shook him. 'Open the main door,' he said. 'Then we can escape.'

This brought Templeton out of whatever trance he was in, but he just shook his head. 'Absolutely not,' he said. 'These things must not be allowed to go free.'

'What?' Reid asked, incredulous. 'Are you insane? This place is lost, we'll die.'

'No!' Templeton yelled. 'We will not abandon our posts.' He turned to his head orderly. 'Mr. Jones, if we cannot retake control of the situation, then we must make our way down below and draw things here to a close.'

Jones nodded and took half a step forward. The horrors he held at bay responded in kind, evidently fearful of what his weapon could do, as some of their brethren lay crumpled, burning, and unmoving on the floor. The smell of cooked meat had already begun to fill the air.

He ignited the nozzle again and sprayed flame forward. 'I'll get things under control,' he vowed, his voice determined.

But he was wrong.

As he bore down on one creature in particular, setting the multi-armed abomination ablaze, other fast-moving beasts circled on either side. They were quick, scarily so, and pounced on Jones, who had no chance to re-aim his cumbersome weapon.

They pulled him down, though not without a struggle as the large man fearlessly fought back, punching at the things that surrounded and overwhelmed him. Even as they bit down on him and ripped at his flesh, he continued to resist. Jones' face soon become a mangled mess as skin was torn free; even when the fight finally left him and he lay motionless, he still did not scream.

But instead of finishing the mortally wounded man off, something curious happened. All but one of the creatures backed away.

The one that remained, a crawling thing with a wide mouth that pulled itself along on needle-thin arms, moved over Jones. With long, spindly hands it tore open the man's mouth, wide enough for Reid to hear a snap as it dislocated. This, eventually, brought a grunt of pain from Jones.

The creature then moved its head down and opened its mouth. Reid expected it to bite down and feast.

Instead, it began to heave. A stream of black fluid erupted from the maw and splashed down into Jones' own. He coughed and gagged, but the constant flow of foul liquid continued to pour, splashing and coating his face, and he could do nothing but swallow and drown in it.

The vile purging went on, and Reid was sure Jones should have choked to death by now. Certainly the man was no longer moving.

Eventually, the creature ceased its vomiting and moved back, and Reid now expected the other monsters to continue their attack on the rest of them.

But they all held off.

They watched the body of Jones... which soon began to twitch. Small, sudden movements that quickly turned into full-on convulsions. A gurgled sound came from his mouth, one that sounded... wrong. Not human, and it grew louder as Jones began to thrash about.

Then the changes began.

Jones' muscles swelled to inhuman proportions, threatening to burst through his skin. In some areas his skin even split, and red sinew pushed through. The man's form grew in length as well—the straps holding the tank to his back snapping and letting the metal object drop heavily to the floor—and his head was pulled down closer into his massive torso. The mouth on his skinless face widened to reveal rows of razor sharp teeth.

This new nightmare then stood to its feet, easily over nine feet tall, a hulking mass of muscle and strength. It let out a bellowing roar and started to attack the other creatures around it indiscriminately. One was crushed underfoot as the raging beast took a step, pushing down with trunk-like legs. Another was scooped up and torn in two as it squealed in protest.

This walking nightmare that Jones had become let out another deafening bellow.

'We need to go,' a voice said. Again, it was Adrian James. Reid took out his keys and ran to Ward B, heeding the advice. Patients and orderlies alike all ran with him, even Templeton. 'Quickly,' the director yelled in a panicked voice.

Reid fought with his keys as the monsters behind, led by this new behemoth, made their way forward. Eventually, he pulled free the correct one and managed to unlock and heave open the door. He was forced forward by a mass of bodies behind him and pushed to the floor as the keys spilled from his hands, skidding off ahead.

'No,' he yelled. 'We need to lock it.'

He rolled to his back as more bodies ran over him, fearing for their lives. Through the doorway, he saw it—the mass of creatures growing closer and, beyond them, Director Templeton, who had fallen to the floor and was swarmed by a group of monsters. At the same time, he could see the door to Ward A give way on the opposite side of the Main Hall, allowing even more of these terrifying creatures to spill through.

And they would soon make their way in here and kill him.

Reid closed his eyes, certain this was the end.

A metallic slam rang out.

He opened his eyes again and saw that Adrian James had slammed the door shut and was now locking it with the very keys he himself had dropped, moments before violent bangs and crashes reverberated through the metal. The heavy door shook and rattled in its hinges as the denizens of hell on the other side fought to get through.

But for now, it held.

Adrian James then backed up.

'It won't hold for long,' he said, and Reid tended to agree.

38

'WE NEED TO GET FARTHER BACK,' Adrian said to the large group squeezed into the hallway. All eyes were on him now, looking for guidance. 'They'll be through soon, so our best bet is to lock ourselves in the Communal Area for now.'

'All we are doing is boxing ourselves in,' Seymour said.

'I agree,' Adrian said, 'but we don't have much of a choice, do we?'

He looked to the doctor, who was now getting to his feet, and the other orderlies, who looked as scared and lost as he felt. One stocky orderly, with dark, messy hair, stepped forward—apparently unwilling to let a mere patient give the orders.

'No,' he said. 'We do not follow you. We follow Brother Templeton.'

Brother? He'd heard that term uttered recently and had a suspicion that the people who worked at the asylum were not as they first appeared.

'Then go and ask him for instructions,' Adrian said. 'Last I saw of him, he was being hauled away by those things. Monsters that you people created and set free.'

He was well aware that there were only three patients—himself, Seymour, and the sick-looking Sean—against the large gathering of orderlies, so they could be quite easily overwhelmed. But then again, what exactly would the orderlies do to him? Isolation seemed a little unfeasible, right now.

An idea formed that he hoped could even things out if he could just keep these orderlies at bay for long enough. Fortunately, help came from an unlikely source.

'He's right,' Doctor Reid said. 'In case you all missed it, we have lost control of this facility. If we stand around here much longer, those things are going to get in here and rip us apart. So can we stop the grandstanding and make a move?' The orderlies looked to each other, unsure of what to do. 'Now!' Dr. Reid snapped.

It seemed to work. Whether he had any real authority, Adrian wasn't sure, but Reid had at least appealed to their survival instinct enough for them to retreat through the short, connecting corridor they were in to the main ward beyond. As the crowd of people moved, Adrian, Seymour, and Sean kept pace, with Sean struggling but pushing himself to keep up. His skin had taken on a horrible shade of yellow, and he was sweating profusely.

Adrian felt uneasy running beside the men who had once acted as guards and bullies to them, but right now he had no choice. They filtered through the next secured door, and Adrian locked it behind him as the vile creatures from the Main Hall continued their barrage.

As they set off again, Adrian heard a voice.

'What's going on?'

It came from behind one of the closed cell doors, and Adrian recognised it immediately. His first instinct was to set the man free, but then he stopped himself. Could they really take a chance of letting *him* free right now? Adrian walked to the door and dropped the viewing hatch, seeing Trevor's scared face appear from the other side.

'What's happening?' Trevor asked.

'It's hard to explain,' Adrian said, 'but we are all in a bit of trouble.'

'With the orderlies?' he asked, then peered past Adrian, seeing patients and orderlies standing together. A frown formed on his face.

'Not exactly,' Adrian said. 'There are... things here that are loose. And they are attacking and killing people.'

Trevor's frown deepened. 'I don't understand.'

'Me either, Trevor, but that's what's happening. Now, I'm going to let you out, as long as you are feeling like yourself. Because, to be honest, right now we can ill afford for Mother to show up.'

'I... think I'm fine,' Trevor said in a soft voice. Adrian took this meekness as a sign that he was telling the truth, and that Mother was not in control right now. How long that would last, of course, was another matter entirely. Still, it didn't seem right to leave him locked in his cell—trapped, with no way to even attempt an escape. He deserved the same chance as the rest of them, slim though it was.

So, Adrian acted. He marched up to Dr. Reid, who cowed away slightly, and relieved him of his keys. He then walked back to Trevor and opened his door.

'I'm not sure I want to be out,' Trevor said, surprising Adrian, but still took a tentative step from his room. 'I told Seymour earlier that trying to get out would end in trouble.'

'Trouble is already here,' Adrian told him as chaotic noises still reverberated from the Main Hall. 'Things have changed.'

Even now, Adrian could see tendril-like strings of flesh

forming on the walls, floor and ceiling. They were thinner
and less noticeable here than in Ward A, but he knew they
would soon grow larger and envelop more of the
surrounding space.

'So what do we do?' Seymour asked, angrily. 'You've
brought us down a dead end.'

Adrian ignored him, partly because he didn't want to
listen to Seymour right now, and partly because he had no
way to answer the question—he had absolutely no idea
what they were going to do. Running back into the ward
hadn't exactly been a choice—it was an instinctual act of
survival.

In truth, the only real outcome to this that he could see,
for any of them, was death. They would either be ripped
apart by those ungodly monsters or, even worse, become
one of them. But that didn't mean that the patients trapped
in the building had to sit in their cells and wait for death to
come calling. He could at least give them all a fighting
chance.

Adrian walked to Jack's cell next and pulled open the
door. Jack was sitting on his bed, looking terrified.

'Stop,' the dark-haired orderly shouted. 'You can't just
start letting inmates free.'

Adrian ignored him. 'Come on, Jack,' he said to the
giant, who had his arms wrapped tightly around himself
and was rocking back-and-forth, obviously disturbed at
what he had been hearing. 'It's okay.'

That was a lie, it was *not* okay, but he knew he had to try
to coax the man out gently.

'I know you're scared, big man,' Adrian said, 'but I need
you to come with me. It isn't safe here.'

Jack shook his head, so Adrian stepped inside. He sat
down next to Jack, feeling dwarfed by the giant's frame, and

rubbed a hand on his back in an attempt to comfort him. 'I'm not gonna lie,' Adrian said. 'Things aren't looking good. I know you can hear what's going on out there, and I hear it too. I've seen it. But staying in here isn't safe. I can't guarantee that anywhere is safe, but the more of us that stick together, the better chance we have.'

Jack shook his head again and continued his rocking. Adrian went on. 'I'm not leaving you behind. I want us to at least try to make it through this. So please, will you come with me?'

Adrian felt for Jack. As big and strong as he was, the man was positively childlike, and right now he looked terrified. 'Please,' Adrian coaxed again, 'be brave and come with us. You can do it, Jack.'

After what seemed like an eternity, Jack seemed to make up his mind. He stood to his feet, his body rising up and up, making Adrian feel tiny. The large man still looked scared, but he nodded.

Adrian got to his feet as well and patted Jack on the arm. 'Thank you, Jack,' he said. 'Now let's go.'

They both left the room, and Adrian quickly moved to the next door, unlocked it, and pulled open. Then he did the same with the two opposite and started working his way along the hallway, releasing confused and scared patients as he went.

'Stop,' the same orderly said again. 'I'm ordering you to—'

He was cut off, again by Dr. Reid. 'Be quiet, you fool,' he said. 'The more of us there are, the better. Now just shut up.'

The orderly clenched his fists and curled his lip, apparently unhappy with the way he had been spoken to. However, as instructed, he said no more.

And so, Adrian kept going, releasing more patients.

The hallway started to fill up and become crowded, and Adrian noticed that, even though he didn't fully understand what was going on, Jack was helping as well, beckoning people from their rooms after Adrian had unlocked them.

Then they were stopped by a short, sharp yell from beyond them in the hallway.

'Hey!'

Adrian looked up to see a group of three more orderlies come running from the direction of the Communal Area. They looked angry and confused, all with coshes in hand.

It was the orderly in the centre who spoke.

'Everyone back in their rooms,' he demanded. 'What the hell is going on here?'

'Enough,' Adrian said, sternly, and loud enough for them to hear. Whatever was going on, these idiots had no control over it, and it was time they knew that. 'Listen to that noise,' he said, pointing back towards the Main Hall. 'Those things, whatever they are, whatever you've been trying to bring through here, have taken over. Your colleagues are dead. I saw them get torn apart. Whatever you've been trying to do here, it failed.'

'You're lying,' the orderly replied.

'Am I?' Adrian asked, stepping forward. 'Then go out there and find out for yourself. Or just take a look at your friends here. Why else do you think they would be running alongside us? Because they can't control what is happening, and they have no way out. So, if you don't help us, then pretty soon we'll all be dead.'

Murmurs of discontent rippled through the gathered crowd.

'What do you mean?' one patient asked.

'What's happening?' questioned another.

'Enough!' the orderly shouted. 'I'm warning you all, back in your rooms now, or we'll throw you in there ourselves.'

Then a thunderous, crashing sound rang out around them, and the chaos from the Main Hall grew closer. They were through the first door, and something started to pound relentlessly on the ones behind them.

Adrian knew exactly what was coming. The thought of it terrified him, and his heart began to race. Ultimately, there was nowhere for him to go, but he didn't want to just stand here and wait; he had an urge to keep going to the last, a survival instinct that he didn't know he possessed.

He turned back to the orderlies who were holding them up and saw a look of genuine doubt creep over them. Another two appeared from around the corner behind them, joining their friends.

'What the hell is going on here?' one asked, a question that had been repeated quite a lot recently.

The crashing sounds continued.

'You need to make up your minds,' Adrian said, 'and quick. Those things back there will break through soon, and when they do, they'll come for all of us.'

'Where are Templeton and Jones?' one of the new orderlies asked.

Adrian shook his head. 'One of those things *is* Jones. Or it was. And Templeton is dead. I'm not waiting around for the same thing to happen to me,' he said, and proceeded to open more doors. 'And I'm not leaving these men trapped and helpless here, either.

'Stop,' the stubborn orderly insisted.

'There are more of us than you,' Adrian replied, hoping to push some of the patients—normally so placid—to help themselves. 'So you do what you need to do... and we'll do the same.'

'You'll do as you're told,' the orderly insisted.

'No, we won't,' a patient answered. It was an older man that Adrian had seen in the Communal Area from time to time. Someone who always looked miserable and always kept to himself. 'I never asked to come here, I was taken. Brought against my will. You people are nothing but criminals and degenerates, and I've had enough.'

Others agreed with the older man, and there were some half-hearted shouts of support. Much less enthusiastic than Adrian had hoped, but it seemed at least some were willing to fight back. Enough, he hoped, to overwhelm the orderlies, should they need to.

Thankfully, he saw this new group of guards physically wilt—not used to having people stand up to them. And, of course, the incessant crashing and banging on the weakening door behind them played a part too.

One orderly whispered something to the self-assumed leader of the group, but Adrian was just able to make it out. 'We can't control them all.'

'For the love of God!' Dr. Reid screamed. 'I'm getting tired of this. We are all in trouble here. What this patient is saying is correct. Your friends here have seen it too. We've lost control, and if we don't move, we'll die. Now either come with us or stand aside. I hold rank, and I'm making that an order.'

'You don't give the orders, Doctor,' the defiant orderly said. 'Not unless Templeton approves it. And he ain't here to do so.'

'That's right, because he's dead.'

'He's right,' Adrian said. 'If you have any sense, you'll think about standing with us when that door gives.'

'Stand with you? Why would we do that? We aren't like

you people. We aren't feeble and infirmed. We serve something higher.'

Adrian kept releasing more of the prisoners, getting closer and closer to the orderlies as he did.

'Well,' Adrian said, 'I hope you really believe in what you serve, because you are about to meet it. And I have a feeling you won't like it.'

Then it happened.

Adrian knew it had been coming, and now was the time.

The door behind them finally gave.

Metal crunched and squealed as the door was pulled from its hinges. Then the inhuman sounds became louder.

'They're coming,' Adrian said.

And they did.

Monstrosities barrelled into view, and patients and orderlies screamed in terror.

But Adrian knew worse was to come, and he heard it approach—the booming *thump, thump, thump* of heavy footfalls.

The thing that used to be Jones.

It soon emerged as well, turning the corner into full view —its raging mass filling the corridor, so large that it had to stoop to keep its head below the ceiling. It saw them all and bared its teeth, letting out a nightmarish bellow that seemed to shake the walls around them.

The panic and chaos around Adrian rose to new, unimaginable heights, and Adrian could think to do only one thing.

'Run!' he yelled.

39

DIRECTOR ISAAC TEMPLETON should have been dead.

After he'd attempted to escape with the rest of the crowd in the Main Hall, someone had rushed past and knocked him off his feet. He'd barely had time to roll to his back when one of the creatures—the very things he had nurtured into this world—seized him. It was a grotesque mix of human and spider, with multiple legs that had sprouted from a bulbous, fleshy base. A humanoid torso sat vertically atop this section, with a demonic, alien face melted into its head.

Templeton readied himself for death.

But instead of killing him, the thing hoisted him up and slid him beneath its underbelly, where small centipedal legs lined the underside. These small legs were far too short to reach the ground and be of any use for walking—the long, scuttling appendages to the side of the mass served that function—but Templeton soon realised what these smaller legs were for as he was thrust into them, face up. They then clamped shut over him, hugging him in place, and he could feel the sharp ends penetrate his skin as they pushed him forcefully into the disgusting belly of grey and yellow flesh.

He was then carried away, helpless, as the thing moved, followed by a crowd of other shrieking creatures as well. His screams of terror were lost in the body that his face was pressed into.

With his limited vision, Templeton saw that he was carried down into the passageway below ground, then over to the door that housed Robert Wilson. It was here that the gathering of monsters that had followed got to work on the door, heaving at the great thing. The door was strong, he knew that, but there were simply too many of them. It took a while, but soon the lock gave and the door was heaved open. He was then taken inside and dropped to the floor.

Only things looked radically different in here now.

Robert's form had changed—swollen to grotesque proportions and littered with large, tumour-like sacks that hung down to the floor. His head had engorged as well, the cranium swelling to three times its normal size, with the skin around it melding and changing to resemble something more like a brain. And on this bulbous mass were multiple white orbs, each with dirty yellow pupils that twisted and rolled independently.

The mass of his body spread, stretching out around the room like a virus, winding down to the floor and creeping up the walls and across the ceiling. And it wasn't just the tendrils Templeton had seen before that were growing; most of the room was now coated in what appeared to be pulsating flesh. Within the expanse of this lumpy, writhing tissue were other eyes as well, like the one on the inflated cranium, as well as circular, gaping mouths of various sizes. Indeed, so spread out was the sea of Robert's body, that his original outline was in danger of being lost within.

At Robert's feet sat another tumour-like sack, this one as tall as a person. A mass of eyes covered it, and a large, gaping mouth split it vertically down the centre.

The spider-like creature that had brought Templeton down here, and its friends, all retreated, leaving him alone. Then Templeton saw Robert's eyes open, revealing those black orbs beneath.

And it was only at the last moment he noticed movement. He turned his head just in time to see a long, tentacle-like appendage slither out from the mouth of the sack— long, dark purple ropes of slimy, veiny flesh. Templeton had no chance to move as they wrapped around him, sticky and warm to the touch, and quickly tightened, trapping his arms to his side. Templeton let out a scream as the wriggling lengths tightened and constricted him.

'*Come... my... child,*' the voice from Robert's body said. '*It... is... time... to... ascend.*'

Templeton, fighting the whole time, felt himself pulled towards the open mouth, now larger than Templeton's entire body. The pit beyond looked fleshy, wet, and dark. The smell that drifted from the insides that were lined with needle-like teeth was foul, like rotting meat. Templeton fought and kicked against his organic bonds, but there was no give.

No hope.

He was pulled into the wet, stinking pit, and the light cut out as the mouth closed around him, pushing the putrefied, gummy flesh onto his face, smothering him completely. He felt like he was being eaten alive, like he'd fallen prey to a Venus flytrap.

The pressure was immense, and he felt teeth puncture his skin, causing excruciating pain. Templeton's screams were then muffled as something he could not see slithered into his mouth, forcing its way down his throat to his stomach. He could feel this invading, phallic thing expel something inside of him—and it burned.

The pain from the foreign sludge that pumped into him —coupled with the pressure of the sucking mouth—was simply too much to take. Certain he was in the throes of a horrific death, and in absolute agony and torment, Director Templeton lost consciousness.

And even after he did, the Great Being continued to use his ruined body as it wished.

Changing it.

Shaping it.

The entity had a specific purpose in mind for this mortal and his shell of flesh. It would use the husk to birth something. Something different from its other children.

Something truly unique.

40

IT WAS A STAMPEDE.

Adrian struggled to keep his footing as the bodies of terrified inmates around him surged down the corridor. If he fell, then no one would stop to help him—he would be trampled and left to the horrors that now chased them all.

So he concentrated on keeping his footing and making it to the Communal Area, even though he knew was pointless in the end.

Because after that, there was nowhere else to go. No escape lay ahead, and those things would eventually get through and show them a gruesome end.

They soon reached the large Communal Area, and the mass of people started to filter inside, fighting to get in, all acutely aware of the beasts that chased them, snapping at their heels.

After he was through, Adrian turned and saw that Sean had dropped to the floor just outside the door and was screaming in agony. Others ran over him and he grabbed the leg of one of the patients close to him. The patient tried to pull away, but lost his balance and fell to the floor.

'Help me,' Sean said, desperately, as he started to convulse.

The patient in his grasp kicked out at him. 'Let me go!'

The approaching creatures grew ever closer, but not everyone was inside yet.

'Close the door,' someone yelled, and those nearest the entrance obeyed, forcing them shut.

'Wait!' Adrian yelled, but it was too late—Sean and four other patients were locked out, on their own and the first to die. 'You cowards!' Adrian yelled, but through the glass of the door he saw that their actions may actually have been wise.

The four helpless men began frantically pounding on the door, begging for a mercy they were not afforded.

Before Adrian's very eyes, Sean began to change, still holding the leg of the struggling patient. The creatures stormed into view as well—the behemoth standing tall above them all—but held back, watching as the transformation occurred.

Sean screamed in agony as he began to fatten and stretch, his face turning into a round, open mouth containing a ring of sharp teeth that circled round and round, disappearing into the black gullet beyond. His arms and legs melded into the long mass of his body, until he became more worm than man, one of grotesque size. Its skin was a dull brown—tumorous and lumpy with a sheen of slime. Small, milky eyes pinpricked the wriggling form, and it began to move forward, crawling towards the patient Sean had been holding. He was backpedaling but had nowhere to go. The other creatures still held back, happy to let their new addition have its first kill.

And kill it did.

The monstrous worm opened its mouth wider than

should have been possible, even considering its girth, and it lunged forward, taking the man's kicking legs into its maw.

It bit down.

The patient screamed and kicked and writhed as the ten-foot worm began to suck him into its mass. Fighting all the way, the patient was dragged up to his waist, then to his shoulders, as he screeched in pure agony.

His head was the last thing to disappear inside, swallowed up by the slimy thing.

The other remaining men outside screamed for help, but they were left alone.

Abandoned.

Then things took an unexpected turn—if indeed anything that had come before could be considered *expected*.

After holding its food within its bulk, the fat worm turned itself to face the door that separated it from the rest of the patients. It opened its mouth and purged, regurgitating the man it had just swallowed whole.

The screaming inside the Communal Area increased as everyone—Adrian included—saw what was left of the poor patient spill out and slop out to the floor. Amazingly, he was still alive, though was writhing and moaning, mostly dissolved and melted.

He was devoid of skin and his body was a pinkish-red in tone, his flesh gooey and dribbling down over his bones in streaks of sickly yellow. One side of his face was gone, revealing the workings beneath, the eyeball still present but sagging and losing its roundness. Steam rose from the screaming man as he lifted a deformed arm, pleading to the people hiding behind the door.

'Heeeeeellllgh meeeeeeee,' he cried, not able to properly form the words.

The agony must have been unimaginable as whatever acids that coated him continued to melt and dissolve him.

And it appeared this was a signal for the other creatures, allowing them to get to work and indulge themselves as well. And the first, of course, was the monstrous behemoth that used to be Jones.

The other entities circled around it, seemingly fearful to get too close, as it reached down and grasped one of the unfortunate, abandoned patients. It clasped a huge hand around his throat and lifted him up. So large was the meaty paw that, when it closed, the patient's neck actually seemed to stretch up to an unnatural length, his jaw crushing and cracking as it did, to allow the mass of the hand to form a fist. The man seemed to be trying to scream as the monster lifted him higher, but he could only form a strained sound, given the lack of airway available to him. He kicked and fought in the grip of the terrifying giant.

The hulking thing raised another massive hand and grabbed at the man's torso and then, in a slow, painfully drawn-out motion, it pulled.

The man's eyes opened wide as his head rose... but his body did not. Blood poured from between the brute's thick fingers as the head split from the torso beneath, the neck pulling apart into long strings of red meat. The man's mouth still moved, a reflex action of the fading nervous system, as a length of his spine dangled down from beneath the monster's fist.

His body was dumped to the floor and the severed head held high.

The monster bellowed out an ungodly roar, and the others about it screeched excitedly.

'What the hell is that?' one of the orderlies asked, the same one who had done so much talking earlier.

Fearful murmurings rippled around the room. They all watched through the wired glass panels as the beast dropped the detached head to the floor and squashed it underfoot. The remaining three patients were then set upon by the other creatures, who wanted their own chance to kill. One man was thrown to the floor and his stomach torn open, the innards on show feasted upon by a gaggle of smaller abominations, like pigs feeding at a trough.

Another was surrounded by a different group that pulled the skin and flesh from his body in large chunks, leaving crimson-soaked bones glistening beneath. The last man, who was pinned screaming in a corner, lost of all of his limbs, leaving only a torso and head wriggling and squealing on the floor as blood pumped from the bloodied stumps.

Now the behemoth stepped forward, over the melted man who still twitched, and it roared again, before slamming a fist into the door, rattling it on its hinges.

Adrian knew that the door would not hold for long, and the hulking creature struck again, ready to indulge in more carnage.

Everyone inside the room pulled back, running to the outer edges, hugging the wall tight—but there was nowhere left to go. They were trapped in here, and the creatures outside were about to find their way in.

In short order, the door gave way, and the demons of hell came through.

41

It awoke.

Consciousness flooded into its mind.

From nothing came something, and its nervous system tingled to life.

It kicked, finding itself confined in a warm and safe space.

Something in its gut pulled free and slithered from its mouth, relieving pressure in its stomach and throat.

It kicked again, squirming, quickly tiring of its confines, yearning for freedom.

Memories began to surface.

Echoes of a past life.

No.

That was wrong.

It was not just a single past life.

Confusing, contrasting memories fought for attention. Two different beings, on two separate planes of existence.

A temperature change drew the thing's attention, and it felt cold air on its skin as an opening formed in its protective cocoon.

The thing opened its two eyes and could make out light —an ugly yellow hue, seeping in from the opening before it. It crawled forward, reaching for its freedom, and eventually pulled itself out of the fleshy, pulsating surroundings and into a new environment.

It dropped to the hard floor, the cold rushing in to meet it from all around.

It heard a voice, not its own, within its mind.

Stand.

The being complied and pushed itself up, feeling strength start to flow in a body consisting of only two arms, which it felt was restrictive and primal.

Though unsteady, it was able to climb up and stand on its feet.

The room around was covered in flesh, similar to that it had just escaped from.

No, been *born* from.

And at the centre of this expanse was a specific outline —a body similar to its own.

That was the entity, the thing knew, that had birthed it and communicated with it.

Its creator.

And this creator had also transferred its memories and knowledge—though not all was available just yet. It came in gradual waves.

This was frustrating.

The thing wanted more, and it wanted it now, desperate to feed and gorge on the knowledge that was dripping into its consciousness. Sensing this anger, the parental entity spoke again.

Patience.

The newborn laid a hand on the flesh—an affectionate

gesture—and it heard the multitude of mouths that lined the expanse of skin chatter in response.

Then it listened as its creator told of the conflicting memories... and where they both came from.

The being learned of its creator's home—a place of wondrous chaos. And it learned of the place where it now existed.

It was then told its purpose—the reason for its birth.

And when it had all the knowledge it needed, the thing in Director Templeton's ruined body left its creator behind forever.

42

ADRIAN BRACED HIMSELF.

This was it.

He had always maintained he was willing to accept death in the facility, and now it appeared it was before him in the form of monsters and devils.

Punishment indeed.

And yet he found himself pushed back against the far wall with the others, clinging to the false hope of life and continued existence. He realised just how desperate he was to live. Or to avoid a gruesome end.

And what followed was a massacre.

A sadistic orgy of violence, desecration, and depravity, dealt out by beings that had more suffering in mind than simple animalistic instincts of hunting and feeding.

It wasn't just killing, but prolonged torture and torment.

With nowhere to go, it was a matter of sheer chance as to who would be claimed and killed first. Screaming, terrified men were plucked from the false safety of their huddled groups, thrown to the floor and opened up as the creatures swamped the room. The patients' red, wet insides were raised up into the air with what appeared to be excitable glee from of the monsters. Limbs were pulled free and thrown into the cowering men who still pressed themselves against the walls, as if taunting them as their friends were killed.

It was all too much, and Adrian's grip on reality threatened to slip completely as he saw one patient crawling along the floor, screeching and desperate, in a state of utter terror. He didn't seem to be aware of the fact that his body was ripped at the waist, with red, spaghetti-like strands of guts and intestines dragging behind him, leaving a trail of crimson liquid.

A strong smell of copper filled the air—the smell of death.

Adrian hugged the wall behind him as one of the living nightmares approached. It was that vile worm, what used to be Sean, and it wriggled its way closer, arching its centre as it did, its movements like that of a caterpillar. Adrian noticed other features at this close distance as well, including small, stabbing legs that held its weight as it moved. The thing drew nearer, reared up, supporting itself on its hind third, and opened its dripping mouth. But it wasn't facing Adrian... not quite.

Luckily for him.

The thing made a disgusting, gurgling sound, and belched forward a yellow liquid from its mouth in a powerful blast. The fluid coated the patient next to Adrian, and Adrian quickly pulled away from him, feeling a ferocious burning on his arm where some of the liquid had landed.

However, the patient next to him had taken the full hit and was howling in agonising pain. Adrian could smell it before he even looked up—a stomach-churning mixture of sour bile and burning flesh. The man's hands were on his face, but as he pulled them away Adrian saw a melted mess beneath; a mixture of running yellows, pinks, and browns that held the vague shape of a face, but one that sagged and dropped. Adrian managed to put further distance between himself and the unfortunate victim next to him as another blast of the searing liquid coated the inmate. Then another, mercilessly, as he screamed like Adrian had never heard anyone before.

The vile smell grew stronger as the man was coated in even more of the bile-like substance. He dropped to the floor, throwing his arms over his head, but the assault continued. The man's hands soon melted into his bubbling cranium, and his clothing dissolved, leaving his dripping, oozing body visible beneath, now with a consistency of running wax. As his throat oozed away, stripping the vocal cords, the inmate's screams halted, but he still writhed as his flesh pooled below him. A sagging ribcage was exposed as more and more of the liquid was spewed over him. Thankfully, he eventually stopped moving, and the creature moved in, lowering its monstrous mouth to what was left of his body.

Adrian ran when he heard the slurping sounds as the beast started to suck up the watery remains.

He slipped on an entrail and fell to the floor, suddenly feeling far too far exposed out in the open.

Ready to be picked off.

He scuttled backwards, practically crab-walking, and again pressed himself against the side wall. Looking out into the chaos, Adrian saw that poor Trevor had been taken as well. A hunched creature with a bloated, translucent belly showing black blood within had him captured, embraced in a hug. And it appeared to have just finished its act of regurgitating the black substance—that seemed to be at the heart of this madness—into Trevor's mouth, and the poor man was now bucking and spasming in its arms.

It then dropped him to the floor, seemingly finished with him, and moved on to its next victim, joining in with a crowd of other beasts that were literally pulling a man apart. Legs and arms were twisted free, and his stomach was pulled open. Lastly, his jaw was yanked off, leaving a lolling tongue that wriggled in the air before the head was detached completely.

Adrian watched as Trevor then turned.

Like the other transformations he had witnessed, this one, too, caused the victim to twitch and move in sudden, broken spasms. And the process was obviously excruciating, as Trevor screamed in pain while his chest expanded and a gelatinous gut pushed out even further. Grotesque, veiny bosoms formed and sagged down to his sides. His arms and legs engorged as well, fattening out as his body grew, and his head was pulled down towards one fat shoulder. Another monstrous head and face emerged and reared up, taking prominence—demonic, with a round, snapping mouth. Adrian couldn't help but think it had feminine features, with sharp eyes and a thin nose. Trevor's face was now completely melded into the flesh of the left shoulder, still screaming in silence as no sounded emitted from the moving mouth.

This new creature stood high, almost as tall as the behemoth that was now running wild.

But Trevor's transformation was not quite complete.

Something that loosely resembled male genitalia started to protrude from the underside of the sagging, grey gut. The long, stalk-like thing moved and bobbed independently, and even had a snapping mouth of its own—lined with teeth—at the head.

A horrific mesh of male and female, twisted into a monstrous form.

Mother, Adrian thought.

And soon Mother was on someone, and the acts of depravity she carried out on that poor inmate were vile beyond belief. Screaming was of no use as the poor man was violently abused and then killed, his limbs twisted and torn away.

Adrian wanted to give up. Seeing such carnage and depravity was just too much. Part of him just wanted to lie down and wait for death to come, but the fear of how painful that death would be drove him on.

He crawled onwards, trying to skirt the edge of the room to avoid the violence and make it back to the door. Maybe there was a small chance that he could make it unseen, though the odds of that were not in his favour.

Amongst the carnage of all that was happening, the most ferocious came from the hulking beast at the centre of the room, one that towered over everything else.

It held aloft two men, one in each hand. The one in the left was fighting for his life as the paw of the monster engulfed his head, slowly crushing it, taking its time and enjoying his suffering.

In the other, the man was close to death. He was already peeled of his skin, and the monster took periodic bites from the exposed flesh, tearing chunks away.

Mangled bodies lay scattered at its feet.

Adrian moved quicker, circling the room, desperate to escape the notice of the evil creatures.

But soon his luck ran out.

Something tall stepped in front of him, setting a heavy

foot down. When Adrian looked up, he saw one of the more human-looking creatures standing above him. Perhaps one of the first to turn, it seemed stretched out, gangly, with long limbs and bumpy skin. The only other features that marked it as inhuman were the small littering of eyes about its chest and shoulders, and a mouth that split up in the centre of its stomach.

It made an excited noise, almost a laugh, and then reached down for him. Adrian tried to crawl away, but felt its hand wrap around his ankle. It dragged him back, clearly stronger than him, but not as overpowering and dominant as most of the transformed nightmares that tore their way through the remaining residents of the ward.

When it let go of him, Adrian quickly rolled onto his back and looked up at the thing as it stared down at him. Its teeth seemed far too long, and razor sharp, and it reached down again and grabbed him by the throat with both hands. Adrian felt himself heaved up, and he dangled before the demon as his legs kicked below him, trying and failing to find purchase on something.

He felt himself slowly brought in towards the face of his attacker and could feel and smell its hot, rancid breath on his face. A thin, pink tongue slithered from the open mouth and snaked its way towards Adrian. The appendage was ridiculously long, and quickly found its way to his face, licking up his skin.

Tasting him.

A ripple of pleasure seemed to surge through the creature, and it emitted a long moan. Then it opened its mouth further, and Adrian readied himself to be eaten alive.

But that was not the creature's intent.

Long fingers pushed their way into Adrian's mouth and

forced it open, pulling his jaw down. It then moved him closer and started to make gagging motions.

Adrian soon realised what it had planned for him. Whatever criteria these things had to select who would be chosen to join their ranks, he appeared to have matched it.

He was to be turned. He would twist and change and would soon be one of them. And he would commit the same acts of evil they revelled in.

He would be a monster. Thoughts of his father leapt to the fore of Adrian's mind. He remembered those acts of depravity his father revelled in, and the things he did to Adrian as a boy.

No.

He couldn't allow that to happen—he would not turn into such a beast. That fate was worse than any other he had witnessed so far—hell, he would have preferred the end that came to the melted man who had been slurped up by the monstrous worm, and the pain that came with it. He would not become what he loathed so much.

So Adrian fought back.

The monster held him close to it, so Adrian used the proximity to his advantage, reaching out his hands to claw and fight. His attack was a targeted one, and he cut his fingers down the hard skin of the demon, making sure to scrape over the small eyes that covered its chest, driving his fingers into the milky bulbs. He felt some pop beneath him, and to his surprise the creature howled in pain. He continued with his attack, gouging and scratching at the small, inhuman eyes, breaking them open like fish eggs as a yellowy substance spurted free.

Adrian felt the pressure on his throat release as the creature dropped him. As inhuman as these things were, they could still feel pain. He then cast a glance at the tank-like behemoth as it crushed men beneath it.

Okay, so maybe only *some* of them felt pain.

He couldn't imagine anything being able to hurt that giant enforcer.

Adrian moved quickly and made a dash for the exit. Up ahead, in the doorway, he saw Jack beckoning him on. The big man had gotten clear of the room, which Adrian was glad to see. And cowering next to him was that doctor, Reid. They had made it out, and as they were not being attacked, it seemed the hallway outside was clear.

That gave him hope, so he pushed himself, running at full sprint. However, as he neared the door, he felt something grab his wrist and stop him.

Another creature to fend off, he assumed, and he didn't think he would be lucky enough to escape a second attack. But when he spun, he saw that it was Seymour—bloodied and battered—who grasped hold of his wrist.

'Don't leave me here,' the fat man said, eyes wide in terror.

Adrian didn't reply, he just pulled his arm away, then turned and ran. He felt Seymour behind him, and hoped his unwanted companion did not draw attention.

But that proved not to be the case.

As the two men managed to break free of the room and sprint up the corridor alongside Jack and Dr. Reid, Adrian heard something following behind, emitting an awful, hellish screech.

43

Isaac Templeton's mind swam back into consciousness as agony wracked his senses. He felt submerged, somehow, and tried to scream, but a suffocating, scalding liquid flooded his mouth and body, burning him up inside and out.

He kicked and flailed as he felt his flesh burning.

Desperate, he began to swim as hard as he could in a direction he assumed to be *up*.

Eventually, he broke free of the surface and pulled humid air into his lungs. The cold of the environment above the boiling water was a stark contrast on his searing skin. Templeton opened his eyes... and immediately wished he hadn't.

He knew where he was.

He'd seen this place before.

In his dreams after consuming the blood of The Great Being.

The endless, alien sky above dwarfed him, and flashes of red lightning illuminated the surface of the sea he bobbed up and down in. Those stars, circling together to form a great eye, were maddening to look at.

The water continued to scald him, and Templeton looked at his arms to see them ruined and stripped of skin, with only red and black flesh exposed beneath.

He should be dead—perhaps he was—but still he continued to exist. Another flash, and up ahead he saw a landscape. Agony continued to rage as the boiling water cooked him, so he began to swim again, this time towards the landmass up ahead, every stroke causing more and more white-hot pain.

How long it took him, Templeton could not say, but eventually he heaved his ruined body out onto the hard shore—a black, rock-like surface, one that exuded a red substance when pressure was applied. Small pools of it formed around his hands and knees as he crawled from the water, screaming, allowing his steaming, ravaged body to take in the cooling air. He then heaved, involuntarily purging water and chunks from his stomach. As he looked down to the mass that he had expelled, he saw red flesh and stringy intestines.

He began to scream again and, looking up, saw the same landscape from his dream.

Only this felt much more real.

Because it *was* real.

Whatever happened to him back in the asylum had brought some part of him here, and had spat him out in the boiling sea.

To be trapped for eternity.

Creatures and nightmarish visions roamed before him, wandering the terrifying wasteland. A being so big that its head touched the sky scrawled its way across the far distance.

The fear Templeton felt was absolute.

How long until one of these horrors found him and then had their way with him?

He began to sob.

Then a noise caught his attention—the sound of something dragging over the stone ground—and he looked up to see whatever it was approach.

The thing looked human, but without skin—only scabbed, blackened flesh. It crawled on all fours, keeping low.

'So it is,' the thing said, in a strained, gravelly voice. 'I was told that you would come.'

Whatever this thing was, it had a familiarity to it and, as it drew closer, Templeton recognised exactly who it was. But that was impossible.

It can't be him.

The thing grew closer and pulled the ruined flesh around its mouth into a smile.

'Hello, old friend,' said Robert Wilson.

44

THE BEING MADE its way from the chamber where its creator lay and into a large area beyond. It saw rooms off of the central space, all open and empty.

On the floor was a ruined body, one that had been similar to its own, though now it was little more than a mangled husk. It also seemed to be drained of much of its meat.

The entity studied the ruined corpse and felt something twinge within it. Concentrating harder, it felt as though it could reach out with its mind and actually touch the body.

Which is exactly what it did... and the body twitched.

With increased focus, the corpse was lifted from the ground—bobbing at first as the entity controlled the link between mind and matter. With extra effort came more confidence and control, and the body hung limply, unmoving, until it was pulled forward and then hovered above the entity.

The thing with no name, or identity.

Not yet.

Then the being obliterated the hanging sack of meat,

pulling its atoms apart, causing it to burst into chunks of red flesh and a shower of blood, all of which rained down over the thing. It savoured the feeling of blood and meat, which once brought life, slopping down upon it, coating it in the stink of death.

A first step: learning just what it was capable of.

The being then continued through the dark place. The whole environment seemed very familiar—but not from its creator. The memories it now accessed were, it knew, from its original host. A pathetic, weak creature, typical of the kind that inhabited this world.

This plane of existence.

But that sub-creature now existed somewhere else, its life-force thrust over to the home the creator. A home that the entity would never know, but one it yearned for. So, instead, it would have to make the best of this world.

And change it.

Now upstairs, the being felt that a transformation was underway in the environment around it; the creator was spreading its influence, reaching out with its winding, twisting roots, and in doing so was changing the surroundings. Growths had formed on the walls and ceilings, and pods of flesh pumped out small puffs of black spores into the air.

It could hear other, lesser children of the creator close by, indulging in their desires. But it felt no desire to go to them. They were lower than it was.

Beneath it.

Two of them even wandered the level on which the creature now found itself. They were aimless, but steered clear of the being. They were scared of it.

As they should be.

It considered pulling them apart, for no other reason

than to further test its powers; however, it was curious to see something else first.

It walked to a doorway, and with a flick of its head, pulled the door open, breaking the primitive lock in the process. The being then wandered the corridor towards its destination, eager to see the place that the lowly human who had inhabited body before—*Templeton... Isaac Templeton*—was so attached to.

The Chapel.

A place, it understood, that these humans used for worship.

False gods.

The being soon reached its destination and entered the Chapel.

It looked around, taking in the details, less concerned with the overall aesthetics of the room—which even now were beginning to warp and twist thanks to the creator—but more on the smaller details.

The symbols of religion.

The effigies.

A man stuck to a cross, hanging in pain. This was a symbol of hope and virtue to these humans?

The being scoffed.

Hope and virtue were as pointless. They were not the real truths and values of this universe.

It knew what these humans were—small, lowly, and blind. Insects scurrying around without the capacity to understand the true order of the universe.

Perhaps it was a lingering echo of the humanity that resided within it, but the being had a desire to change things here. To violate what was a false place of worship. To cleanse its message from the world and replace it with one much more fitting.

Much more pure.

The being moved to a circular, ornate mirror that was fixed to a wall close to the entrance door. It looked into the reflective surface, gazing at the fullness of its own body for the first time.

And was disgusted by what it saw.

The skin was sunken and greyed, lined with tears and cuts that showed the flesh beneath, and the eyes were milky white, but it was still a distinctly human appearance.

Distinctly weak.

The being knew that this appearance would need to be improved. It grabbed at the skin on its head and began pulling, peeling at the flesh and attached hair follicles, pulling it away to reveal the bone beneath.

It enjoyed the pain.

Then it brought its hands to its lips.

45

ADRIAN RAN WITH JACK, Seymour and Doctor Reid in tow. Behind them, something—he dared not look back to see what—scampered at their heels, screeching as it gave chase. Though danger was rapidly closing in, it seemed the way ahead was clear.

Giving everything he had, Adrian broke through the first ruined door into the small, linking corridor, and then on through to the large Main Hall.

He had hoped this space would be empty.

But he was disappointed.

Two creatures prowled the area. One was a tall, humanoid figure whose skull had split open at the head, revealing a writhing, moving brain beneath that blinked with small white eyes. Its tongue was long, wriggling down to its navel as its mouth hung open like a panting dog. It was accompanied by a small, dwarfish thing, with long arms that touched the floor. Its head had melted into its torso, and it had a wide stomach with a gaping mouth and sharp teeth cut into it. Out of the two, it looked less threatening, but no less horrifying.

Adrian had noticed the two creatures the second he burst into the Main Hall but, as they turned to face him, he saw something else too, hanging above the door to Ward B—a pulsating sack with multiple black eyes, fused to the wall at the junction between the wall and the ceiling. It had no human shape to it at all, only a mass of flesh with large, blank eyes. Tendrils hung down beneath it, ready to snare unsuspecting prey.

Adrian and his group did not break stride as the thing behind them gave chase, and with the creatures ahead of them, they were in danger of being surrounded.

But he had an idea.

Adrian remembered what had happened to Jones in this room when the man was turned, and what he had been carrying when he had been overwhelmed.

So Adrian took a sharp right and continued his sprint, well aware the abominations in the room had noticed him and would soon be upon him. He saw the weapon lying discarded on the floor and prayed it still worked. The small blue flame at the end of the nozzle still burned, and he hoped that was a good sign.

He heard the others—Jack, Seymour, and Reid—all keeping pace with him, wheezing and panting as they ran for their lives. But he also heard the approaching creatures, roaring and shrieking.

Gaining ground.

It would be close.

Adrian hurled himself forward, feet first, and slid along the tiled floor on his rear. As he moved across the ground, he grabbed the nozzle—the end still hot in his hand—adjusted the weapon, and swivelled his body, aiming the dangerous end away from him.

He had just enough time to see the others in his group

run to either side of him, leaving his aim clear, and a half-man half-spider horror leaping in for the kill.

Adrian squeezed the trigger.

A jet of scalding flame erupted from the nozzle and, as it did, he could actually feel the heat from the blast emanating back towards him. The leaping monster was engulfed in flames, and Adrian only just managed to roll to the side as its blazing body crashed to the floor.

Adrian quickly got to his feet and took aim at the other two monsters that were bearing down and pressed the trigger again. This time, however, he cast his aim lower, towards their feet, arcing the thrower left and right to make sure he caught them both in its stream.

Like the creature before them—who was now getting back to its feet as it writhed and burned—these two monsters went up as well, a burning mass of macabre flesh. He hit them again, and they collapsed to the floor, then he turned back to the first beast, which was trying to crawl away as the flames that engulfed it seared away at its skin. Adrian slowly stalked the thing, dragging the tank of the weapon along the floor behind him, and hit it one last time in a prolonged attack.

Eventually, it, too, stopped moving, and just continued to burn like its friends.

After taking a couple of panicked breaths, and feeling his knees grow weak, Adrian dropped to his rear. He felt a large hand land on his shoulder and jumped, but looking up saw the smiling face of Jack. The large man gave him a thumbs up.

Adrian laughed. 'Thanks, Jack. Didn't know I had it in me.'

'I did,' Seymour uttered quietly, but still loud enough for

everyone to hear above the crackling of the burning creatures.

Adrian didn't react to the comment. 'It isn't safe here,' he said to them all.

Looking past his group, he could see the tentacles of that thing that hung to the ceiling above the door to Ward B snap and whip about, apparently aware of what had happened to its brethren.

And knew it could be next.

The thought did cross Adrian's mind, but he had no idea how much fuel was left in this weapon, and had a feeling they would need every last drop.

'So we need to get out,' Seymour said, and he turned to Dr. Reid. 'Don't you have a key for the main door?'

The doctor shook his head. 'No, I was never in possession of one. If I ever wanted to leave for any reason, it had to be arranged.'

'Then what good are you to us?' Seymour said. He stepped forward and shoved the man backwards, a snarl forming on his face.

'Stop it,' Adrian said. 'We don't have time for this.'

'Stop it?' Seymour snapped back. 'Are you serious? He's one of the reasons all of this happened. He's part of it. Tell me why we're helping him again?'

Adrian then realised that Seymour had a point, and he turned to Dr. Reid.

'Wait,' the doctor said, holding up his hands in supplication. 'I was never a part of this. I was here strictly as a doctor and nothing more. I had no idea what these people were doing until recently, I swear.'

'And why should we trust you?' Seymour said and pushed the man again.

'Because,' Dr. Reid said, 'it's the truth. And I may not have a key, but I think I know where we can get one.'

Adrian had a feeling he knew what the man was going to say. 'The Director's office?'

Dr. Reid nodded. 'That's right.'

'Excellent,' Seymour said. 'Now we know where to look. Don't need you anymore.' He let fly with a punch, catching the startled doctor on the chin and sending him sprawling to the floor. Seymour then started to kick the fallen man, and Adrian saw a look of savage delight in the fat man's eyes as he did.

He knew exactly what Seymour was feeling when he let loose like that.

It was a feeling he knew well.

'Stop,' Adrian commanded.

'Fuck you,' Seymour said, continuing his attack. 'Who made you the leader?'

Adrian stepped forward and pushed Seymour back as hard as he could. Seymour backpedaled, pinwheeling his arms a little, but managed to stay on his feet.

'I said stop! We don't have time for this. No one appointed me the leader, but if we stay here, we'll die. We have a plan of action, so let's go.'

'And what about him?' Seymour said, pointing to Dr. Reid who was still groaning on the floor.

'He comes with us,' Adrian said.

'What? Are you serious?'

'I am.'

'Well, I ain't going anywhere he goes.'

Adrian shrugged. 'Fine, you can stay here.' He then hooked his arms under the doctor's shoulders and heaved him to his feet. He looked the dazed man in the eyes. 'This still doesn't mean I trust you.' Dr. Reid nodded his understanding, and Adrian asked, 'Which way?'

The doctor then pointed to a door up from Ward B. 'There.'

Adrian recognised the door; it was an area he had been dragged through before when he had been slung into isolation. He also saw that the door was open, hanging on its hinges.

'Something got through,' he said. 'We need to be careful.' He then looked at the weapon on the floor, knowing they would need it. The problem was, however, that the bindings that would hold the propane tank to one's back had completely torn when Jones had transformed. That meant he would need to carry the tank and try to aim with the nozzle at the same time.

While he was figuring out a solution, Jack reached down and easily plucked up the tank. He then nodded to the connecting nozzle.

Adrian understood.

'Thanks, Jack,' he said, and Jack adjusted his hands to give another thumbs up.

Adrian retrieved the nozzle and checked to make sure the small blue flame was still on.

It was.

'Let's go,' he said, and he, Jack, and Dr. Reid began to walk away. But Seymour did not follow.

'I said I wasn't going anywhere with him,' the fat man yelled. Adrian could still hear the carnage emanate from Ward A and knew that whatever was still happening in there wouldn't keep the creatures occupied forever. When everyone was dead, the things inside would come looking for more.

Which meant Adrian and his group needed to be free of this place before then.

'Stay here on your own, then,' Adrian said. They reached the door Dr. Reid had directed them towards, and Adrian turned back to Seymour, giving him another chance. 'Are you coming?'

Seymour looked furious, but was also clearly considering Adrian's words. Eventually, he started to jog towards them, his mind made up.

46

THANKFULLY, the journey to the office Dr. Reid and the group now searched had been a clear one with no further incident. But that didn't mean they could take their time and rest easy. They'd had to kick in the door to the director's office upon arrival—courtesy of the large patient, Jack—but as much as they searched, they could not find the key to unlock the main entrance.

Reid was worried, as the lack of progress would undoubtedly infuriate Seymour, the one who seemed most volatile, and that could lead to another confrontation. And Reid wasn't confident Adrian James would save him this time. So he continued to search, throwing books from the shelves in desperation, but noticed that Mr. James was entirely focused on something else.

'It isn't here,' the fat man yelled, almost predictably. Seymour held up a small, open case that he'd retrieved from one of the shelves he was searching. Inside was a foam base, with the impression of a large key, but no key to go along with it. 'Shouldn't it be in here? If so, it's gone.'

'I don't know,' Reid replied. 'Keep looking.'

Adrian, however, was currently focused on the folder in his hand, engrossed in what he was reading. Reid kept his head down and continued looking.

Upon entering the room, Reid's first place to look was in those drawers that Templeton kept locked, but it had turned up nothing. However, after grabbing the key from its location beneath the carpet, the others had noticed the director's folders and notes, and it was one of these folders that now so intrigued Mr. James.

'Would you just drop that and help?' Seymour shouted.

But Adrian ignored him, keeping his focus on the file. He eventually looked up at Reid.

'Is this true? What I'm reading here?'

Reid hesitated. 'Depends on what you read.'

'Don't play coy. There are reports here saying the medicine that you forced on us is... blood. How can that be?'

'Let's just find that damn key,' Reid said, but Adrian stepped forward.

'No,' he replied. 'Answer me. What kind of blood turns people into those things out there?'

'How should I know?' Reid snapped back.

'Because you're part of it.'

'I'm not. I swear on my life, I'm not. What I said before was true. This was all going on without my knowledge. I was being used, just like the rest of you.'

'No,' Adrian said, shaking his head. 'Not like the rest of us. You weren't locked up and fed that filth. You weren't turned into one of those things like my friends were.'

The man was growing angrier the more he spoke, and Seymour and Jack stepped closer as well, causing Reid to back up.

'That's true,' he said. 'But I was only trying to make people better, I swear. I didn't want any of this. I told

Templeton that, repeatedly, but he said I could either go along with what they were doing here, or I would die.'

'Go along with what, exactly?' Adrian asked.

Reid sighed, realising he had no way to divert the subject any longer. If they were going to press on and find that damn key, then he needed to get them all searching again.

And now it seemed there was only one way to do that.

'I don't know everything,' Reid said, 'but they did take me down below this place. There is an underground ward where more of those creatures were being held. And... there was something else down there as well.'

'What?' Adrian asked.

'The body of a man, only I don't think it is a man anymore. And I know this will be hard to believe but there is something... possessing it. Some kind of entity. Templeton and the others who work here, they are all part of some cult that worship this thing like a god. They extracted its blood and fed it to the patients here.'

A silence hung over them all, eventually broken by Seymour.

'You expect us to believe that rubbish?'

'I don't know if you'll believe it,' Reid said, shrugging, 'but it's the truth. I swear on my life. I didn't believe it either, but I've... seen things. I've seen it talk, and I've tasted its blood as well. When I dreamt, I saw a place, the place that thing comes from.'

'I've seen it too,' Adrian said. 'It's hell.'

Reid nodded. 'Worse. Because, as much as I hate to admit it, this place actually exists.'

'And this... thing, underground, is the cause of it all?'

'Yes,' Reid said. 'According to Templeton, they had

measures in place that would bring this whole operation to a close, if needed.'

'Well, those clearly failed,' Seymour said.

'What were those measures?' Adrian asked.

'To burn it,' Reid replied. 'He believed that if the host's body was burned, then any link that thing had to this place would be destroyed.'

'And the rest of the creatures?'

'He seemed to think that it would destroy them, too.'

Adrian James looked back to the file and flicked through it, seemingly lost in thought.

'Utter horse shit!' Seymour exclaimed.

'Believe what you want,' Reid said, then continued his search for the key.

'I believe it,' Adrian said.

'Then you know we need to get the key and get out of here,' Reid told him.

'That, I can agree with,' Seymour added.

But it appeared Mr. James had another idea in mind. 'No. Even if we escape, then those things will be free, and if they follow us out then God knows what will happen, or where it will stop. We've all seen what they do, how they kill, but also how they turn people. Who knows how far it could spread? We have to stop it.'

'Excuse me?' Seymour asked, incredulous. 'You're insane, aren't you? You deserve to be here. Think about it, you fool, if we stay here, then we die. At least if we get out, then we have a chance.'

'Not for long,' Adrian said. 'I've seen the place this thing comes from. It is chaos, hate, violence, and death. We can't let it infect our world.'

'It won't,' Seymour argued. 'Because it's not real.'

'I'm not arguing with you about this, Seymour,' Adrian

said. 'We have a chance to put an end to this whole thing, but we need to work together.'

'And what do you have in mind?' Seymour asked, throwing his hands up into the air in exasperation.

'We go down to the host and use that,' he said, then pointed to Jones' weapon that lay on the floor. 'Then all of this stops.'

'We don't even know if that will work,' Reid said. 'Templeton couldn't know for sure.'

'We have to try,' Adrian replied.

'No,' said Seymour. 'I refuse.'

Adrian shrugged. 'Then you're on your own.'

'Says who?' Seymour asked, defiant, then looked up at Jack. 'Don't tell me you're with him? He's going to get you all killed.'

Jack took a step forward and stood next to Adrian, side by side, and folded his arms over his broad chest. His decision was clear.

'You fucking idiot,' Seymour spat. He then turned to Reid. 'And what about you? Eager to die as well?'

The truth was, Reid was not eager to die at all. He regretted telling Adrian James so much, and he knew that going back down there to face that thing was suicide. But without that weapon of theirs for protection, he wouldn't last long on his own. Especially if they couldn't find the key to escape.

Reid felt like his whole world had fallen apart completely. He had leapt from one impossible choice—join a mad cult or die—to another; he could either wait around up here, unprotected, and likely die, or go down with them to try to end things... and likely die.

'I'll go,' he said, hoping there was safety in numbers.

'Idiots!' Seymour said, laughing. 'Fucking idiots.'

'Stay here on your own then, coward,' Adrian said. He picked up the nozzle of the weapon as his large friend retrieved the connected tank. 'Or come with us and help. Either way, the rest of us are going to end this.'

'You'll die trying, you know,' Seymour told them with a smile.

Adrian shrugged. 'Maybe so. But it's better than hiding and waiting to die. And to be honest, I'm tired of waiting for death to find me. Time to meet it head-on.'

47

ISAAC TEMPLETON WAS BEING PULLED along by someone who should not exist.

'Come,' Robert instructed in a hoarse voice. 'We must be quick.'

Robert had a tight hold of Templeton's left wrist, and dragged him quickly along as Templeton scampered to keep up. Templeton kept himself low, like his guide, and his exposed, blackened flesh scraped across the harsh ground, sending searing pain through his exposed nerves. He let out a pained grunt.

'Quiet!' Robert admonished. 'We must not be heard.'

'What happened to me?' Templeton asked in a panicked whisper. The noises that rumbled all around them were horrifying; thundering roars, guttural growls, and even shrieks of pain were the ambient sounds in this hellscape.

A flash of red lighting cut through the cosmic sky, illuminating more of the horrific landscape. As it did, Templeton's eyes were drawn to one of the massive, cylindrical towers—and he almost screamed. A huge, multi-legged monstrosity with a fat body at its centre clung to the side of the titanic structure, like a monstrous spider waiting for its prey. Another flash, and he saw it move, its many legs working independently as it scuttled to the hidden side of the tower.

'I'm going to die here,' Templeton said, sobbing.

'Already dead,' Robert replied, still pulling him quickly along.

'So what happens here? Can we die twice?'

Robert just chuckled. A horrible, manic sound. But no definitive answer was given.

Robert led Templeton farther along until they reached a split in the ground, a crack that grew wider and wider as it ran down before them, cutting deeper into the ground. They dropped inside and followed the slope down as jagged walls rose up around them. Templeton saw someone clinging to the sides of this wall, hiding in the cracks. His flesh, like Robert's, was devoid of skin—dark and scabbed with yellows and blacks. Templeton's own, in contrast, still dripped with blood, raw and fresh.

'Who is that?' Templeton asked.

'Another.'

'Like us?'

'Like us.' Robert confirmed, yanking Templeton forward again.

They continued further, and as they did Templeton saw more like them, all hiding and fearful. Poor souls who had been brought here, somehow, to exist in this nightmare.

Farther into the perceived safety of the underground cavern, Templeton saw groups of the poor wretches gathered around small fires, or hiding away in the shadows. One, he noticed, was tucked away in a corner, sitting on the ground with her knees drawn to her chest. She looked miserable, but very different from the rest of souls here.

While thin and dishevelled, she was at least in possession of the skin on her naked, sagging body.

'Who is she?' Templeton asked, unsure as to why she was so different from the rest of them.

'A woman I have spoken to, on occasion. Margaret Hobbes.'

'Why does she have her skin?'

'Different things exist here, and she is protected by one. She just waits until her master needs her, then she is pulled away and just disappears.'

Almost on cue, the woman's eyes opened wide, and she let out a scream as her form dissipated before Templeton's eyes.

His lungs burned as Robert pulled him on, relentlessly.

'Where are you taking me? Shouldn't we stay here where it's safe?'

'Not safe. Never safe. We must go. The Great God Ashk-laar demands to see you.'

'Great God?'

Robert just started his manic chuckling again as tremendous roars boomed from behind. Something big was coming. Shrieks from the gathered souls rang out as they all ran in panic.

'Quickly,' Robert said.

Heeding Robert's words, Templeton pushed himself on.

48

SEYMOUR HATED that he was so reliant on this group of misfits.

They should have listened to him; his way would have led them to safety. Led *him* to safety, at the very least. But they had ignored him, and more importantly, they had the weapon. On his own he stood little chance of survival, so he went against his nature of leading and followed.

He hated it.

And he hated the people that circumstance had lumped him together with, and he hated that he followed them like a dog out into the corridor. As they moved, Seymour heard something—a door opening—and looked back.

He shrieked at what he saw stepping out into the hallway. It was of human form, dressed in a blood-soaked gown, with grey skin and white eyes. The skin had been peeled away from the top of its head, revealing the skull beneath, and the flesh from its lips had been torn free, showing a grimacing smile of teeth and red gums.

'Run!' Seymour yelled and pushed past the others as he broke into a sprint. Panic rose as the rest of the group laid eyes on the thing that resembled some kind of dark, twisted priest, and they matched his efforts to flee. Seymour cast another look back, but this Dark Priest simply watched them, head cocked to the side like a curious dog. It followed, but at a slow, deliberate pace.

They bolted out from the corridor, out into the Main Hall.

Into hell.

In their panic running from the strange thing behind them, they hadn't paid any attention to what was ahead and entered a room full of horrifying creatures that had moved away from the carnage of the Communal Area.

And while trying to stop, Seymour slipped, lost his footing, and fell into one of the monstrosities that was roaming about close by.

One of the biggest in the room.

The thing turned and looked down to Seymour as he lay on the floor at its feet. An appendage hung down from the monster's groin, a phallus complete with a mouth of its own that snapped at Seymour as he scampered backwards.

Seymour had seen this thing before. He knew the person it once was and had seen its transformation take place. Even now, he could see that familiar, pathetic face frozen in horror within the massive shoulder of the beast. Above that, a nightmarish, feminine face looked down at him.

Mother.

Seymour screamed as it reached down and grabbed him by the throat with a massive paw. He twisted his head to look back, desperate for help, but the others had already fled towards the door to the basement, leaving him behind.

Leaving him for dead.

Cowards!

Panic flooded his senses as terrifying noises rang out throughout the hall. The gathered acted as one, rushing towards the fleeing prey, and the booming footsteps of the behemoth overpowered everything as it overtook the rest of the pack in great strides, trampling some underfoot as it moved.

The chase was on.

But Seymour would play no part in it.

He saw the three men disappear through the doorway moments before the powerful creature started to squeeze itself into the opening as well, pushing and cracking the frame as it forced its sizeable bulk through the gap. The rest of the creatures snapped and shrieked at its back, eager to participate in the hunt.

Eager to feed.

Seymour struggled in the grip of Mother, but felt himself lifted into the air. The bitch brought him up so that it could look into his eyes, and he swore he saw a smile form on its hideous face.

It exhaled, and a rush of foul, sickening air washed over him. A long tongue snaked from its mouth and pressed its wetness against his cheek. The tongue then rolled up his skin as the foul thing licked him.

Savouring the taste.

'Please don't,' Seymour begged.

Then, to his surprise, he was dropped to the floor.

Before he could even think of scampering free, the creature reached down and pressed his back and shoulders to the floor.

Then it mounted him, and Seymour began to scream again.

The weight of the thing was immense, and Seymour felt his ribs cracking as it let its bulk settle atop him.

To his eternal horror, he then felt something else as the monster moved its huge hips around.

No! Please, God, no!

But God didn't listen.

Seymour felt the gnashing appendage bite at him, eating its way into his body, tearing through between buttocks and genitals. He shrieked in pain, but the torture continued as Mother pressed more weight down on him. No matter how much he fought and squirmed, it did no good—he was helplessly trapped.

All he could do was endure... and feel.

The force of the appendage that ate its way through him was frightening and unrelenting. Blood pushed its way from Seymour's mouth as his insides were torn and forced upwards. More blood spurted free and drowned out his gurgled screams. His ribcage cracked even more, causing searing pain to ripple through his chest, all while the devouring organ continued its march upwards with every thrust from Mother.

And as Seymour was eaten away and mashed up internally, the blood that ran from his mouth was replaced by red meat as his intestines and guts were pushed up through the small opening, splitting open his mouth at the cheeks in the process.

He bucked and writhed, utterly desperate, but the mass above him kept him pinned in unimaginable agony—one that went on and on until, eventually, Mother gave a final push with her writhing genitals, forcefully enough that it burst through his throat with a shower of gore.

As Seymour's vision faded to darkness, he saw Mother stand back up to her full height—a malicious smile on her face.

Pleased with her work.

49

THE CARNAGE that the newborn entity witnessed was glorious.

It had followed the lowly human beings as they fled from it, only to see them run into more of the creator's children. While most of the humans ran, chased by the children, one poor wretch was torn in two in an exquisite sight. The wretch's still bleeding body was opened up and exposed, ruined and mashed insides on display.

The great child that stood over the mangled body looked over to the entity. It took a single step back. Then another.

And then it fled, jogging away with heavy footsteps.

Afraid of the entity.

As it should be.

The newborn sensed that down below a chase was on— these pitiful humans were racing towards the creator, intending to burn the vessel it inhabited. To scorch it from existence.

The entity felt no compunction to go down to stop it, however.

What they were trying to do was irrelevant.

For the creator's will was already done.

50

ADRIAN PUSHED on through the basement, racing as fast as he could with Jack and Reid keeping pace beside him. He gripped the nozzle of the weapon in his hands as Jack held on to the tank, each of them linked together via the connecting tubing.

Adrian heard the sloshing of liquid within the metal tank as they moved, but it sounded alarmingly low.

But that could well be the least of their worries.

Behind them, the rampaging sounds of hell bore down, led by those booming footsteps from the behemoth. It let out a roar of pure rage, gaining ground with every moment. Adrian was also able to hear the screeches and howls of other abominations that followed in the titan's wake.

Adrian tried to keep his focus up ahead, on the door to the chamber at the end of the passageway.

The one that supposedly housed the body of Robert Wilson—the vessel behind all of this.

The door had already been pulled wide open, looking slightly bent and twisted. Whatever had gained entry into that place before them had obviously not been gentle in doing so.

Which presented another problem.

Once they were inside, how would they then buy the time to do what needed to be done? He could only hope that they would be able to force the door shut and somehow keep it closed long enough to burn the body inside to cinders before the legions of hell poured in behind them.

And given the strength of the behemoth alone—even ignoring the combined might of the other creatures—he did not think the odds were close to being in their favour.

Yet they had nothing left to do but try.

And so they ran, harder, with the deafening chaos pursuing them from behind.

Gaining and gaining and gaining.

Adrian's thighs and calves burned and his chest ached, his body begging him to stop, close to exhaustion. Jack, to his right, was cumbersome in his movements, but had a longer stride so was able to keep up. In fact, Adrian thought the larger man was holding himself back to let Adrian keep pace with him. And Dr. Reid, to his credit, was actually pulling ahead.

'When you get through,' Adrian wheezed, 'pull that damn door shut after us.'

But he wasn't sure if Reid heard him at all. The man looked absolutely petrified. His face was a mask of terror, wide eyes focused on the door ahead.

Adrian didn't have the breath in him to tell Reid again, so just concentrated on pushing himself harder, praying he didn't trip and fall.

Boom, boom, boom.

The behemoth closed in.

Please, please, please. Let us make it, Adrian pleaded to any god that would listen.

Well, perhaps not any god.

The doorway grew closer, painfully so.

They were going to make it through, but Adrian didn't think they would have time to force that door shut.

'We're going to be killed,' Dr. Reid panted, almost crying.

He crossed the threshold, followed by Adrian as the titanic demon closed in behind. Adrian was about to stop and look back when he felt something push him farther into the room. In the same moment, he saw the tank of the weapon fly past him and hit the floor with a loud clank.

As he fell, Adrian turned to see that it was not the creature that had nudged him, but Jack.

The towering man had made sure Adrian and Reid made it through and was now forcing the door shut... from the other side.

'End it,' he said, his voice—the first time Adrian had heard it—soft and gentle.

But as big as Jack was, the sight behind him positively dwarfed him. Adrian could only watch as Jack gave a mighty strain and was able to press the door closed.

Adrian had no time to process what was happening, and he spun around, still gripping the nozzle of the weapon. As he turned, he saw that Reid was huddled into one corner of the flesh covered room, looking horrified.

'Wha—' Adrian stopped as he felt something wrap around his leg. He looked down to see a vine of black and purple, lined with small teeth, take hold of his calf. He grunted as he felt the teeth penetrate his skin. Adrian was then pulled to the ground and dragged forwards by the writhing tentacle, to a large, man-sized growth that lay close to the body, the one he presumed to be Robert Wilson. It

had not escaped Adrian's notice that this body was almost
lost in the mass of fleshy growths that surrounded it. The
vine continued to pull him in, towards the large sack, and
Adrian felt the nozzle slip from his hand.

'Help!' he screamed over to Reid, but the man seemed
paralysed with fear. Adrian then heard a sickening shriek
from outside of the room and, in short order, the door began
to open.

'*Welcome, my child,*' a voice said, coming from the open
mouth of Robert Wilson. '*I look forward to tasting your pain. I
will make sure you get what you desire. Your mother will be
pleased.*'

'Reid!' Adrian cried out. 'Please!'

But the coward did not listen.

JACK KNEW that they would not all make it out of this alive.
Even if they reached the room that his friend Adrian was
heading towards, the monsters that he did not understand
—things that terrified him—were too close and too
powerful.

So Jack knew what he had to do.

He was sad and didn't want to die, but he knew that,
eventually, everyone had to leave this life behind.

Just like the man he had killed four years ago.

Jack had been locked up for that, and the director had
found him in prison, miserable and alone. He'd offered Jack
a chance to stay somewhere better. More comfortable.

But he had lied.

However, Jack knew he did not deserve any better. The
man that he'd strangled was mean, and had continually
harassed and teased Jack, but hadn't deserved to be killed.

Jack had let himself down.

He didn't like being violent.

And yet, he had killed someone.

So, he decided that while he stayed at the asylum, he would keep quiet and keep his head down.

It was an added bonus that he had actually made friends. They had all been as troubled and sad as he was, but that was something they'd had in common. And Adrian James had always been kind to him.

Adrian was a nice man, Jack thought, and as they raced through that passageway, Jack decided that Adrian deserved to live. He was smart enough to perhaps put an end to this madness that was spreading.

And Jack didn't think he could do that himself.

But he could help.

So he had pushed Adrian through the doorway and hurled the metal container he was carrying into the room with him.

Then he had pulled the door closed and given Adrian a message.

It was the first time he had let himself speak in years, the last time being when he screamed in the man's face as he had strangled the life from him four years ago.

Jack then turned around to face what was coming for him and saw that they were closer than he expected.

And that massive, monstrous thing reached him first. Jack linked his arms through the metal handles on the doors and closed his eyes.

He knew this would hurt.

But he didn't realise just how much.

He felt the thing grab him by the throat. Jack's eyes opened instinctively, and he looked all the way up to the face of this monster that snarled down at him. He saw it bring its other arm back, then swing it forward into his gut.

Through his gut.

He felt the thick, muscular arm push its way through his stomach, snapping his spine, into the door behind.

Jack screamed. The pain was horrible.

Blood ran from his mouth. He knew he was going to die.

Still, he kept his arms linked through the handles of the doors. He needed to give Adrian more time.

He started to sob.

'I'm sorry, I'm sorry, I'm sorry,' he repeated over and over again, to no one in particular, gurgling as he did. Jack knew he deserved this for killing that man.

And he was sorry for it.

The beast before him pulled its arm from his guts as the lesser creatures jumped and moved impatiently behind it.

Jack felt his legs buckle and had to fight to keep himself in place. The giant monster before him leaned closer to him, and he could feel its hot, nauseating breath on his face. He heard a deep chuckle rumble from its throat.

'I'm sorry,' he said again, feeling his strength leave him.

Jack felt two large hands grip either side of his head. Then an immense pain spiked as the appendages pressed together, crushing his skull completely as grey brain-matter and red mush burst forth from between the creature's thick fingers.

51

ADRIAN REACHED for the barrel of the weapon as he was dragged farther towards that disgusting open sack.

He fought against the pull of the stalk-like thing that held him, but try as he might, the metal weapon lay agonisingly out of reach.

'Reid,' he yelled out again. 'Please.'

The door to the room was forced further open, and Adrian saw a flow of blood run from between the open gap.

He looked again to the doctor, desperate, but Reid was useless to him, crouched, sobbing in a corner.

Adrian was on his own and he was going to die.

Whatever this large, tumour-like thing was, he was confident it was going to kill him, and then likely bring him back as one of those things. The creatures here would then break free, spilling out into the world.

The words uttered by Robert Wilson—or the thing using his body—hung in Adrian's mind. What it had said about him receiving a penance that he deserved, and also that his mother would be pleased.

Was that true? Would his own mother really be happy that he was about to meet his death?

Of course she would.

Adrian could still remember the look on her face before he'd smothered it under that pillow. Caring for her after she'd been stricken with that damn illness was hard.

Too hard to bear.

It had stripped the life from her, making her a shell... a husk. Always in pain and always miserable. He'd loved her so much, and yet he could do nothing to help her.

Or so he thought.

But a solution did present itself, and he had taken it, and now that decision meant he was forever wracked with guilt and shame. He would never forget the feeling of holding that dirtied pillow over her face—ravaged, pale, and sunken—as she fought meekly against him.

Adrian had killed his mother like he had his father before her.

He truly was a monster, worthy of the pain, suffering, and death that was now waiting for him. So why bother fighting it? It's what he deserved.

But was that fate what everyone else deserved? Everyone outside of this damned asylum?

Jack had given his life so that they would have a chance to end this. And given what a disappointment and monster he'd turned out to be—just like his father—shouldn't he at least strive for one moment where he did something good? Something worthwhile that actually helped people?

Even if no one would ever know.

Though perhaps, if his dear mother did now exist somewhere, and she was looking down on him, she might feel something like pride for him.

He clenched his fists together and clenched his teeth,

readying himself. Adrian dug the balls of his feet into the floor and pushed his body forward, fighting against the strong pull from the alien vine that worked against him. The thrust managed to gain him a little ground, but as he looked up, he saw the door to the room open fully, and Jack's ruined body flop to the floor in a pool of blood.

Adrian pushed again, his fingers brushing against the warm metal of the nozzle, but he was not close enough to take hold fully.

Another tentacle wrapped around his other leg.

No. I won't let you.

The force working against him was greater now. And to compound things, the giant beast entered the room with a deafening roar.

No.

Adrian pressed his palms into the floor and arched his back a little, like a sprinter ready for the firing gun, and with every ounce of strength he could muster he pushed off his feet and again flung himself forward, arms outstretched.

This time, he managed to grab hold of the nozzle with a firm grip. Working quickly, he manoeuvred it in his hands, turning it as the great behemoth made its way over to the cowering form of Reid, a swarm of other monstrosities flooding in behind it.

The tank beside Adrian squeaked across the floor as it was pulled along with him. Adrian had now given up fighting against the pull.

He had what he needed now and took aim at the form of Robert Wilson—the thing he hoped was the centre of this ever-expanding nightmare. He then held his breath... and pulled the trigger.

A stream of fire burst forward.

The behemoth and its brethren stopped upon seeing the flames arc through the air, and it growled in protest.

But Adrian kept up the assault, despite still being dragged back. He saw the flesh at the centre of the room ignite, then he gave another burst as he felt his feet pulled into that foul, fleshy sack.

Again and again he fired the weapon, as he was dragged completely into the darkness, and the sides started to close around him, trapping him inside the slimy, pungent growth. However, he managed to keep his arm free of the opening after the sack closed around it, painfully trapping the appendage.

Another prolonged squeeze. And another. Firing blind.

Eventually, it would fire no more, now out of fuel, and he was forced to drop it as he heard the screams of the creatures outside.

Adrian had no idea if the plan had worked or not.

Then he felt something slither to his face and force its way into his mouth.

52

REID CONTINUED to press himself into the wall of pulsating flesh behind him, crying out in terror as the vile creatures made their way towards him. The fire that Adrian—who had disappeared into that tumorous sack—had thrown around the room had stopped the monsters momentarily, but as Wilson's form burned, they seemed to find renewed vigour.

And they turned their attention to him.

The giant thing at the head of the pack took a couple of huge steps towards him, and Reid cried out, not yet ready to die.

Especially not like this.

But as the fire spread and the room became engulfed with searing hot flame, the behemoth faltered.

Its huge legs seemed to wobble.

It growled as it tried to take another step forward, but only succeeded in losing its footing completely. It then crashed to the floor, its head falling at the feet of Reid.

The other monstrosities seemed to be faring no better, all dropping to the ground and writhing around before finally falling motionless. The great hulk before Reid gave a few more spasms, trying in vain to cling to life, but finally expelled a long breath, and soon it, too, was still.

The only sound now was the incessant crackling as the room continued to burn. Reid felt the heat and smoke gather strength around him.

Run!

This was his chance.

Perhaps it was now all over, and Adrian James had succeeded. Which meant that Reid was the last one left alive.

He took a tentative step forward, needing to pass over the massive body of the behemoth that blocked the way before him. He slowly climbed atop its back, the enormous body holding firm beneath him.

It did not stir.

He made his way from the room, scrambling over the piled bodies of impossible creatures of nightmarish compositions, and as he did, he looked over to that sack of flesh at the foot of the burning mass. Adrian's arm still protruded from it, but was unmoving.

Perhaps there was a chance he was still alive? If so, shouldn't Reid help?

But the fire was growing stronger, and quickly, and Reid felt a sense of horrible familiarity. He remembered the burning room from his past, and his pleading wife and child. He knew at the time that if he had tried to save them, he would have been killed as well.

And the fire here was growing too strong.

The hell with Adrian James.

Reid continued climbing over the lifeless bodies, seeing the remains of the towering fool Jack beneath them all, and made his way to the corridor beyond. It was cooler here, the air—while still heavy—much cleaner. There were a few motionless creatures scattered about the ground, now empty husks.

Reid broke into a jog, a feeling of freedom washing over him.

Considering the position he had found himself in not long ago, having to choose between being a prisoner or being killed, the turnaround in his fortunes had been drastic.

Up the stairs he ran and out into the large Main Hall. He knew he would still need to find that key to escape, and that would take time, but if he was the only one left alive in Arlington Asylum, then it mattered little.

However, as he made his way forward, he noticed that the key would not be needed at all.

The main door to the facility lay on the floor—twisted, bent, and ruined. The remaining doorframe was cracked and misshapen and the way through free and unobstructed. Something had forced its way out.

Reid hesitated, instinctually, but quickly realised that whatever it was, it would now be dead, too, given what had happened down in the basement. So his escape had been made that much easier.

He felt his heart lift, and he let out a laugh as he sprinted forward, passing the sloppy, gory mess of Seymour's body, and on towards the cold air that spilled in from the opening.

Towards his freedom.

He burst free from that damn asylum—finally—and out into the night, ready to continue his run back into the normal world.

The sane world.

But as he broke clear of the threshold, he stopped.

There was a flight of grand stone steps outside of the

facility that led down to the lower ground level outside. At the bottom of the steps stood two stone pillars, and it was between those pillars, on the bottom step, that something stood with its back to him.

Something Reid recognised—that thing from the corridor before.

The Dark Priest.

And it was very much alive.

Impossible, he thought, *it should be dead.*

He heard a chuckle come from the thing as it turned to him, showing its mangled face.

'*Killing the link to the creator has no bearing on me, wretch,*' it said as if reading his thoughts.

Then he realised that was exactly what had happened.

'What are you?' Reid asked, his voice quivering. Freedom stood just behind that thing, out beyond the stone driveway that led off between the trees and into the darkness, where the exit sat within the boundary walls. The walk to a populated area would take hours and hours, but it was something Reid could certainly do.

Now, however, his escape seemed infinitely far away.

'*I am the purpose of the Creator. Its goal in this world was to create me, so that part of it could live on, free from the decay and death it is suffering in its own existence.*'

'But the other... things? They're all dead,' Reid said.

'*Those mongrels were nothing. Merely a result of the Creator spreading its influence, gaining enough strength here for what it needed to do.*' The thing opened its arms wide to either side. '*To birth me unto this world. And it succeeded.*'

'What will you do?'

The thing shrugged, which Reid saw as a very human gesture. '*Whatever I wish. I will wait and learn... and then mould this world into what I wish it to be. A place like the home of my creator. And I will reside atop a throne of bodies and blood.'*

It then began to laugh—a horrible, demonic sound.

'Please,' Reid begged, 'please let me go.'

The thing continued to laugh, but gave a simple answer.

'*No.*'

It raised an arm towards Reid, then flicked up its hand. Reid felt himself suddenly rise up from the ground, pulled upwards by some unknown force... farther and farther until he was about twenty feet in the air, hovering.

He cried out.

'No! Please!'

Then the Dark Priest below held both arms straight out before it and started to slowly pull them apart. It took a moment for Reid to feel the pain begin to rise in him, and he groaned and squirmed.

And then the pain increased even more, growing stronger, and he started to *really* feel it.

His skin, the very make-up of his body, began to pull itself apart, and Reid could do nothing, only feel every tiny ounce of absolute agony as it happened.

His skin began to separate, splitting and pulling away from his body, dragging his clothes with it, leaving the meat and flesh attached to his bones, nerves and muscles now exposed.

The skin fell to the ground like a discarded pelt, slapping to the stone with a wet squelch. Blood poured down from his body as the tendons and muscle began to pull away as well.

He continued to screech in hellish torment as he saw the glistening red meat rip off of him and plummet below in bloody chunks.

The Dark Priest continued its incessant, mocking laughter as Reid suffered an unimaginable hell.

His guts and intestines pulled themselves free and hovered for him to see. One then wrapped around his neck, with another snaking into his mouth, choking him.

All the while, the demonic conductor below orchestrated the desecration upon his dying body.

One eye was pulled free, and the optic nerve severed. It, too, plopped to the ground, into the pile of gore that was building up.

His pain was absolute.

And finally it ended, but only when the Dark Priest allowed it to end. The thing pulled its arms out wider, and the last thing Reid felt was his body exploding in a shower of meat and blood.

THE ENTITY HAD TRULY ENJOYED itself.

It felt the wretch's fear, pain, and suffering, and it was truly exquisite.

It then turned and looked out to the world it intended to one day rule.

For now, though, it was time to leave this place behind.

The building—where it had come into the world—meant nothing to it.

It needed to find a place to dwell, to grow, while it formulated the downfall and subjugation of the pathetic human race.

The entity did not follow the path out, instead choosing to turn to its left, heading into the welcoming darkness of the trees.

And it kept going.

53

THE WRIGGLING THING that had forced its way painfully down Adrian's throat had become still. The compressing walls of the pod had eased, and the teeth that covered the internal lining no longer worked into his skin.

Outside of his fleshy cocoon, he heard the crackling of fire. He could even feel its heat emanate through the pod that held him.

And he was alive.

A sliver of flickering light made its way through into his surroundings from outside, wedged open by his aching arm. He could smell burnt meat and thick smoke.

Adrian moved his arms as best he could in the tight space available and grasped hold of the alien thing that was lodged in his oesophagus. He heaved at it and felt it slowly start to pull up from his gut, making him gag. It caused a horrible, burning sensation in his throat, but still he continued, tears running down his face.

Eventually, the slimy tentacle was pulled free, and Adrian emptied the contents of his stomach as the head of it slopped from his mouth.

After taking a moment, he then forced both arms through the small opening and started to squeeze himself through. It was a struggle at first, but eventually the walls of the pod gave, opening just enough for him to flop to the floor outside.

Into an inferno.

Flames coated the room and were close to the cocoon he had just escaped from. The heat was almost unbearable and the smoke overpowering, making it hard to see as the fire scorched the monstrous bodies that littered the floor.

Adrian sucked in whatever air he could, though he couldn't help but draw in smoke, causing him to cough and dry-heave again.

With a spinning head, he knew he would not last long in this place. So he pushed himself up to unsteady feet, got his bearings, and then ran through the flames, feeling them lick at him as he went.

He shielded himself with his arms as best he could, but soon became aware that the ruined clothing he wore had caught fire at the waist.

But he didn't have time to stop. So, instead, he stomped over the fallen bodies, careful of his footing to try to avoid the worst of the fire. He stumbled slightly, but was able to keep his balance and pushed on as the flames burned at his already stinging skin.

Finally, Adrian managed to stumble out of the chamber, into the relatively clean, cold air of the passageway beyond. He ripped off his burning clothing and dropped them to his side, now completely naked.

Not that he cared.

After a few more stumbling steps, Adrian let himself fall the ground, pulling in mouthfuls of oxygen. He allowed himself a moment to rest—to allow his body to stop shaking and head to stop spinning.

And in that moment, he was unable to stop his thoughts from running to his mother.

To his last moments with her as she had begged him to end her suffering.

She had hated that she was such a burden. And the constant pain was unbearable, so she had asked of him the unaskable. He had tried to dissuade her—begged her not to make him do it, but she had insisted, pleading that he be brave and do this one last thing for her.

And, in the end, Adrian had obliged—reluctantly giving her the release she had so desperately wanted.

But the woman at the time had been close to delirious, such was the pain she was in, and Adrian could never convince himself it was what she had actually wanted. He didn't hold out long enough to find out for sure and had been too quick to kill.

Again.

And if it had been the delirium talking, then he had murdered his innocent mother, the one person in this world who had ever loved and cared for him.

Then there was her struggle as he held the pillow over her face. Why would she fight back if she wanted to die? Adrian had taken it as a natural reaction, but was that really it?

He would never know the answer to that, and he knew he would never find peace.

It took a while, but eventually enough strength returned so that Adrian was able to drag himself to his feet and push on. He staggered through the passageway and then up the stairs to the Main Hall above.

When he got there, he saw what was left of Seymour—a desecrated mess smeared about the floor.

Adrian wasn't exactly said to see what had happened to him, though he did feel bad for Jack, and the idea that his body would stay down below with those monsters did not sit well with him. He knew that soon enough, however, what was left of Jack would burn to nothing, along with the other lifeless creatures down in that hellish ward.

Up ahead, the door to the exit had been ripped from its hinges, revealing the open air of the night outside. Something had broken its way through there, leaving the ruined door on the floor in the hall.

But Adrian paid it no mind, too exhausted to care, feeling all but broken.

He walked out into the night, finally stepping free of the wretched place that had so tormented him for so long.

Freedom was his.

As he stepped outside, he almost slipped on a pile of gore that covered the stone floor. Something had met a nasty end here. He trudged through whatever it was and continued down the stone steps to the wide gravel driveway below.

The air was biting cold on his naked skin, and he realised he wouldn't last long without some form of clothing.

But perhaps that wasn't a bad thing. He was tired, so very tired, and considered lying down to let exposure claim him. Considering what could have happened to him, that wasn't a bad way to go. At least he was out of that God-forsaken place, dying on his own terms.

But a rumbling sound up ahead drew his attention.

Lights appeared as the sounds came closer.

Headlights.

Soon a convoy of automobiles could be seen breaking through the darkness, and they pulled up to close to the building, the gravel popping and cracking under their tires.

There were five cars in all, and a large truck at the rear.

What now?

The doors opened, and people spilled free, all of them wearing odd, dark-red gowns.

'Who are you?' Adrian asked of the first man who approached. He was tall and gangly, with thin white hair and a hooked nose.

'Are you an inmate?' the first man asked, with a gravelly, old voice.

Adrian didn't know how to answer, so he just nodded.

'Where is the man in charge? Isaac Templeton? Or any of the others who work here?'

'All dead, I think,' Adrian said. He brought his arms around himself in an attempt to ward off the cold.

The man just nodded, solemnly, and turned to some of the others who were with him. Adrian saw that many of them were equipped with the same type of weapon he had used down in the basement earlier.

'As I feared. Brother Templeton did not check in when he should have. I told him things were progressing too quickly to be properly controlled.'

'I think you were right,' Adrian said. 'Now if you don't mind, I'm going to continue past you and go on my way.'

The man just laughed and then shook his head. 'I'm afraid not.'

Adrian had expected that answer. 'Then what happens now?'

'We cannot allow knowledge of what happened here to get out, and will therefore purge all evidence, so that nothing can be discovered. No loose ends.'

'Figured as much. Does that mean you're going to kill me?'

Two other men approached, flanking the first. 'No need for that,' the man said with a smile. 'You'll come with us.'

'Just give the word, Mr. Ainsworth,' one of the men said. He was tall and broad, cutting an imposing figure. Another joined him.

'Whenever you are ready,' the hook-nosed man said with a smile.

In an instant, the large man dove on Adrian and grappled with him, while the other pulled a burlap sack over his head. Adrian fought against them, but was quickly overpowered. He felt his arms tied behind his back, and his legs were bound together as well. He was then lifted and thrown over a shoulder.

He then heard the hooked-nosed man again. 'There are other facilities that you will be able to call home. Though I'm afraid it won't be much of a life for you. Goodbye, inmate.'

Adrian was carried away and thrown to the metallic floor in the back of the truck. Heavy doors were closed behind him as he screamed in anger. But it was useless—he was a prisoner again.

Now and forever.

54

For Isaac Templeton, the journey he was on with Robert Wilson seemed to take days; but it was impossible to tell as no sun ever rose here.

There was only the eternal night.

He had been pulled through cracks and valleys ripped into the ground, up over rolling hills of obsidian, and through moving forests of flesh. And he had seen horrors that had almost shattered his sanity.

There were times when he tried to talk to his old friend, to apologise for what he had done and to find out where he now was. And, more importantly, if he was stuck here.

Robert's answers ranged from muddled and vague, to entirely non-existent. One thing Templeton found strange was that Wilson seemed to harbour no ill will towards Templeton for what he had done. For, in truth, it was because of Templeton that Robert Wilson was here.

But Robert's concentration seemed focused purely on getting them both to where they needed to be.

Wherever that was.

And so they continued, and Templeton's raw body was

ravaged further over the harsh ground as he was forced to crawl—the exposed nerves and muscles becoming coated in black dirt as the flesh started to puss, then scab.

The pain of it all never left him for a moment.

Templeton's body was ruined, and he was exhausted, but Robert still dragged him on, telling him that the Great God had the answers Templeton searched for. When Templeton grew tired of not knowing, he threatened to stop completely.

Robert simply shrugged. 'Then you will be left alone to torture and damnation here.'

That was enough to get the terrified and confused Templeton moving again.

Eventually, after cutting through yet another deep ravine —where he saw something unholy emerge from a wall and pull in a group of skinless people—they started an ascent. High above, towering in the sky at the head of the climb, Templeton saw a titanic monolith—the top of which was impossible to discern.

The massive object was too wide to know for sure, but Templeton sensed it was cylindrical in shape. As they grew closer, he was able to make out details on the surface.

While it had looked smooth and black from a distance, and indeed the material of which it was formed was of an obsidian appearance, other characteristics could be seen here too.

For one, behind the glass-like structure, Templeton could see shards of red light trapped within swirling pools of black. There were also alien markings and depictions on the surface.

But those details paled in significance to what Templeton saw lining the structure.

People!

Fused to the surface, they writhed and screamed in

agony. Most were misshapen and melted, almost to the point of being unrecognisable, but some features could be made out—a sobbing face, the odd limb, a trail of intestines. A few seemed more whole, perhaps newly grafted to this thing.

These poor souls stretched all the way up into the distance.

Robert kept dragging Templeton closer, but now Templeton resisted.

'What is it?' he asked.

'Ashklaar,' Robert said, with a sense of reverence. 'This is the god that wishes to speak to you.'

'I don't want to,' Templeton said, feeling a further swell of dread bubble up inside of him.

'No choice,' Robert replied. 'He has summoned you, and he will give you the answers you need. There is a way to survive in this place, and he will give it to you.'

'I'm scared,' Templeton admitted, and began pulling against Robert. The man let go of Templeton's wrist and turned to him.

'You cannot disobey the will of the god. You learned of The Great Ailing one, correct? The thing beneath the boiling sea? Well Ashklaar is feeding on that god, slowly digesting its very existence. The thing under the boiling sea. You believed that was a powerful being? Ashklaar burrows deep within the bowels of this place and it will continue to grow in strength, perhaps one day gaining enough power to eventually ascend, to reach the heights of the eternal nightmare Vao!'

Robert pointed to the sky above, to that impossible, swirling mass of stars. And to that great, terrifying, cosmic eye.

'What will happen to me?' Templeton asked.

'Whatever Ashklaar wishes. But now is your only chance. You can see what happens to those who attempt to turn away from its knowledge.'

Robert gestured to the poor souls fused to the surface of the tower.

Of Ashklaar.

Templeton's head dropped. He had no idea what to do and was completely overwhelmed.

He felt like he was in a nightmare, only he knew better.

This was real.

Robert grabbed his arm again and pulled. Templeton submitted, not knowing what else to do, and allowed himself to be dragged onwards again, up to the base of this gigantic thing. The red light inside was mesmerising to him, every bit as much as the melted, eviscerated bodies that still lived were terrifying.

'What do we do now?' Templeton asked.

In response, Robert pushed him from behind.

Templeton let out a shriek as his body made contact with the scorching surface. He tried to pull away... but could not.

He felt himself pulled into the smooth face of the tower, and a white-hot pain shot through him.

'Robert!' Templeton screamed. 'What have you done?'

Pain engulfed him, and Robert began to laugh as Templeton's body moved upwards—dragged along the surface, sliding between the other poor souls stuck here.

'Getting my revenge!' Robert shouted from below. 'It was you that cast me out here, and Ashklaar promised me this moment. Enjoy your eternal damnation, Isaac. You have earned it!' The man started to bellow out a mad laugh as Templeton was pulled farther and farther up.

Finally, when he was miles into the sky and could look

out over the hellscape before him, he felt his body drawn deeper into the tower. His flesh started to dissolve and split painfully, and his insides ran along the searing surface, held fast by some unknown force.

The pain was unimaginable, but he did not die.

He never died, even as his body lost most of its form, becoming little more than pools of smeared gore as he was slowly melded into the form of Ashklaar. Time had no meaning for him because his existence like this would never end.

There was no respite.

Only eternal torment.

HORROR IN THE WOODS

Horror in the Woods

FINDING THAT DESE-CRATED BODY WAS ONLY THE BEGINNING...

For Ashley and her three friends, it was supposed to be an adventure-filled weekend. A chance to get away from the hustle-and-bustle of city life, and experience the peaceful tranquility of nature.

But when they ventured into those woods, their trip turned into a horror far beyond what they could have ever imagined.

Because these four friends have wandered into the terri-tory of the violent, grotesque Webb family. A group of psychopaths who have a taste for human meat. And they are hungry!

Ashley and her friends must face this evil head on, and

worse, discover the shocking secret behind the family's existence...

In the vein of THE EVIL DEAD, TEXAS CHAINSAW MASSACRE, and WRONG TURN - HORROR IN THE WOODS will leave you exhausted and drained. A brutal, violent tale that hurtles along at break-neck pace—one that horror fans should not miss!

THE DEMONIC

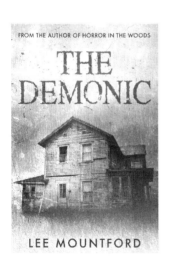

The Demonic

Years ago Danni Morgan ran away from her childhood home and vowed never to go back. It was a place of fear, pain and misery at the hands of an abusive father.

But now Danni's father is dead and she is forced to break her vow and return home—to lay his body to rest and face up to the ghosts of her past.

But Danni is about to realise that some ghosts are more real than others. And something beyond her understanding is waiting for her there, lurking in the shadows. An evil that intends to kill her family and claim her very soul.

Experience supernatural horror in the vein of THE CONJURING, INSIDIOUS and the legendary GHOST-

WATCH. THE DEMONIC will get under your skin, send chills down your spine and have you sleeping with the lights on!

THE MARK

The Mark

A SATANIC CULT. A WOMAN'S BRUTAL ASSAULT. CAN SHE FACE HER DARKEST FEAR BEFORE A DEMON IS UNLEASHED FROM HELL?

Kirsty Thompson is no stranger to trauma. But when a vicious attack leaves her drugged and disoriented, she never expected to wake up to a permanent scar. She starts having demonic visions, all linked to the ancient symbol carved deep into her back...

With the help of her best friend Amanda, Kirsty discovers that the mark originates from The Devil's Bible and forges a connection between her and a terrifying creature. As they track the man who assaulted her to a satanic cult, the beast hunts them from the shadows. Can Kirsty escape the devil worshippers and her bond with the heinous creature to save herself from eternal damnation?

The Mark is a terrifying standalone horror novel. If you like mysterious depraved forces, tales of the occult, and stories that will have you looking under the bed, then you'll love this gripping tale!

THE DEMON OF DUNTON FARM

Sign up to my mailing list for free horror stories...

Enjoy The Demonic?

Find out exactly what happened on that cursed land in Bishops Hill all those years ago, and relive the most grisly events in its history.

The horrifying truth surrounding the demon that dwells on the farm will be revealed in this prequel to The Demonic.

To sign up to my mailing list go to www.leemountford.com and get your free books.

ABOUT THE AUTHOR

Lee Mountford is a horror author from the North-East of England. His first book, Horror in the Woods, was published in May 2017 to fantastic reviews, and his follow-up book, The Demonic, achieved Best Seller status in both Occult Horror and British Horror categories on Amazon.

He is a lifelong horror fan, much to the dismay of his amazing wife, Michelle, and his work is available in ebook, print and audiobook formats.

In August 2017 he and his wife welcomed their beautiful daughter, Ella, into the world. Michelle is hoping she doesn't inherit her father's love of horror, but Lee has other ideas...

For more information
www.leemountford.com
leemountford01@googlemail.com

ACKNOWLEDGMENTS

Thanks first and foremost to my editor, Josiah Davis (http://www.jdbookservices.com), for such an amazing job.

The cover was supplied by Debbie at The Cover Collection (http://www.thecovercollection.com). I cannot recommend their work enough.

Thanks as well to fellow author—and guru extraordinaire—Iain Rob Wright for all of his fantastic advice and guidance. If you don't know who Iain is, remedy that now: http://www.iainrobwright.com. An amazing author with a brilliant body of work.

And the last thank you, as always, is the most important—to my amazing family. My wife, Michelle, and my daughter, Ella, thank you for everything, you are my world.

ISBN-13:

978-1986211291

ISBN-10:

1986211290

❧ Created with Vellum

Made in the USA
Middletown, DE
10 March 2019